Nest or Invest

ENNI AMANDA

2nd edition, 2023

ISBN 978-0-473-56207-6 (paperback)
ISBN 978-1-99-116506-0 (hardcover)
ISBN 978-0-473-56208-3 (ebook)
Designed by Yummy Book Covers
Typeset in PT Serif, 10pt

To my husband, who makes it all possible

Nest or Invest

Chapter 1

Shasa sank into her worn-out wingback chair and let out a deep sigh. Afternoon nap time. For the next ninety minutes, she could ignore the floor covered in dirty clothes and crumbs and just sit. She had nothing scheduled. Nothing but the scent of lemony green tea rising from her cup and a phone she could use to read her emails – if she had the stomach to open the last one.

The message was from Ollie, her partner and the father of her child. He'd spent the last two years working on the Greenpeace ship somewhere in the Pacific Ocean, extending his stay twice. In three weeks, he'd return to New Zealand. That was the plan, anyway.

Over the last two months, their relationship had become more and more strained. The distance between them felt longer than nine thousand kilometres of ocean. Now, this ominous email had landed in her inbox. Nothing good ever followed a subject line 'Something you should know'.

She dropped the phone on the floor. She didn't need to know anything. Not yet. She could sit for a moment and admire how the afternoon sun played with her net curtains, exposing a sprinkling of mould, illuminating the dust particles dancing in the air. She focused on her breath, inhaling for one, two, three...

Before she reached 'four', someone knocked on the door, loudly enough to break her concentration and wake up her daughter. The telltale whimper carried down the hallway, making her muscles clench, and a hot burst of anger propelled her out of her chair. She marched to the door, flinging it open.

"Hi! Mac McCarthy. I'm here for the property valuation. Were you expecting me?"

Damn! A week ago, Shasa had received a text from her property manager, informing her of the valuation. Why hadn't she marked it in her calendar?

She eyeballed the guy standing at her doorstep. His suit and tie exuded success. A branded pen stuck out of his pocket.

A real estate agent.

He had a stupid name, deep brown eyes, and a dazzling

smile, which quickly turned cheeky. His gaze dipped down, scanning her from head to toe, no doubt noting the overgrown dreadlocks and colorful bracelets. It wasn't a style befitting a 32-year-old, her mum had announced during one of their video chats, later sending her a gift certificate for the hairdresser. The rest of her outfit was equally questionable. She wrapped her arms around her chest to cover the threadbare, food-stained tank top from the guy's roaming gaze. Was he here to evaluate the house or her?

Lilla's high-pitched wail rang through the house, demanding attention.

She nodded towards the bedroom. "That's my daughter."

The agent's eyebrows shot up in an animated show of sympathy. "Poor little one!"

Shasa glared at him. "You woke her."

He smiled brightly. "Don't worry, this won't take long. She can go back to sleep in a jiffy."

"No, she can't. She takes ages to fall asleep." The low hiss of Shasa's exhale sounded like a tiny Darth Vader. If only she had a scary mask and were two feet taller. Being petite meant guys tended to underestimate her.

She spun on her heels and hurried to the bedroom across the uneven wood floor. Her three-year-old, Lilla, stood in her cot, her doll face contorted in despair, wailing like she'd been abandoned on a desert island. She had her father's blue eyes and Shasa's dark, wavy hair, self-styled with far too many pink and purple clips.

Careful of her lower back, Shasa scooped her up and carried her to the lounge. Even if the ritual of bum-patting and water-bottle-suckling worked to put her back to sleep, she'd get another half-an-hour at best. With a stranger snooping around the house, nap time was officially over.

She adjusted Lilla's skinny legs on her waist, letting her shoulder get slimy from the tears, and strolled around the house. The old villa had plenty of creaky doors that, when opened, created a handy loop. Gradually, Lilla's wailing turned into sniffling, allowing Shasa to hear another sound.

The real estate agent cleared his throat, still standing at the entrance. Couldn't the dude just do whatever he was here to do and get out of her way?

"What?" she barked.

The guy flashed her a bright smile. "Is it okay if I look around now? Or would you rather reschedule?"

"I'd rather you were done already."

Sensing an intruder, Lilla halted her sniffling. Her arms tightened around Shasa's neck, and her head lifted in curiosity.

The agent beamed at her. "Hi, there! Sorry I woke you."

Shivering at his sugary voice, Shasa backed away from the door. Lilla, the traitor that she was, decided she was done with hugs and squirmed out of her arms, onto the floor. She followed Mac-whatever down the hallway, straight into the laundry.

A sight to behold. The mountain of dirty clothes had

grown to the point where it could no longer be contained by the cupboard-sized room and spilled freely into the narrow hallway, meeting a row of recycling containers lined up along the wall. Hurdling a heap of washed Styrofoam prepared for special recycling, Mac nearly stepped on a pair of dirty underwear.

Shasa shuddered, squeezing her eyes shut. She was desperate to run away, but first, she had to catch Lilla. The girl had attached herself to Mac's side, fascinated by the stranger taking photos of their laundry pile.

"Mummy's panties," she explained, lifting the frayed, purple underwear.

Could the earth please swallow her now?

"You're right," Mac replied, nodding appreciatively. Was he looking at them? She leapt in, grabbed the panties from her daughter's hand, and stashed them behind a bag of dirty towels.

"Look—" Lilla picked up a T-shirt with a big spaghetti stain "My unicorn shirt. It's dirty."

"Yes, I'm sure your mum will wash it, at some point."

Shasa's fingers curled into tight fists. For the last two weeks, she'd worked long hours at the community house to make up for the lack of volunteers. She'd stayed behind to pack food parcels and call local businesses to secure more donations. With no family around, she always had her child with her, sometimes even at work. If she didn't have time to tackle laundry, so be it. Who was this guy to pass judgment?

Mac reached into his jacket pocket and pulled out a bag of chocolate frogs. He glanced at Shasa.

"Do you mind if I give her one?"

Shasa huffed her consent. Anyone who showed a child a treat before asking the parent was playing a dirty game. How could she say no? Lilla was so excited she practically levitated towards the chocolates.

"Say thank you," Shasa grumbled, grabbing Lilla's non-chocolate-holding hand, pulling her to the kitchen. "Do you want a snack?"

Lilla wrinkled her button nose. "You have scary eyes."

Shasa tried to relax her face. "Can you save that chocolate for later? Have some kiwi fruit first."

Lilla shook her head.

By the time Shasa had peeled the kiwi fruit, the chocolate was gone, and Lilla accepted the healthier snack. Watching her daughter munch on fruit, Shasa allowed her shoulders to drop. She fetched her previous teacup, now lukewarm, and settled at the table. For a glorious moment, she forgot about the intruder – until she saw him outside the window, holding a tape measure. A layer of cold sweat formed on her neck.

The landlord had sent property valuers before, to borrow more money from the bank. The last one had stayed for two minutes, confirming that the house hadn't burnt down. So why was the real estate agent strolling around her backyard with a tape measure, recording the width of her driveway, the distance from the boundary to her garden shed, the girth of the magnolia tree? Property valuations weren't based on the circumference of trees, were they?

She knew she paid way below market rent. She had a lot of space – two bedrooms, a study, and a huge, fenced backyard. Last summer, her blueberry bush had produced the first decent crop. She'd planted it five years ago when they'd first moved in. This year, she was planning to stock the community pantry at her workplace. Blueberries were so expensive in the shops.

From behind the curtain, she kept her eye on the guy. He stopped in the middle of the lawn and typed something on his phone, a self-satisfied smirk on his face.

She wanted him gone, but she needed answers. Was the owner planning to sell the house?

It'd be easier to confront him outside, without the dirty laundry or carpet stains casting judgment on her.

Shasa wiped her daughter's mouth and hands with a tea towel. "Get your shoes, let's go outside!"

She leaned on the old key just-so to open the back door and located him by the rear boundary, partially hidden by the compost bin and their abandoned chicken coop. They'd given up the chickens when Ollie had gone vegan, dragging them all in with him. The day he'd left for his first voyage, she'd driven to the supermarket to buy eggs and yoghurt. With no grandparents around, it was hard enough to be a single mum without maintaining complicated shopping and meal planning.

Lilla stuck her feet into her glittery ballet shoes. "Swing?"

She loved the swing they'd hung off the magnolia tree. In the spring, huge, floppy flowers formed a magical, pink ceiling. Now, in late summer, the ceiling was green, contrasting with the yellow grass that had seen little rain in weeks. The council didn't charge for water, but Ollie had always been adamant they shouldn't waste town water on the garden. Right now, the collection barrels were empty, and she only used the hose for her blueberries. When Ollie returned, she hoped he'd see the yellow lawn as a sign of her dedication and would forgive her for not sticking to a vegan diet. If he returned. That ominous email still sat on her phone, unopened.

Lilla ran to the swing. "Push me!" she yelled before even sitting down.

Shasa gave her a couple of shoves. Leaving her squealing with delight, she approached Mac, who was now taking a photo of her house, and as it appeared, her child. "What are you doing?"

He jumped. "Don't worry, these are just for reference."

"Why are you taking measurements? Is the house going on the market?"

He averted her eyes. "I'm just here to do a valuation."

Shasa's voice rose in alarm. "Please, don't bullshit me. I need to know what's going on."

Mac tapped on his phone. "If your landlord's planning to

sell, he must give you a ninety-day notice. Or, if they're not getting new tenants, forty-two days. Either way, you'll be notified."

He spoke like a robot, rattling out a rehearsed script.

Desperation tightened Shasa's chest. "Forty-two days is nothing! There are hardly any rentals out there and rents have gone up so much! I'm a single mum on a part-time salary. I won't be able to find anything."

"I understand it's tough, but with good references, there's always something." He still wouldn't give her more than a cursory glance, but his voice sounded more strained.

Panic swirled in Shasa's stomach. She had to get through to this guy. She stepped closer, forcing any anger out of her voice, pleading with all she had. "Mac? Please tell me what's going on. I'm begging you."

He looked at her, his face frozen in a strange, half-baked expression. She had an odd sensation of peeking behind a curtain, like she was seeing an actor moments before they stepped on stage. Something flashed behind his brown eyes, something human that gave her hope. She held his gaze, her nerves raw, fingertips aching.

He glanced at Lilla. A quick smile passed his lips, then disappeared like it was chased by the wind. He turned back to his phone. "I'm sorry. We don't discuss property deals with tenants."

So, that was it? A black cloud swallowed her thoughts, her voice pouring out like acid. "It's all about making money for you and your clients, right? Nobody cares about the tenant."

He straightened his spine. "I don't make money. Money makes money." The reply sounded rehearsed, but at least she had his attention.

Shasa squared her shoulders to match his posture. "What if you don't have any money?"

He shrugged. "Plenty of people start with nothing and make millions."

Her blood boiled. "And millions of people start with nothing and make nothing! The system's not fair!"

Mac's mouth twitched. She caught a light behind his eyes again, a flicker of fire. Engagement. It felt better than the half-arsed brush-offs.

The twitch in the corner of his mouth grew into a proper smile. "Life's not fair. Doesn't mean you give up, sit on your bum and whine about it."

Shasa folded her arms. "I'm not whining! I'm asking you to tell me what you know, so we can avoid becoming homeless. Isn't that what I'm supposed to do in your capitalist utopia?"

"Capitalist utopia?" He raised a brow and cocked his head, baffled. "I'm on your side. I love seeing renters get on the property ladder. In fact, you might be interested in—"

"Oh, spare me the spiel! I'm not your buyer. I'm not your competition, either. I'm just a single mum trying to survive. All I'm asking is a fair warning. Do I have to move? Is it possible the new owners might keep us on? We're good tenants." The picture of her laundry pile flashed behind her eyes and warmth engulfed her face. "I mean, we pay on time."

Mac's eyes softened. He slipped his phone into his pocket. "I'm so sorry, but my client's looking at developing. It's a decent sized section, enough for several high-end townhouses. Makes more sense than trying to renovate ... that." He gestured apologetically at the old villa. "The location's perfect. Close to town, close to the lake, on a popular street. You're right, Hamilton is short of rentals. When you think about it, this is great for everyone. Multiple apartments instead of one."

Great for everyone? Her stomach roiled. This was her worst nightmare. She stared at her perfect garden, all the fight seeping out of her. "Is it final yet?"

Mac shrugged. "It's looking good. The house is on stilts, easy to move. No reason it wouldn't go through."

Her gaze landed on her big blueberry bush, surrounded by nets she'd painstakingly installed last summer. "Do you think they'll destroy the whole garden? The blueberries, the fruit trees, everything?"

Mac gave her an odd look. "Why? You won't be here."

"I know. But I've put in so much work, I don't want to see it all die." She bit down on her lip to stop it from quivering.

This was the worst news, and she hadn't even read Ollie's email yet.

Mac looked at the blueberries. "If the garden is in the way, it has to go."

Lilla shouted from the swing, asking for someone to push her. Shasa tried to move, but the devastation of the news had nailed her to the ground. She fought the sting behind her eyes, but it only got worse.

Mac stepped in and gave Lilla a push. Her giggle rang across the yard.

He returned to her, shifting his weight from one foot to the other. "I was going to take one more look inside the house, but..."

Shasa squeezed her eyes shut, tears now flowing freely. "I think it's best you leave."

She'd expected him to run at the sight of her tears, but he simply stood there, head slightly tilted, his brown eyes radiating concern.

"Hey. It'll be okay." The sudden kindness in his voice made her shiver. "Maybe you'll find something better. Plant another... blueberry bush."

When his hand landed on her shoulder, she jerked. "It takes... five... years... to produce any berries," she hiccupped, trying to get her tears under control.

Despite everything she found obnoxious and disagreeable about him, from that fancy suit to his arrogant rhetoric, Mac seemed completely at ease with her emotional outburst.

"Five years is a long time." He stroked her shoulder with his thumb, his voice soft.

She should have shaken off that hand and slapped it away for good measure. But something deep inside her hummed to life, responding to the warm, reassuring touch. She noted the weight of it, that subtle vibration that spread through her body, flooding her with confusing warmth. She hadn't been touched for a while, at least by a man.

The sheer unexpectedness of the physical comfort held her spellbound, until doubts slowly entered her mind. Why was he comforting her? He didn't care about her or her child. He was simply easing his own guilt over making them homeless.

With a bout of resolve, she wiped her eyes with the back of her hand, pushing his hand away. "It's okay. You're excused." Her voice wobbled as she lifted her chin to confront him.

His arm lowered, fingers grasping the air like they were unsure of where to go next. "Well, Thanks for having me. And good luck with... everything." He held still, looking at her for a little too long, a little too intensely, as if trying to decide something.

Finally, the turned around and left. Through her tears, she watched him exit through the gate, get behind the wheel of a huge black pickup truck and tear away.

Lilla took her hand. "What is it, mummy?"

Shasa wiped her eyes, trying to calm down. "Just a hard day, baby. But we'll figure it out."

How, she had no idea.

Chapter 2

Shasa stretched out across the bed and turned on her pink vintage nightlight. Lilla snuggled up against her like a heat-seeking missile. The girl accepted her cot for afternoon naps but slept next to Shasa at night. She didn't mind. Without Ollie, she no longer needed privacy. This way, she felt less alone.

Her arms ached. After the real estate agent had left, she'd scrubbed the entire house. She needed to prove to herself that the state of her home had been temporary, that he'd just happened to step in moments before her weekly (okay, monthly) clean. By clearing the tabletops and mopping the laundry room floor, she'd been redeemed. Yet, sleep eluded her. She had to read that email.

Shasa grabbed her phone and brought up the message. It began with well wishes and greetings to Lilla, his little bean. She wondered if Ollie called her that because the last time he'd bonded with his daughter, she'd been the size of a bean. He'd been great during the pregnancy, but once they entered the daily grind of parenthood, his interest waned, and his feet itched.

She kept reading, her heart in free fall. Ollie always wrote eloquently, but his beautiful words couldn't hide his intent. He wasn't coming back. On the ship, he felt like he was finally contributing in a meaningful way. As much as he'd miss Lilla (not her), he needed to do this for the planet, for their future. And he didn't want to stop her from realising her dreams.

Shasa shrank as though someone had sucked the air out of her lungs. Forcing her eyes back on the phone, she read the message again. There was no way around it. He'd already let her go.

She hugged her knees, willing her churning gut to settle. This didn't change anything, right? She'd practically been a single mother for two years, only now it was official. She was officially alone. At college, her parents had split up and returned to their respective home countries, Finland and South Africa, while she remained in New Zealand. They stayed in touch over Skype but visited infrequently. Ollie's parents live in the South Island, too far to be of any help.

She looked at her wrists, covered in colorful, woven bracelets. Some were from second-hand shops; others Ollie had given her during his brief visits. She'd worn them proudly, happy for the way they brightened her wardrobe and connected her to him and his causes. Just like the dreadlocks. Hers were dark to Ollie's dirty blond, but they matched, signaling to the world that they belonged together.

She sat up on the bed, running her fingers through the thick, woolly strands. That was it. If he let go of her, she'd let go of the hair.

It was a petty thought, but it gave her a sense of control. She tiptoed into the kitchen, looking for scissors. The dreads were overgrown, so she didn't have to do a close shave, only snip them off one by one. It would look terrible, but she could get someone to tidy it up later. Until then, she'd wear a scarf or something.

After twenty minutes of frantic scissor work, she had a sink full of matted hair and the most awkward pixie cut ever seen. She looked in the mirror, picturing the horror on Ollie's face. She'd always fallen short of his standards – veganism, plastic-free life, exclusive breastfeeding... The chopped off hair was the perfect cherry on top of her half-hearted efforts. It made her look exactly how she felt – someone who didn't fit in anywhere.

She scooped the loose hair into a paper bag, wondering how to dispose of it. She'd heard it could be used to clean up oil spills, but how? Maybe she could compost it. Without

Ollie, did she still care about the planet? Would she abandon the compost bin? Buy a packet of plastic spoons?

That was the truly hard part. She agreed with most of what Ollie said: Recycling made sense. Helping the less fortunate was important. It was part of her job, too. As much as she hated Ollie right now, she couldn't align herself with the greedy, self-serving people like that Mac-something, who bought and sold properties for maximum profit, never mind the tenants. After all, she had a conscience. She hadn't lopped it off with the dreadlocks.

As she returned to the bedroom, she marveled at how light and cool her head felt. Sliding under the covers, she snuggled against Lilla's warm back, taking solace in her soft breathing. She would find her own way, a way of doing the right thing without Ollie's nagging voice in her ear. She didn't need him. She didn't need a man at all. Men couldn't be trusted – as fathers or anything else.

She wrapped her arm around her daughter and imagined them lying on a floating raft in the middle of the ocean with no land in sight. Ollie had thrown them overboard, and they needed to find land. A place to anchor.

Chapter 3

Mac stepped into the busy cafe on Victoria Street and ordered two drinks – a flat white for himself and a short black for his friend and business partner, Rick, who was running late. He suspected that Rick's perpetual tardiness was part sloppiness and part power play, but he didn't care. He would have happily waited for hours.

Three years ago, Rick had let him in on a property deal that made a year's wages in a couple of months. Mac still remembered the thrill of it, the realisation that he no longer had to survive on a property manager's salary. He could invest and grow his wealth, like Rick. Despite what his parents had always told him, money wasn't evil; it made things possible. If he ever wanted to do something good on a larger scale, he needed money. He hadn't quite got to the doing-good part yet, but it was only a matter of time. He wasn't the bad guy, and he wouldn't let the big, fat tears running down that beautiful face tell him otherwise.

He huffed, trying to shake the frustration. He hadn't been bothered by thoughts like these in months, happily working on lucrative property deals. Having to defend his morals to a woman whose rundown house brimmed with dirty laundry… how had she managed to get under his skin? He knew her type, but there'd been something about her… something had given him pause and forced him to pay attention, allowing her words to slip through the cracks and make a home in his mind. Did he only care about money? Had that become his number one goal or was he still working towards a better world?

He shouldn't have touched her. The memory of the warm, smooth skin of her shoulder still made his fingertips tingle. He'd expected her to react in anger, but she hadn't. Not right away. She had every reason to hate him, but she'd allowed that moment of contact, and the way his body reacted scared him. He would have stood there forever. Some primal part of him wanted to save her. And he couldn't. He couldn't think like that.

Mac sat down on an aluminum chair and balanced three folders, a phone, and a laptop on the wobbly table. Despite the hot sun, summer was almost over, and they were running late finishing the drawings for buildings that had to be weather-tight before the rain started pouring. Every cloudless day pushing papers was a wasted construction day.

Rick arrived as their drinks were served, lifting his designer sunglasses on his forehead. “How’s my prodigy?” He grinned, sitting down and picking up his coffee. “Are we making progress?”

“We are.” Mac opened the top folder and handed over a pile of smudgy scans he’d obtained from the council. “Everything looks good. It’s freehold. We can build one point five metres from the boundary, two levels up. The soil has never been tested, but there shouldn’t be any issues.”

Rick lowered his voice. “And the owner?”

“He’s on board, we should settle quickly. But I don’t want to push it, he might get suspicious.”

“Of what?” Rick raised his brow in mock innocence. “We’re saving him agent fees and a lot of the trouble.”

“Yeah, I meant... never mind.” Mac slid the papers back in the folder and smiled.

It wasn’t shady. They’d offered a decent price, on par with what a first-home buyer would have been able to pay. But if the vendor knew what he stood to make, he’d feel duped. This project was a license to print money – something Mac desperately needed after a fiasco involving a leaky townhouse. He’d learned his lesson and wouldn’t make the same mistake twice; he wouldn’t touch an old house with a ten-foot pole. It was far safer, not to mention more profitable, to build new with reputable companies.

"How's it going on the ranch?"

Rick rolled his eyes. "Missus wants to get chickens."

Rick's family lived on a vast lifestyle property right outside of town.

"And ... you don't want chickens?"

"They destroy the lawn and we're hosting the balloon this year. Every man and their dog will be there. I don't want the place full of chicken shit."

Rick's company sponsored Hamilton's annual Hot-air Balloon Festival, the highlight of the year for local families –and even more so for Mac. Rick made fun of his passion, but he didn't care.

Mac flashed a cheeky smile. "If I get my own balloon, can I park it at your house too?"

"You'll have your own land by then. And a family."

He forced a laugh. It's not that he didn't want a family, but women were high maintenance. The last one had exhausted him. Charlotte had been on a mission to perfect his appearance, his home, and his social standing. There had been a lot of shopping. A lot of donating. They had to be seen at every event, wearing the right labels, dropping tasteful hints of his success. Every room they entered, she'd sized up the competition and socialized like it was a sport. She'd insisted she was looking out for him, but he didn't want a never-ending makeover. He didn't need help throwing out old towels. He still missed the well-worn terry ones she'd given away, far more than he missed her.

Rick's wife was great, but even she expected diamonds a couple of times a year. Mac sighed. It must have been his upbringing, having a mother who never expected more than a hand-drawn card from her children, or her husband. There was something sweet about that, something he wanted for his family. If that wasn't available, he'd gladly stay away from commitment.

"The kids must be excited about the balloon," he said, hoping to steer the conversation back to Rick.

"You have no idea."

He'd met the nippers, but still found it hard to imagine Rick with children. He never had ketchup stains on his clothes.

Rick finished his coffee with one gulp, stood up, and grabbed the folder off the table. "Cheers. I'll look it over and let you know if I notice anything. But I think it's solid. This'll get you into the big leagues."

Mac swallowed. "I got lucky."

Rick shook his head. "Luck is when preparation meets opportunity."

He wished he could have sounded as confident, but he had too much riding on this. Sleep at night was becoming elusive.

Rick gave him a long look. "You haven't spoken to anyone about this, right?"

"Of course not."

After Rick left, Mac thought about the tenant. She wasn't worth mentioning. Her biggest concern was finding another rental, and he knew why. He'd checked with the vendor and found out she was paying well below market rent. If that was all she could afford, her options were slim. It was a shame, but he couldn't get sentimental about her or her daughter. He had to look at the big picture. If he made this work, in a couple of years, he could achieve something far better than helping one tenant. That was the plan, anyway.

She was so cute though, even with those dreadlocks. He hadn't been able to stop staring at her huge, brown eyes... and to be honest, he'd stolen a few glances at the nipples poking under the threadbare tank top. He'd happily ignored the clothing in favour of imagining what was underneath, so much so that he'd nearly missed her words. And she'd been talking some crazy stuff.

What kind of tenant got that attached to their garden? Why on earth had she put in so much effort to raise the value of someone else's investment? He shook his head, looking across the cafe table at the busy downtown street. Maybe she didn't think about those things, not like he did.

Still, the little girl had been adorable. For her sake, he hoped they found a decent new home.

Chapter 4

"We'll figure it out."

Shasa smiled with gratitude as Marnie, her best friend and colleague, slid a steaming cup of tea across the desk. Her soothing voice mixed with the scent of peppermint and the unventilated air of the community house, creating the perfect cocktail of comfort. Familiarity. Things that remained.

They kept their voices down so they wouldn't disturb the ladies' Pilates class they were observing through an open doorway. The class was targeted at new mums and seemed to focus on breathing in and out.

Marnie sipped her coffee, a distracted look on her face.

Shasa could tell she was listening to the instructions, breathing out and squeezing her pelvic floor, as the instructor's serene voice told them to imagine sucking a blueberry up in their vaginas.

Shasa's cheeks blazed as she remembered her dream. Both blueberries and lady parts had been involved, but in a very different capacity. She'd been behind the blueberry bush, in the dead of night, approached by a man with brown eyes and dark hair. If she closed her eyes, she could still feel his hand resting on her shoulder, then moving down, his other hand joining in, firing up her skin, peeling off her clothes one by one. He'd pulled her flush against him, to straddle an erection that made her gasp from pure anticipation. Everything was so simple in dreams, subtext written across the night sky as she surrendered to the dark stranger, no questions asked. Grass didn't tickle her back. Wind didn't chill her skin. There was only arousal. A beautiful, overwhelming sensation that built up until she shuddered in his arms.

It wasn't the real estate guy, she told herself as she woke up with her heart racing. She'd just been alone for too long, and his brief touch had reminded her body of that.

"You look a million miles away." Marnie's voice brought her back to present.

Taking a deep breath, Shasa adjusted the headscarf that concealed her homemade haircut. The late summer heat made it far too hot for a scarf.

"Just... thinking of the blueberries. It's such a shame," she said, trying to neutralize her expression.

"I know, sweetie." Marnie rubbed her back.

She was one of the best people she knew. Despite being only six years older than Shasa, she'd once been mistaken for her mother, maybe because she dressed in long tunics and orthopaedic shoes. Or it could have been the drop earrings that often got tangled in her chestnut perm. Shasa didn't mind her style. Their friendship made the poorly paid work a million times better.

She stirred her tea. "I think they're a couple of weeks away from finalising the sale, so I hope we have more than forty-two days to find a new rental."

"It'll be more than that! Those things always take time," Marnie reassured, reaching for a muffin.

Shasa sighed. "I just thought next time we'd move into our own place, not another rental. I've saved everything Ollie sent us. We've been lucky to have such low rent, most people can't save anything. But it was such a pipe dream."

Marnie straightened up. "Are you sure? With the interest rates still low..."

"Prices have gone up faster than my savings. And my pay is too low for the banks."

Marnie carefully removed a white chocolate chunk before taking a bite of the muffin. "What about that cohousing thing?"

A month ago, they'd hosted the chief architect of a

cohousing community in Auckland. She'd shown countless slides of the building process and the finished village with its community garden and rammed earth houses. They were beautiful and solid, a far cry from the standard new builds in Hamilton.

A wistful sigh escaped Shasa's mouth. "It looked amazing, but did you hear how long it took?"

"Eight years? But..." Marnie lowered her voice, "I reckon it was because they couldn't agree on anything. They came up with that colored card system just to manage people talking at meetings. Our parliament's more agreeable than that lot."

Shasa chuckled. The cohousing community mirrored the mix of characters they saw at the community house. Some were all about the environment, others protected cultural heritage, followed religious or dietary rules, or complained about the cost of anything that wasn't free. Wrangling them to do the smallest thing together took a lot of patience.

"It's human nature," she said. "If you have thirty people all putting in their life savings, it gets complicated."

Marnie threw up her hands, nearly knocking over her mug. "That's it! Scale it right back! You don't have to do it with thirty people. Do it with... I don't know... five? You can still get a larger piece of land and design the space the way you want. It's much easier to get five people to agree on things."

"True." A flicker of hope woke up in the pit of Shasa's stomach. Was it possible? Could she get some people together to buy and build something?

Marnie beamed. "You already have one."

"One what?"

"One person who agrees with you and thinks you'd be the perfect project lead. And who'd happily move into one of the houses to get away from a certain ex-mother-in-law."

Marnie's divorce had left her in the family home with her two teenagers. The downside? Her ex-mother-in-law lived right next door. Not by accident. They'd bought the neighbouring property, hoping to get regular babysitting help. Instead, the demented grandmother of her children now wandered over daily, firmly believing Marnie and Steve were still married. Steve didn't want his mother in a nursing home, but he had the luxury of living in another town with his new girlfriend.

Marnie sighed. "I'd move right in! Since Tom's in college, I'm thinking of downsizing. Tanya and I can fit in a two-beddie, easy! Even if we built some smaller townhouses, I'd be keen."

"Seriously? If we built like ... four or five apartments and leave space for a shared garden?"

"Totally! I was going to put the house on the market and was looking at those new townhouses in Greenhill Park, but honestly, I can't afford anything in there. This could be my chance, too! I'm sick of that old house, it's falling apart and Steve's not there to do any maintenance. I hate it."

Shasa's heart leapt as she considered the possibility.

Marnie tilted her head, catching her earring on her linen

tunic, pulling loops out of the stitching. "Just promise me I won't have to raise a blue card to make a suggestion."

Shasa rolled her eyes. "Or a red one for a toilet break?"

They laughed, and a smile lingered on Shasa's lips. It felt nice to dream about something, even if it was completely unattainable.

"Would any bank touch it?"

"Why not?" Marnie shrugged. "They funded those mud houses in Auckland."

"Rammed earth houses," Shasa corrected, suppressing a giggle. "Remember the spreadsheets, though! They had those complicated calculations, I mean budgets... that's not my strong suit." Her shoulders dropped.

"I can help with that. Plus, we can let the builders and the bank worry about the numbers. That's their job."

Shasa loosened her headscarf to let in some air. "Okay."

Marnie rested her hand on Shasa's arm. "Promise me, you'll think about this. It'd be so good for your family to finally get out of renting."

Shasa's family. Tears sprung to her eyes without warning. She'd been doing so well, pushing the thoughts of Ollie to the back of her mind to focus on work.

Marnie frowned. "What is it?"

Shasa fidgeted in her seat. Marnie could see right through her. She had to tell her. "Ollie. He's not coming back. He's signing another contract, for another year."

"And..."

How did Marnie know there was an 'and'? Shasa inhaled a lungful of warm, stuffy air. "He's breaking up with me."

"Oh, girl!" Marnie pulled Shasa into a side hug. "I knew there was something else to this new haircut."

Shasa offered a weak smile. "I meant what I said. I am tired of maintaining it. But yeah, when I read that email... he couldn't even tell me face to face, he's just starting another contract."

"Is there someone else? Another activist?" Marnie spat out the word 'activist' like they were talking about child molesters.

"He didn't say anything. I hate the way he worded that email, though, like he was being charitable, thinking of what's best for me. He said he wants to 'release me' to live my life in total freedom with whoever I wish."

Marnie's expression shifted. "Okay. So, he's already embracing his total freedom with someone."

Shasa winced. It made sense. Why hadn't she thought of that? She finished her tea and got up. "Lucky me, I'll have something else to focus on. I get to worry about becoming homeless."

"Oh, shush now! If you run out of time, you can always move in with me."

"Thank you."

As much as she loved her friend, the thought horrified her. Marnie's kids were older, well past the daily tantrums and sticky fingerprints. She'd done the work and deserved her peace.

Marnie picked up her cup and the plate of muffins and followed Shasa to the staff kitchen. Afternoon sun streamed through the small window above the sink, heating anything it touched. She stopped at the window, staring into the distance. Shasa recognized her plotting face; she'd seen it many times before. Marnie wrote romance novels set in faraway locations. To escape, she said, and to replace her ailing marriage with an imaginary love life. No dating, no heartbreaks. An example Shasa was tempted to follow, if she could write.

Marnie rinsed their cups and began stacking the tray that was waiting to go into the industrial dishwasher. "Ollie would make a great villain. I mean ... he can be such a prick but thinks he's saving the world. Can I use him in my book, please?"

Shasa shrugged. "Just make sure you include a self-righteous lecture – a page-long monologue about dolphins."

"Will do! You'll have to help me with that, though."

Shasa laughed despite the stab of pain. "I'm not sure I can survive another lecture. If he ever comes for a visit, you should see him. Bring a can of tuna." She chuckled at the thought, wringing a dishcloth over the sink.

"I can finish up here." Marnie nodded at the pile of dishes sitting in the sink. "Leave early, take Lilla out for an ice cream? Maybe get a haircut?"

Shasa smiled, fighting the stubborn tear that tried to

squeeze out of the corner of her eye. Marnie had a way of lightening the mood. Her solutions were often food-based but surprisingly effective. The heat made the thin fabric of her pants stick to her sweaty legs. Ice cream sounded heavenly, and Marnie was right about the haircut. She plucked her canvas bag off the floor and leaned her weight on the swing door, edging out of the kitchen.

Marnie's voice stopped her. "Hey, let's organize a meeting to see if anyone else is interested in the cohousing. Can we do that?"

Shasa exhaled. "Okay. Let's."

At the front door, she bumped into the ladies leaving the Pilates class. Ladies and one middle-aged man, Lando.

"They let me join the ladies' class. I did pelvic floor exercises," he gushed without a hint of embarrassment.

Shasa tried to keep her gaze from dipping too low. Lando had the physique of a racehorse and wore skin tight cycling shorts that left little to imagination. He was one of the community house regulars – an out-of-work landscaper who turned up every day and joined any class they had on offer. She had to admire his attitude.

Lando blew kisses to the giggling women and jogged towards his car. So, he hadn't even ridden a bike today. The shorts must have been purely for the ladies, Shasa thought, and couldn't help smiling. She had to find that spirit, that ice-melting shamelessness to go after whatever called for her.

Shasa thought of the bitter words that had spilled out of her mouth at the real estate agent. Despite his annoying attitude and disagreeable views, he had a point. She'd sounded like a victim, and it didn't sit right with her. She was a doer, someone who made things happen.

If she attempted this cohousing thing, where would it lead? Would someone eventually stop her? A current of fear and excitement travelled up her spine, making her shiver. Shasa crossed the parking lot, feeling a new sense of purpose. This is what she needed. Action. Something that she was in charge of.

Chapter 5

Elsie Joyce took one last look in the mirror and adjusted her Lululemon top. At sixty-two, she needed her daily walk around Hamilton Lake to keep her spirits up and her figure slim. Her dachshund, Stina, needed it too. The old girl had a healthy appetite and a pot belly that hung dangerously close to the ground.

Snapping a lead on Stina's collar, Elsie made her way across the manicured front yard and through her cast iron gate. Behind a row of pitched roofs, the lake glistened in the distance. She'd chosen the building site for its position, perched on top of a hill, the highest point overlooking the lake. It was her universe, the crux of her new independence, decorated exactly to her liking. After the divorce, they'd sold the sprawling lifestyle property on the outskirts of town. After decades of pleasing her husband, she was finally free to choose for herself.

Stina pulled her towards the lakeside path. It was Saturday, and the playground was packed. The recently opened outdoor gym attracted youths and fitness junkies. Elsie studied the two girls spinning on a carousel, so happy and carefree. Yet, she couldn't enjoy their smiles, not with the cloud of regret hovering over her. She was a childless woman – not by choice. As much as the thought still stung, she'd also been saved from a lot of heartache. Her sister had lost a child in a driveway accident. Elsie would never experience that pain. Nor would she ever know what it was like to love someone that much.

It is what it is, Elsie told herself firmly. That's what the therapist had said.

It is what it is.

So simple, so underwhelming, but in the end the thought comforted her. She had to let go of things she couldn't change. The horrible thing about the divorce at her age was the space it created for introspection. For so long, she'd been consumed by Jeff, his business ventures, his goals, his legal battles. Without Jeff's drama, she had to look at her own life. What did she want to do? Who did she want to be? It was terrifying.

Elsie picked up speed, and Stina complied, her belly

wobbling from side to side. Pounding the pavement always helped. She could almost outrun the darkness. A bead of sweat trickled between her shoulder blades. The morning was gorgeous.

She'd find a direction. She could get into volunteer work and be remembered for fighting for her own causes, not as the discarded ex-wife of property guru Jeffrey Alders.

Elsie's thoughts were cut off by a flash of green, followed by a screeching sound. Within seconds, she hit the asphalt and tasted blood. White papers floated around her like giant, square snowflakes.

It took her several seconds to put together the chain of events. The green flash had been a speeding Lime scooter. The papers belonged to a young woman with a man's haircut, who was taping notices onto the brick feature wall. She must have also been on the scooter's path, but remained standing.

The young woman helped Elsie up. "Are you okay?"

Elsie brushed her clothes, embarrassment running through her veins. Had anyone seen that? There were no other people in close vicinity, thank God.

Where was Stina?

The lead was still in her hand and the dog seemed fine, moving about her feet. Her face hurt. Had she hit it against the ground?

The young woman looked at her with a strange expression, as if searching for words.

"What is it?" Elsie demanded.

The woman rummaged through a purse that looked like Middle Eastern camel saddlebag and pulled out a packet of tissues. "Here. You're ... bleeding."

Elsie accepted the tissues. The packet was opened, but they seemed unused. A mirror. Was there a mirror somewhere?

As if reading her mind, the woman handed her a scratched-up powder container. The 'vegan makeup' advertised on the cover was all but gone, but Elsie wiped the mirror with a tissue and peered in.

"Oh, my God." The side of her cheek was bleeding. She dabbed the blood with a tissue, revealing a long graze along the left side.

The young woman studied her with concern. "I think he hit you with the scooter handlebar. He should've stopped. But he was under-aged, maybe twelve. They're not allowed on Lime scooters, so they're scared to get caught riding."

Was this woman making excuses for the rascal who ran her over? Elsie huffed in disdain and handed back the sorry excuse for makeup. She exhaled and turned around, ready to return home. She needed a bath and a strong cup of tea.

Elsie pulled on Stina's lead, but found her dog out on the lawn, enjoying enthusiastic attention from a young girl with dark ringlets.

The young woman, who she detected was the mother, urged her child to say goodbye to the dog. "Lilla, sweetie, let's go. You can help mummy hang these posters."

Elsie wondered how she'd missed the child. How lucky she hadn't been in the path of the wretched scooter.

"I love you, cute doggy," the girl gushed, trying to give Stina an awkward hug.

Elsie had to admire her dog's patience, not the least bit bothered by the smothering display of affection.

The young woman picked up the last one of her discarded papers, sliding them in her bag. She wore a pair of yellow parachute pants and countless bracelets. She must be one of those alternative types, the kind that believed in vibrations and burned incense in every room. Elsie eyed the little girl's outfit – pink, purple, yellow and green, like a walking rainbow.

The young woman smiled and handed her one of the papers. "I work at the nearby community house. We're putting up flyers about this cohousing meet up. It's early days, we're just gauging interest."

Maybe it was the recent hit in the head or the pang of affection for the little girl hugging her dog, but Elsie didn't do her usual gracious hand wave, the one she used to stop the fundraisers and campaigners in their tracks.

Instead, she stared at the flyer. She could easily afford to live on her own. In all honestly, she could afford several houses, but couldn't be bothered with property investment, the field her ex-husband dominated, so she'd put most of her money in conservative funds. Yet here she was, reading a home-printed flyer on cohousing. The absurdity of the situation almost teased a laugh out of her.

The young woman, encouraged by the smile she misinterpreted as interest, spoke with enthusiasm. "It's such a great idea, building houses to serve the community rather than the other way around. Have you ever thought about how the property developers get to decide everything? They aren't the ones living in those houses, but they make all the calls. What if I don't want a double garage? What if I want a community garden, instead?"

Elsie gave her a level gaze. "Developers make decisions based on what sells, what the buyers want." That was exactly what Jeff would have said, she thought with a shiver. Had she any thoughts of her own?

The girl flicked a short strand of hair away from her eyes. "How would they know? If the only type of house available is the one with a double garage, surrounded by a two-metre fence, that's what people buy. I never thought there could be a better way until I heard about this village in Auckland—"

"Okay, okay." Elsie waved her hand to shut down the sales pitch. "I appreciate your enthusiasm, it sounds lovely. But I have my own home, which I've designed to my liking. I suppose I'm lucky to be that comfortable." She tried to sound gracious, but her throbbing face made smiling difficult.

The young woman's face lit up. "That's great. You don't happen to know anything about property development? We could really use someone with expertise."

The throwaway comment carried such underlying exasperation that Elsie felt a tug at her heart. Hadn't she just thought about volunteering? She did have expertise, and she had to admit, the idea of helping others by sharing her knowledge was rather appealing.

"I was in the property business for two decades, with my ex-husband."

The young woman's eyes widened as she took in her tentative admission. "Wow! You'd be a treasure trove to us. Would you please consider coming along, even once? We have so many questions..."

Elsie carefully folded the piece of paper. "I'll think about it."

Ten minutes later, as she opened the door to her empty house, she'd made up her mind. She would join this meeting. If it worked out, she could end up doing something worthwhile, something memorable. This could be her legacy, advising young people on how to get onto the property ladder. She wouldn't be a rich, old divorcee, wasting long days with a book and a glass of wine. She'd achieve something.

Chapter 6

Mac winced as the loose gravel on his parents' driveway peppered the bottom of his ute. Nothing ever changed around here. His family tolerated things. They were experts at it, patient like saints, prone to enduring and mending rather than changing and rebuilding. Mac was convinced he didn't take after either of them.

Despite the less-than-ideal entrance, he still enjoyed visiting his parents on Sundays. The scent of lamb roast wafted from the house, drawing him closer. As he reached the door, two neighbourhood kids caught up with him.

"Tawhiri! Manaia! What up?" He high fived the boys and let them in ahead of him.

His mother had a reputation for feeding half the street, and Mac never quite understood how she managed to do so on his father's modest pension from pastoring a small church.

"Mac!" Mum greeted him with a hug, holding a spatula covered in chocolate cake batter.

Mac made a mental note to check his shirt for stains. Stepping over the threshold, he noted the threadbare flowery carpet and yellowing wallpaper that gave the dining room and lounge a time-capsule vibe. Had it always been this bad? Well, good thing he had a plan.

The table was set for ten. Despite having two children, his parents always managed to fill the seats. After Tawhiri and Manaia were seated, four more kids showed up.

Mac's younger brother Isaiah had cancelled hours earlier, claiming he was stuck in the edit suite. The edit suite being the basement flat he never left, and stuck being his general state of mind. Their mother was probably the last person still inviting Izzy to social gatherings. Others had given up a long time ago.

Mac could have made up an excuse, too, but this time, he had an agenda. So, he'd typed an enthusiastic response in the family Facebook chat, letting Izzy off the hook.

As everyone took their seats, his dad entered the room. "If it isn't the prodigal son!" He peeled off a pair of greasy gloves, grinning.

He must have been working on the car. In his retirement,

Dad had become a self-taught mechanic, although he never seemed to fully fix the car, which kept breaking down. It was a 90s Volkswagen, so the issue was likely more with the car than his skills.

"What's wrong with it now?" Mac asked, narrowing his eyes.

"The fuel gauge stopped working. Left me on the road this week, had to call AA. The tank might have a dent in it."

"You ran out of petrol?"

"Well, yes. I thought I had heaps, but the needle had stopped moving."

"He thought God was making the same petrol go longer," Mum chimed in, her eyes wide with amusement as she carried a tray of roasted potatoes and carrots to the table.

"But he wasn't?" Mac asked in mock horror, sitting down.

Dad rolled his eyes. "I think he was teaching me about the importance of renewing my AA membership. And now I get to learn about petrol tanks."

"Exciting." Mac had to laugh.

Fortunately, his father didn't take himself too seriously.

Mum took her seat, reaching for his hand. After a long-winded freestyle prayer that mentioned each child and their families by name, she opened her eyes at Mac. He mouthed 'Amen', making sure she noticed.

After the meal, Mac took his plate to the kitchen, timing his exit so that he ended up alone with his mother who was taking a chocolate mud cake out of the oven. "Mum, I need to talk to you about something."

She left the cake to cool and followed him out the back door.

"Did you hear about those neighbours in Auckland teaming up, selling their properties together, and making a huge profit?"

Mum cocked her head. "I saw it in the paper. Can't see why anyone would pay that much, but Auckland's a bit crazy, isn't it?"

"It makes sense for developers. Trust me. If you can combine the sections and put fifteen apartments on them, you make it back quickly. Those homeowners thought they were getting a good deal, but the developers are the ones winning big."

His mum made a non-committal sound.

"Mum, listen. Your neighbour's house is going on the market. I'm talking to the owner, and he's interested in selling together with you."

Mum's eyes widened. "But this street is our—"

"Mission field? I know. That's the best part! You wouldn't have to move away. You could move into one of the new townhouses, right here! I'd make sure you get a good deal and the best views. You'd still be here, but in a house that's new and healthy to live in!"

He saw a flicker of interest in her eyes and pressed on. "Wouldn't it be nice to wake up in the winter without seeing your breath? Not having to constantly bleach the bathroom walls and curtains? You wear a beanie to bed!"

"I'm more sensitive to the cold than your father. It's a genetic thing..."

"No! It's a sign of poor housing!" Mac tried to hold back his anger, but he hated the defeatist attitude of fellow Kiwis, explaining away living conditions that wouldn't have been acceptable anywhere else in the developed world.

Mum patted his arm. "I hear you. Thanks for thinking of us, but where would we live while you're building the new houses? And what would happen to the garden?"

What was so magical about gardens?

Mac swallowed his frustration. "I'll organize a short-term rental for you. And part of the garden would need to be redone, but it'll grow again."

"Which neighbour's selling? The apartments?" Mum's voice rose in concern as she looked at the rundown apartment block where some of her beloved neighbourhood kids lived.

"No, not that one. The other side." He led them closer to the fence, up the gentle slope. "If we build on two levels, you'll have lake views! Joining these sections will open a big, beautiful yard. It'll look much better than ... this."

Through a gap in the ramshackle fence, Mac saw a slice of the blueberry bush the feisty tenant had protected so fiercely. His mind wandered back to her, conjuring a vivid image of those fiery eyes framed by dark lashes. Beautiful eyes. And a beautiful body, his dirty mind added, distractingly well on display. If he had to be accosted, which in his line of work was inevitable, he wished it always came with a see-through tank top. He'd tried to be subtle about it, but considering how vividly he remembered every detail, he must have leered at her with his tongue hanging out.

Mum joined him at the fence and peered through it. "Look at that blueberry bush! It's grown so much!" She turned to him. "What's going to happen to Shasa and Lilla?"

Mac started. He wasn't surprised that Mum knew the feisty girl and her daughter, but he'd assumed that lifestyle or political differences might have kept them from getting too close. She'd commented on the 'dreadlock-couple and their poor child' when they'd first moved in, but she'd never mentioned them since. Based on his ill-fated visit earlier that week, it seemed the woman was now sans a partner.

"They're tenants, they'll move to another rental."

"What about her blueberries? It's a shame, such a beautiful bush. She shared some with us last summer. That's when I learnt her name. Shasa. Such an odd name, isn't it? But she's a lovely girl."

"Hello!" A high-pitched voice startled them both.

The little girl had wedged her head in the narrow gap in the fence, eager to get their attention.

Mum gasped. "Oh dear, Lilla! Don't do that, you'll get stuck!"

Too late.

Lilla's face flashed with panic as she tried to move her

head. “I’m stuck!”

Mac tried to wiggle her head free, but her ears were already on their side and going backward would have caused her pain, so he worked as gently as he could, helping her through the gap onto his parents’ backyard. Her hair stuck out at the back, and she wore another unicorn shirt, this one purple. She didn’t cry but looked rather spooked.

“Silly girl! What did you do that for?” Mum combed the girl’s dark curls with her fingers.

Mac pointed at her shirt. “You really like unicorns, don’t you?”

The girl nodded in earnest and pointed at the gap in the fence. “Can you push me on the swing?”

Mac laughed. “Sweetie, we’re not going to fit through there. And it seems neither can you. Let’s go back through the gate, shall we?”

He led them toward the front yard.

Mum halted, gesturing at their house. “You go ahead. I have to serve the dessert!”

Lilla turned around, her eyes giant blue saucers. “Dessert?”

Mum glanced at Mac, then at the neighbour’s house. “Ask her mum if she can join us, will you?”

He nodded, biting his lip. The thought of going back to the tenant’s door made his skin prickle. He filled his lungs with warm, thick summer air and let the little girl pull him along the footpath towards the run-down villa she called home.

Chapter 7

Shasa lifted a tray of muffins out of the oven, inhaling the sweet aroma. She planned to put them in the freezer until Tuesday night for the cohousing meeting. They hadn't advertised catering, but now that she had invited the fancy lady, she felt like she had to make an effort. Covering the muffins with a tea towel to keep the flies away, she glanced out of the window to check if Lilla was still on the swing.

The backyard was empty, the swing still.

She dropped her oven mitts and ran outside, urging herself to stay calm. Her girl was in the fenced backyard she knew inside out – a safe environment they'd likely have to exchange for unfamiliar hazards of a new rental. The painful thought squeezed her chest as she meticulously checked each of Lilla's usual hiding spots.

But there was no sign of her. Her daughter had vanished.

A distant knock made her freeze. It came from the house. Was someone at the door? Lilla couldn't possibly have reached that side of the house – she couldn't scale a six-foot fence. Shasa ran through the gate into the front yard.

The sight knocked the wind out of her. Lilla stood at the front door, holding hands with the smarmy real estate agent and the star of her sex dreams, Mac.

He flashed his pearly whites and waved like they were old buddies. "Hi! I found your daughter."

"Mum! Can I have dessert? Please!" Lilla skipped down the steps and yanked at her sleeve.

She ignored her. "Mac? What are you doing here? Where did you find her?"

"She got through a gap in the fence."

Lilla jumped up and down, pointing at the neighbour's house. "Mum! Dessert! Can I go?"

Shasa tried to make sense of the situation. At least her daughter was safe, if a bit hyper.

"Mac, tell her!" Lilla demanded. "Dessert." She folded her arms, expectant.

She raised her brows at Mac. He shifted his weight. "Erm... my mum's serving dessert to the neighbourhood kids. She thought Lilla might want to join?"

Her mouth fell open as she put two and two together. Her

elderly neighbours were Mac's parents! "Your mum?"

Mac flushed. "Yes, my parents live next door."

Shasa's pulse picked up. This was more than a little coincidental. "Does this have something to do with the property valuation?"

A hint of alarm crossed Mac's face before he regained his composure. "Of course not."

"So, how did you meet my landlord? By coincidence?"

Mac shrugged. "Clients find us through many channels. We have a website, email, a phone..."

She studied his face for any further clues but came up with nothing. He must have been taught slippery sliminess at the real estate academy – or wherever they trained these guys.

"Dessert!" Lilla's voice hit a new pitch.

"Okay, let's go then." Shasa took her daughter's hand.

She heard Mac's footsteps behind them. He'd probably expected her to say no, but she couldn't back down. There was something fishy going on with this property deal, and her curiosity grew with every step.

Besides, he'd invited her daughter, and she couldn't let a three-year-old run off to the neighbours' by herself.

As Shasa made it across the footpath, she felt a fizzle of anticipation. Oh, the sweet distraction, how she needed it! Anything to take her mind off Ollie. She'd eventually replied to him with a short, polite, cryptic email she knew would drive him crazy. It was only fair. If he didn't have the balls to come home and talk to her face to face, she didn't have to engage. Besides, if they got into an argument, even via email, it would prove what Ollie claimed to be true – that they were a terrible match and couldn't live under the same roof. Ultimately, that would soothe his conscience, and she wasn't going to give him that. He could live in his happy ship bubble with his new ship girlfriend, but she wanted him to know that he'd abandoned his family.

It was vindictive of her, and not entirely true. She knew, deep down, that Ollie and she were mismatched. She'd never been a true activist like him. He'd been the one doing research late at night, pulling her into his orbit. While she agreed with him, on principle, she'd never had the capacity to maintain outrage over what was happening on the other side of the world, or to other species. Her world had always been smaller and focused on her own family.

Lilla sprinted through the open doorway to the neighbour's sixties brick house. Neither of them had ever been inside, but Lilla took her place at the long dining table without hesitation, joining four other kids already licking their plates.

Shasa halted at the doorway. After a moment, Mac caught up with her. Every hair on her arms stood up as she felt the heat of his body. Why wasn't he moving past her? Why was he standing so close?

Mac's mother appeared from the kitchen, smiling brightly in a colorful apron that featured native plants. She placed a piece of chocolate mud cake on the table. "Here you go,

Lilla."

She noticed Shasa and Mac at the doorway. "Oh, hi! Come on in! We've met before, haven't we? I'm Sue." She shook Shasa's hand. "It's always great to meet the parents. I like your new hair!"

Shasa nodded, instinctively brushing her fringe. A visit to the hairdresser had improved it, but she wasn't used to it yet. She glanced at Mac and caught him staring at her.

"What?" she asked, suddenly self-conscious.

"Nothing. It looks great." He gave her a genuine smile that made her even more nervous.

She settled by the doorway, waiting for Lilla to finish eating.

"Would you like some?" Sue asked, lifting another plate of mud cake. "Plenty to go around."

Shasa shook her head and tried to smile.

"I'll have it." Mac gently touched her shoulders, moving her to the side to get past. He grabbed the plate and took a seat at the table, right next to Lilla.

Shasa tried to hide the full-body shiver his passing touch had ignited. It was her own fault. She'd been partly blocking the doorway. But still. Did he have to do that? Wouldn't one hand be enough to move someone her size out of the way?

"Yummy, eh?" he grinned at the girl.

Her mouth full, Lilla nodded with the largest range of motion her neck allowed. They looked so cozy together, like old friends.

During the last video chat with Ollie, Lilla had wandered away after a couple of minutes. Then again, she couldn't expect a three-year-old to engage with a two-dimensional person on a computer screen. They hadn't had any three-dimensional males around, not since Ollie's last visit three months ago, which had lasted three days. Enough to remind Lilla of his existence, but not enough to close the distance. This real estate jerk was the first man her daughter had connected with in months. Her chest tightened at the thought.

Shasa was starting to feel weird standing at the doorway, so she joined them at the table, gingerly lowering into the one available chair next to Mac.

Sue came back from the kitchen as the kids started getting up. "I'll take care of the plates, don't worry. Go play!"

Lilla's head whipped from side to side as she watched her newly discovered friends run out the door. Shasa could tell she wanted to follow them but didn't want to leave her dessert.

"How about I push you on the swing after?" Mac suggested, then looked up at Shasa as if he'd just remembered the child was tethered to an adult. He flashed her a charming smile. "If that's okay with your mum?"

Shasa stared back in confusion. "Are you sure you don't have anything more important to do?"

"No. I'm enjoying a Sunday lunch at my parents' place."

He seemed infuriatingly relaxed, leaning against the table

as he shovelled mud cake into his mouth. His fitted T-shirt exposed muscular arms. Without a tie, he seemed more relatable, like someone she could almost be friends with.

"Don't real estate agents work all weekend? Gotta get your commissions and so on? It's a dog-eat-dog world, right?" She punctuated her words him a cheeky smile, wondering if she could ever get under his skin.

It'd only be fair. In such a short time, he'd managed to mess up her whole life and infiltrate her dreams. She hated that she couldn't tear her eyes off his arms. They made her all wobbly inside, reawakening something she needed to keep buried.

Mac licked his spoon, studying her face. "Okay. I can tell you have issues with real estate agents, but maybe you should take up those issues with, you know, real estate agents. Not me."

Shasa frowned. She thought back to their first meeting. He'd worn a tie with those colors, and that pen with a logo. What was it? "Harcourts! You work for Hartcourts!"

Mac looked dumbstruck. "Never worked for them in my life."

"No, seriously. You had a pen sticking out of your jacket. I saw the logo. Dark blue and light blue..."

"Like this one?"

Mac unearthed his wallet and pulled out a business card. It was indeed navy blue with light blue stripes, but the company was McCarthy Developments.

"Maybe it's not the most original branding," he admitted. "But we didn't copy Harcourts, not intentionally at least."

Her cheeks flamed. "So, you're a property developer?"

The corner of his mouth tugged upwards. "I get the feeling you're not a fan of those either?"

She bit her lip, not wanting to start another argument. "I suppose you're a... necessary evil."

He laughed. "Wow, that's... encouraging."

She smiled along, wishing she could swipe the last piece of cake off his plate. "I just think people should have more say on how their living spaces are designed, which materials are used and all that."

Mac looked baffled. "You can always buy a section and design your own house."

"How many people have that option? Houses are so expensive, even the bog-standard ones you guys do."

"How do you know what I do?"

"Well, generally speaking..."

Mac picked up his and Lilla's empty plates and stood up. "I build what sells. You know why it sells? Because people want it."

She stood up as well, though she couldn't match his height. "Want it for themselves, or as investment properties?"

"What difference does it make?"

"When people buy for themselves, there must be a backyard and a nice big deck. If it's for tenants, a tiny patio with nothing green is fine, right?" Anger seeped into her voice.

To her surprise, Mac shrugged his shoulders and smiled. "That's true, I suppose. And it's not always nice to the tenants, like you."

His tender voice diffused her fury, replacing it with an unsettling buzz.

"Can you push me on the swing now?" Lilla piped up, sliding off her chair.

Mac cast Shasa a questioning look, and she nodded, surprised that he still wanted to hang out with them. A small part of her was pleased, although she would have never admitted that to anyone. He was so different from anyone else she knew, like a window to an alien world. She wanted to keep him around, to prod him and poke him, to find out what he'd say next. And keep staring at those arms.

Mac took the plates to the kitchen and joined them at the door. Lilla insisted on holding his hand as they walked through the gate into their backyard. He helped Lilla on the swing and gave her a gentle push.

"Higher!" she yelled.

"I don't want to freak out your mum." Mac glanced at Shasa, his expression far less self-assured than when she'd first seen him right there, measuring their backyard.

She wanted to hate him. He'd waltzed in and upended her whole life. She didn't know what else to feel. Hate felt appropriate. But he was also standing right by the blueberry bush, looking a lot like the man from her dream, resulting in a bewildering mix of emotions that welled like a nauseating soup in the pit of her stomach.

She huffed, her cheeks blazing. "Just make sure she stays in one piece, okay?"

Sunlight filtered through the leaves overhead. The sweet scent of ripening blueberries wafted on the breeze. The crop was going to be amazing. Her last crop.

Shasa thought back to their first meeting, back to when she'd thought of him as a real estate agent. A thought popped up, chilling her blood. "Wait. You're a property developer, but you spoke about the buyer, or a client, or something like that. Who's buying this house?"

Mac averted his eyes. "My company."

"And how many people are in your company?"

"Um ... one. But I have a business partner who's investing."

Her heart thumped in her chest as the realisation took hold. "So, you? You're buying my house to turn it into some tiny flats with no backyards?"

His eyes flashed. "Not tiny! And they will have backyards."

"Whatever! You misled me."

Mac raised his arms in surrender. "I didn't tell you everything because it's none of your business. I told you about the plans because you were so upset about moving. We don't usually discuss these deals with tenants at all."

Shasa's throat tightened. Was she supposed to be grateful? Surely there were plenty of other old properties he could have been ripping up and rebuilding. Maybe even ones that didn't have a blueberry bush. But she knew she didn't factor into the decision-making. Not with him. Not with Ollie. She pressed her lips together, desperately holding back the tears, trying to replace them with anger. She couldn't cry in front of him, again.

Mac stared back, his eyes gently inquisitive. "Does it really matter who's buying the property and building on it?"

"I don't know," she sniffed, hanging her head. "But it gives me someone to blame, I suppose."

"Go ahead. Blame me. But I can't cancel a multi-million-dollar deal because of a blueberry bush."

He gave Lilla another big push on the swing. She squealed in delight.

Shasa could swear the girl had cartoon hearts in her eyes. The soup of emotions in her stomach now boiled like a witch's potion. She stepped closer and lowered her voice, making sure Lilla couldn't hear. "I don't understand what you're doing here. Do you always push little girls on a swing before you make them homeless?"

She shouldn't have stood so close to him. Her arm brushed against his, and she caught his scent. There was a hint of aftershave, but also something else. Something masculine and real that made her skin bristle.

Mac matched her volume, his mouth so close that she felt his breath on her ear. "The way I see it, I'm spending time with my parents' neighbours. Where I grew up, which is literally next door, that's completely normal."

Of course. The neighbour's house was Mac's childhood home. She didn't know how to respond. Maybe she would have if she weren't inhaling his scent, his warm breath tickling her cheek, conjuring flashbacks of the dream. She lived in an all-female household and spent her days at a mostly female workplace. The way her body reacted to him felt mortifying. She needed to bottle that scent and use it daily in smaller doses, to build up a resistance.

"And I'm not making you homeless," Mac continued, with a smile in his gruff voice. "If you get stuck, I have a couple of rentals vacating soon. Unless it's against your principles to accept help from the necessary evil?"

Was he drawing out the words? Her breath quickened as his voice lingered in her ear. Every breath sent a wave of heat down her spine, gathering more warmth down south. Holy crap. She needed to get rid of this guy before she did something she'd really regret. Something worse than offending him, or even letting him witness her disastrous housekeeping skills.

She looked away to hide her flushed face. "Why would you help us?"

"How about, yes please? Or thank you?"

"But why?"

He flung out his arms in mock outrage. "Can't a guy help a girl in need?" he bellowed. "And the girl's annoying mother?"

The stupid joke and its theatrical delivery caught her off

guard. It didn't fit with anything she'd thought of him.

Shasa burst into nervous laughter. "You're so weird."

Mac smiled. "I'll take that as a compliment."

She huffed, trying to straighten her face. "I still hate you, though."

"Go ahead." His smile turned into a grin. "That's what I'm here for."

Sunshine kissed her face, warming her, making her see purple floaters. Lilla leaned her weight back and forth to keep the swing going. Shasa could tell her daughter was happy. She wished she could feel like that, hang onto that lightness the laughter had momentarily brought.

His gaze hovered on her lips so briefly she wasn't sure if she'd imagined it, but she couldn't stop imagining. What would it be like to kiss him? His hands looked strong, like they could easily lift her off the ground. Heat rushed through her body, all the way to her hairline. The air between them vibrated. Could he feel it?

Lilla's scream brought her back to reality. She'd fallen off the swing.

Guilt punching her gut, Shasa ran to her daughter. "Where does it hurt?"

She wailed in response. A sound of shock, more than pain. The girl stared at Mac through her tears. "You fell me!"

Shasa hugged Lilla to her chest, harder than was necessary.

Mac lowered himself to their eye-level. "I did. I'm so sorry."

She glanced at him. "She'll be fine. Just go." Her raw voice betrayed her. She'd been the one daydreaming. She'd let her daughter fall.

He nodded, getting up. "If you want to talk about the rentals." He placed one of the blue business cards in her hand.

The sound of his footsteps faded as he disappeared through the gate. She stared at the card, her insides swimming, a weird sensation squeezing her heart. Was he serious about helping them? Would he negotiate on price? And, most importantly, did she have the nerve to ask?

Chapter 8

“Where do you want these?” Lando asked as he lugged two folding tables into the community hall.

He’d volunteered to set up the hall for the cohousing meeting.

“In the far corner,” Shasa instructed. “That way, if you want the food, you come all the way in, right? No snacking at the doorway.”

“I never snack at the doorway! I participate.” Lando grinned as he began setting up the tables, eyeing the food over his shoulder.

Shasa had dug up an old Edmond’s cookbook and baked far more than she’d planned. Lilla perched on a chair next to the catering table, waiting for the treats to be set out. She knew Marnie would let her eat anything.

Shasa left to boil another jug of water to fill up the pump thermoses, trying to mentally prepare for the evening. She should have been excited; she'd put in a lot of effort, distributing posters and baking. The previous night, she'd spent hours preparing her presentation.

Yet, her mind wandered, returning to the Sunday afternoon in the garden. Nothing had happened. Just a daydreamy moment. Although, if Mac had made a move, she wasn't sure how it might have played out. He hadn't, of course, because it was all in her head. She had been alone for too long. Was it any wonder her mind cooked up these delusions? She could certainly appreciate why Marnie preferred fictional men to real ones.

Returning to the hall with the full thermos, Shasa heard a commotion from the front door. The first guests were arriving – an Indian family with three teenagers. She urged them to find seats. Three more ladies arrived, holding an animated conversation about kids or dogs. Their bubbly laughter filled the space.

Lando prepared a cup of chamomile tea, his tight, shiny ass framed by a bum bag. Shasa wondered if the man owned any pants. She also wondered if her long dry spell would eventually make her consider him as a romantic prospect. The guy was in impressive shape, even if he did resemble a horse, down to his long face and hairy nostrils, which quivered when he spoke.

"You must be... Sasha?"

Shasa turned around and stifled a gasp. The rich lady from the park stood right behind her, wearing a crispy white shirt and the most luxurious pair of pants she'd ever seen. Her cheek showed a faint scar, covered so expertly with makeup one could only find it if they knew where to look.

"It's Shasa."

"Shasa, of course! I'm Elsie." The woman gave her a tight and cold handshake.

Shasa stared at her diamond wath. "I'm so glad you made it. Can I get you a cup of tea?"

"That would be lovely." Elsie smiled and chose a seat in the far corner.

Shasa brought her a cup of black tea with a dash of milk, as instructed. She offered her the baked goods, but Elsie politely refused each item. Maybe she was worried about getting greasy crumbs on her expensive outfit. More for Lilla, Shasa thought with exasperation. As soon as she left the catering table, her daughter reached for her umpteenth cinnamon roll.

With everyone seated, Shasa picked up her notes and stood at the front. She didn't hate public speaking; she regularly made announcements and ran events at work, but this wasn't work. She was representing herself, and that notion woke the butterflies in her stomach. She took a deep breath. In a way, it felt good to be nervous, to have that sizzle of energy. Just like when she'd locked eyes with Mac, which she definitely shouldn't have been thinking about.

"Welcome, everyone! I'm so glad you all made it. Tonight, we plan to go over some basics of cohousing and discuss a possible building project for those who are ready to move on soon. We're looking to kick-start with a smaller scale one, something called a pocket neighbourhood..."

Worried about boring people, Shasa rushed ahead with her presentation, flicking through slides of images she'd found online of other cohousing communities. They came in all shapes and sizes, from tall apartment buildings to individual cabins in a rural setting. Once she made it to one of her favourite subjects, the parking, she relaxed.

"You may have noticed the lack of garages. It's not by accident. Many cohousing communities chose to leave their cars at the edge of the property and keep the grounds completely car-free. This makes it safe for the kids to play in the common areas and saves space."

One of the visitors, a middle-aged man in a Ramones T-shirt, raised his hand. "How do you get groceries to the house? Or deliveries?"

"I understand most people just carry their groceries. If it's a larger cohousing village, they might have a cart. And if someone needs to get a larger item delivered, the houses are usually accessible by vehicle."

"But, what if—"

"My sister lost her child to a driveway accident," Elsie's

commanding voice echoed behind him. Everyone fell quiet, shuffling to stare at her.

Elsie kept her chin up, unfazed by the attention. "I used to think we just needed to keep kids in fenced backyards. But New Zealand has the highest reported rate of driveway accidents in the world. Our current model doesn't work. We've chosen our own convenience over our children's lives."

The Ramones man sat down, his mouth hanging. Shasa gave Elsie a grateful smile and continued her presentation. When she got to the last slide, her stomach lurched. What now? She didn't know these people. How could she start talking about building something together?

As if sensing that she needed help, Marnie stood up. "Thank you, Shasa, for preparing this amazing presentation."

After some scattered applause, Marnie explained that they were planning a small-scale cohousing project. "So, if you're interested and ready to take the next step, please stay back and let's chat."

Silence filled the room. Shasa's heart hammered so loudly she was sure everyone could hear it.

The Ramones man stood up. "Yeah, that's all good, thanks. I'm not looking at buying right now, so..." He made his way to the door, followed by the Indian family and a couple of others.

With two people left, Shasa's shoulders sagged. One of them was Lando, who she knew had nothing to his name.

He bagged two mini quiches in his bum bag and headed out the door.

The other was a young woman with a tight ponytail and a bright blue blazer. She stuck out her hand. "Barbara Bell, Waikato Times. If you get this project off the ground, I'd like to interview you. It'd make a great story."

Shasa shook her hand, trying to hide her disappointment. Barbara handed them a business card and left, her heels clicking against the hardwood floor.

Shasa looked at Elsie and Marnie with Lilla in her lap. So that was it? A big, fat zero.

Elsie cleared her throat. "You asked me here to advise, so … There's a real shortage of large sections in the city, and you're competing with the property developers. I wouldn't worry too much about finding the people. Securing the section is the first step."

Shasa stared at her, recalling Mac's words. A thought struck her. "My rental! It's on a large section on Marama street, close to the lake, and it's for sale. The developer's going to build apartments on it. I don't think the sale is finalised yet. Is it possible to, you know, swoop in and make an offer?" She explained the state of the current house, and what she'd found out from Mac.

Elsie's eyebrows lifted at the mention of his name. "McCarthy? He's done some high-profile deals. Frankly, I'm surprised he's told you that much about his plans."

Shasa flushed. "Maybe he didn't think it would matter,

since I'm just the tenant."

"Mac has done business with my ex-husband. It sounds like he's trying to keep this on the down low and not get into a bidding war. Maybe he's made a low-ball offer? That could give us an opportunity."

Shasa took a deep breath, a flicker of hope in her heart. "Could we save the garden?"

Elsie lifted a shoulder. "Maybe. A good architect can plan around existing structures. I happen to know a great one."

Her confidence was infectious. Shasa found herself smiling. "That would be amazing. My blueberry bush has just started producing."

Lilla yawned, leaning on Marnie's chest, who gestured at the girl. "I think she's ready for bed."

Elsie held up her hand. "Before you go ... I wasn't planning to get involved, but a lot of what you said tonight resonated with me. It never occurred to me to challenge the way houses are built, even after my nephew died..." She took a moment to compose herself. "I like the concept. I couldn't live in a two-bedroom unit, but I'd be happy to invest, especially if we can secure a section on Marama Street."

Shasa stared at her, speechless.

Marnie straightened up. "So, you wouldn't buy one of the units, but you'd own part of the entire property?"

"I could buy the land and offer you a long leasehold. What way, you'd only need to finance the build. We can sort it out with the lawyers."

"And you'd be part of the decision-making?" Shasa asked.

Elsie smiled. "As an advisor, not to overrule you."

Shasa glanced at Marnie. Was this for real? Could they trust this lady? Her friend gave her a slight nod.

"Honestly, that sounds wonderful."

"What are the next steps?" Marnie asked.

Elsie stood up. "Council. We should go and find out as much as we can about the section."

Shasa took a deep breath. "Would it be possible to go together? I'm not sure I'll ask the right questions."

Elsie reached out her hand, as if to pat her on the arm, but before she made contact, her fingers curled up and she grasped a fistful of air.

Her smile didn't waver. "Sure. We can go together."

Chapter 9

Elsie led them down the council corridor, into a room that smelled like a filing cabinet. An elderly man behind a messy desk looked up from his computer screen. “Come in.” His face was weary but his eyes kind.

Shasa sat down with Lilla on her lap, leaving the other chair for Elsie. The town planner only had eyes for Elsie. “Mrs. Alders.”

“Hi, Earl,” Elsie said softly. “It’s Miss Joyce now.”

“Right. Right. What can I do you for?”

Elsie grabbed a sticky note off his desk and wrote down Shasa’s address. “We’re looking at building on this section and need to check the basics.”

Earl typed on his computer. "How have you been?"

"Very well, thank you. You?"

"Can't complain. So, here's the section..." Earl angled the screen so they could see the aerial map. He talked at length about water, power, and wastewater connections, pointing at colored lines crisscrossing the map.

Shasa held onto Lilla, who fidgeted in her lap, struggling to follow the conversation. Were they even speaking English?

"I'll print these out for you," Earl said, then lowered his voice at Elsie. "Are you ... needing the neighbouring section as well?"

Shasa opened her mouth to answer, but Elsie placed her hand on hers. "Yes, that would be great," she replied with a charming smile.

The printer whirred to life. Shasa whipped her head left and right, trying to figure out what was going on. Weren't they investigating one section? But Elsie's firm hand remained on hers, keeping her silent. The printer churned out a pile of maps and documents, most of which had distorted text and dark edges, like they'd been scanned from ancient microfilms, then xeroxed to death.

Moments later, they stepped out of the sliding doors.

"What was that?" Shasa hissed.

Elsie led them towards the lifts leading to the underground carpark. "Let's talk in the car."

Once on the road, Elsie pointed at the pile of papers in Shasa's lap. "Earl and I go way back. He ... um ... he's been watching out for me. My ex-husband Jeffrey and I have different approaches to business. He does calculations, I trust my instinct. Jeff started keeping things from me and I'd find out when it was too late, so I asked Earl to let me know which properties Jeff enquired about. As a public servant, he was uncomfortable about it, so we came up with a shorthand. I'd see him about a property, and he'd ask if I wanted to print out the other one I'd enquired about earlier, and that would be the one Jeff had seen him about."

A lump rose in Shasa's throat. "Oh, my God! Is your ex-husband buying the house next door?"

Elsie slowed down to stop at traffic lights and turned to face Shasa. "I don't know. He has a connection to Mac, which makes me suspicious. But they haven't done business together for a while. Not since Mac started his own company..."

"Wait! Which neighbour is it?" Shasa flipped through the papers in her lap and uncovered the two maps. "Mac's parents' house! Of course!"

"What?" Elsie glared at her.

Shasa's cheeks flushed. How had she missed this? Elsie would think she was keeping things from her. Or worse, think she was stupid.

"Mac's my friend! He pushed me on the swing," Lilla announced happily from the back seat.

Her cheeks blazing, Shasa explained how Mac had shown up with her daughter the second time, and how they'd ended up eating dessert.

"Then he pushed me on the swing!" Lilla yelled out again.

Elsie smiled. "If I didn't know better, I'd say he was infatuated with you."

"But you do know better?" Shasa cringed at her own question.

Did it matter what Mac thought about her? Still, she couldn't help her stomach tightening as she studied Elsie's face for clues.

Elsie's hands tightened around the steering wheel. "If he's anything like my ex-husband, he most likely has an ulterior motive."

"You mean like ... getting me into bed?"

Elsie laughed. "No! Don't get me wrong, you're a pretty girl, but you're not his type. I mean, maybe he's looking at you as a prospective tenant for one of his properties. It's hard to find reliable tenants, and it sounds like you've done a lot of gardening..."

Shasa shuddered. She'd thought Mac had offered to help them find a new rental as a favour, wondering if he maybe liked her. What an idiot she'd been. She'd definitely imagined that moment in the garden.

"So, what happens next?" she asked Elsie. "Do we just make an offer?"

"First, we need a solid plan and buyers who are ready to sign a contract. Maybe you should hold another meeting at the community house, cast the net wider?"

"But what if Mac buys the section?"

"Give me your landlord's details, and I'll make sure he knows there's another interested buyer. He won't sign anything if he thinks he can get more."

As agreed, Elsie parked outside Lilla's daycare, down the road from Shasa's house. From there, Shasa had a ten-minute walk to the community house, something she now appreciated more than ever. What if they had to move to the outskirts of town and drive everywhere? She barely had enough money to keep her car on the road. If she had to start filling up the tank twice a week, she'd have to dip into her meagre house deposit and give up the home ownership dream altogether.

After helping Lilla and her temporary booster seat out of the car, Shasa turned back to Elsie. "Thank you so much! I'll set up the next meeting. How about this weekend? People might be more available on a Sunday afternoon."

"Sounds good. Send me the details, and I'll be there. Let me know if I can help distribute the flyers. I can do it when I walk Stina."

Shasa blinked, attempting to keep a straight face. She couldn't imagine Elsie putting up posters in public, but she wasn't going to refuse any help. They made plans to do a walk together, so Lilla could play with the dog.

As Shasa waved goodbye to Elsie's shiny Maserati, she couldn't help wondering if her new friend also had an ulterior motive. Why was she helping them? But Shasa couldn't look the gift horse in the mouth. She'd already pinned her hopes on this crazy plan.

Squeezing her daughter's hand, she headed towards the blue gates of the daycare, hoping against hope that it would all work out.

Chapter 10

“Shit. Shit. Shit.” Rick’s voice blasted from my earpiece. “How did she find out?”

Mac focused all his energy into emitting the correct emotion. Baffled. Flabbergasted. Absolutely stunned. “I honestly have no idea. She must have psychic abilities.”

It sounded convincing, at least over the phone. Rick couldn’t see the sweat stains under his armpits or the panic in his eyes.

“Elsie Alders?” Rick repeated.

“Not Alders. They divorced last year.”

“Fuck! So, she owns half the empire now? We can’t even go to Jeff?”

He was right. Jeff might have been willing to negotiate, but Elsie was a different story. From what he'd found out online, the divorce had been acrimonious. She wouldn't pander to her ex-husband's business partners.

Mac stopped at the traffic lights and picked up his empty takeaway cup. Coffee. He needed more coffee.

"Don't worry," he told Rick. "I'll figure it out. I'll take care of this."

Rick's voice rose an octave. "How?"

"I ... have an idea." He ended the phone call with a sick feeling.

There was no question. The pixie-haired tenant had blabbed about his plans. She was the only one he'd talked to, apart from his parents. He found it hard to believe she knew someone like Elsie, but anything was possible.

After a few minutes, Mac turned onto Marama Street. He slowed down well before the house and parked behind a van. He had no plan, but he'd start with her. Shasa. A ridiculous name. He'd double checked the spelling from the tenancy agreement, not trusting his mum's pronunciation.

As he stepped out of his truck, the gate opened, and she stepped out, holding her daughter's hand, wearing a pair of bright red pants, or was it a skirt? Maybe she didn't own any regular pants, like jeans. The inside of her house had looked like an ethnic second-hand shop.

Mac considered confronting her, but she turned away, heading towards the lake. In her free hand, she held a stack of papers. He followed, keeping them in his sights. It wasn't hard; her red pants flapped in the breeze, catching the golden evening sun like they were on fire. He could tell she had a nice body under all the draping, though. He trailed behind the duo as they arrived on the lakeside path and turned left. The evening horizon glowed pink with clouds of sandflies on the move.

Shasa stopped and scooted in front of a rubbish bin. Mac's heart lodged in his throat. Was she a dumpster diver? He stared at her, unable to look away, like watching a roadside accident. If she pulled out a half-eaten pizza, he wouldn't be able to help himself. He'd drag them both to a restaurant. He'd take them shopping and fill their fridge.

To his relief, Shasa didn't stick her hand into the bin but attached a piece of paper to it. When done, she got up and chased after her daughter, who'd run ahead of her. He waited for them to disappear behind a cluster of gum trees and approached the rubbish bin.

What could the poster be about? A new rental? Why didn't she just search online like everyone else? Why tape posters on bins around town? These alternative types were weird, though. Maybe she thought wi-fi caused cancer.

When he reached the rubbish bin, the penny dropped. This was the answer he'd been looking for and he knew exactly what to do.

Chapter 11

Shasa arrived at the community house an hour early on Sunday to air out the hall. She had no idea how many people to expect. They had distributed twice as many flyers and posted in a couple of online groups. The Facebook event showed ten confirmed guests and another fifteen 'maybes', but she knew better than to trust Facebook commitment.

Lilla ran in ahead of her, dancing to music only she could hear. Shasa went to the kitchen to boil the jug. This time, she had kept the catering to a minimum – tea and biscuits. Twenty minutes later, Marnie arrived, closely followed by Elsie. Five minutes to four p.m., the chairs were set up and Shasa spotted the first attendee. Lando. His smile waned as he eyed the catering table.

A steady crowd followed him, a mix of ethnicities, old and young. A buzz of conversation filled the room. Shasa took her place by the projector, feeling more comfortable than the first time. She knew her presentation inside out. They had a plan, and it was all thanks to Elsie. She'd briefed her architect and spoken to Shasa's landlord, who had agreed to wait for their offer, but wouldn't divulge how much Mac had offered him.

Elsie's confidence must have rubbed off on her. For the first time in months, Shasa felt excited. Her excitement must have taunted fate because that's when the door creaked open, and he stepped into the hall.

Mac McCarthy.

For the first couple of seconds, Shasa almost didn't recognize him. His outfit of worn jeans and a soft T-shirt looked like a disguise.

Elsie appeared by Shasa's side; her eyes wide. They had no time to voice the questions hanging in the air as Mac strolled across the floor.

"Ladies," he touched the brim of an imaginary hat, smiling widely.

"Mac!" Lilla shouted from the other side of the room and ran to him. She hugged his legs and looked up with practiced doe-eyes. "Will you play with me?" She raised her arms, and Mac picked her up, cradling the girl on his hip like her favorite uncle.

Shasa found her voice. "What are you doing here?"

Mac's eyebrows arched in perfect innocence. "I saw a flyer taped on a rubbish bin, and it piqued my curiosity."

She huffed. The whole thing stank to high heaven. "Seriously. What's going on?"

Mac dug up one of their flyers and pointed at it. "It says here 'all welcome,' but I guess that's just marketing talk?"

Shasa filled her lungs, ready to give him a piece of her mind, but Elsie stepped in. "Of course you're welcome, Mac. Have a seat. Would you like a cup of tea and a biscuit?" Speaking in a honeyed, commanding tone, she seated him at the far end of the front row.

She returned to Shasa, lowering her voice. "Don't panic. Just do your presentation the way you planned. I'll handle the bit after, okay?"

Shasa nodded, still holding her breath. Her earlier confidence had been drowned by a surge of nerves. Could she do this with him watching? Part of her brain worked on connecting the dots. Why was he here? Why was he dressed like that? But she had no time to find the answers.

Marnie dimmed the lights and took her place in the front row, coaxing Lilla to sit next to her. Was the energy in the room different, or was it just her? Shasa fumbled with her notes, her fingers sticky. The projector whirred to life, blasting its light on the blank wall, leaving the rest of the room in relative darkness. Better. She couldn't see anyone.

She settled on a slower pace than the first time, lingering

on the best photos and ideas from existing cohousing projects, especially the community gardens, safe play areas, and the lack of garages. Shasa doubted Mac had ever built anything without a garage. After a while, she almost forgot about him until she arrived at the last slide and powered down the projector.

As the lights turned back on, the small crowd looked at her expectantly. All except Mac, who leant back in his chair, an inscrutable expression on his face.

To her relief, Elsie took the stage. "Thank you, Shasa!"

The applause was more pronounced than the first time, making Shasa's cheeks flush. She sat next to Lilla, who'd curled up sideways, staring at something on Marnie's phone.

Elsie joined the clapping. "I know it's a lot to take in. We're inviting you to think differently about living and building community. The next part is for those who are further along in your journey and looking for the right community to invest in. If you're ready to talk numbers, please stay. As for everyone else, thank you for coming!"

Shasa sighed. They'd originally planned to pitch their building project to the entire group straight after the slideshow, but this was better. The faster they got everyone, including Mac, out the door, the better.

As people began trickling out of the room, Shasa looked pointedly at Mac. He sat back as if he had no intention of leaving. Soon, he was the only one left. Shasa's shoulders sagged. The dream that had kept her up at night was slipping away.

Elsie approached him, her voice ice cold. "Thank you for coming."

Mac looked around the empty room, his eyes wide. "Can't believe no one's interested. How many investors are you after?"

Elsie held up her hand. "Come on, Mac. You're not going to get anything more out of us. It's time to go home."

"Wait, is this Mac?" Marnie asked, slowly catching on.

Shasa cast her friend an apologetic look. She'd forgotten Marnie had never met the guy.

Mac got up and offered his hand to Marnie. "Mac McCarthy, pleasure to meet you." His smile and gaze lingered. Was he flirting with her friend?

Mac turned to Shasa. "And thank you for the lovely presentation. You were very engaging. Great presence."

He held her gaze for so long Shasa began to feel hot and had to look away.

"Bye, Mac!" Lilla shouted, hugging his knees.

Mac scooted to her level. "Another unicorn shirt? How many do you have?"

Lilla held up three fingers, then five, then seven, staring at them in confusion. "A fifteen hundred million," she announced with all the confidence of a three-year-old.

She was likely to be as bad at maths as her mother. Laughing, Mac high fived the girl, got up and left. They stood in stunned silence, waiting for the front door to click shut.

Marnie's eyes were huge. "What was that about?"

Elsie shrugged. "Your landlord must have told him about my phone call and somehow he's figured out what's going on."

Shasa groaned. "Why does he need two sections, anyway? We're building on one, can't he just build on the other?" She started stacking the chairs, bristling with frustration. Marnie leapt in to grab the chair from her, likely to stop her from destroying it.

Elsie's soothing voice filled the room. "It makes sense. If you combine the two sections, you only need one driveway. You can remove the fence and fit in more units. More units, more profit."

Marnie stopped mid-task. "Wait! Which side section is he after?"

Shasa gave her an odd look. "I thought you knew. The brown brick house on the left where his parents live."

Marnie stared at her in shock. "Sue and John are his parents?"

"You know them?"

"Everyone knows them! I'm sorry I didn't connect the dots. I just assumed it was the other side. I never imagined he could be Sue's son. They're so... different."

Elsie's eyes moved fast, like she was calculating a chess move. "How do you know his mum?"

"She used to volunteer at KidsCan." Marnie's previous job, before the community house, equipped kids from low-income families with food and clothes. "I've bumped into her a couple of times outside your house since then. She's always so lovely."

Shasa's heart sank. "Does that mean we can't go ahead? We don't want to mess up things for John and Sue."

Marnie pursed her lips. "If Mac wants to build a new house for his parents, he can do that on their section. If we stop him from buying Shasa's, it just means he can't build the condos."

"Okay. We'll keep going, but no more public meetings. We'll find the right people another way."

"Online?" Marnie offered. "I can do some scouting."

Hope flooded back to Shasa's chest. It meant so much that Marnie was on her side.

Elsie's eyes sharpened. "We should also try to find out as much as we can about Mac's plans."

"Why?"

"If we find out how much he's offered for the section, we can outbid him without overpaying."

"We could talk to the people he hangs out with," Marnie suggested.

Shasa frowned. "How would we find them?"

"If we find out his hobbies..." Marnie trailed off, a blank look on her face.

"I know!" Lando stood at the doorway, smiling.

His voice made Shasa jump. "I thought you left."

Lando grinned. "Nah, I just went to the loo. I told you I

can't invest, but I'm hoping you might hire me to do the landscaping, so I wanted to stay in the loop." He crossed the floor to get closer. "You're talking about Mac, right? The guy who was here?"

"Yeah," Marnie confirmed. "You know him?"

Lando reached the catering table and swiped the last biscuit. "You know I have a lot of time on my hands, and I'm big on personal development—"

Shasa's mouth twitched. "You'll join any class, as long as it's free?"

She'd heard him say that before, asking about the next term schedule at the community house.

Lando offered them a good-natured smile. "Very much so. As soon as that guy stepped in, I knew I'd seen him before. I was racking my brain to remember where, but then you said his name and it all came back."

Enjoying his rapt audience, Lando rolled the last biscuit inside a napkin, hid it in his bum bag, and launched into a story.

Within five minutes, Shasa knew what they had to do. The idea scared the life out of her, but she steeled her nerves. It was time for Mac get a taste his own medicine.

Chapter 12

Mac arrived before everyone else, making his way through the creaky double doors, into the hall that smelled of dust and stale popcorn. The dark theater stage with one spotlight beckoned him like a magnet. He loved its otherworldliness, the way it transported him to another reality. Especially today.

It was Wednesday, but the week seemed endless. Mac could tolerate risk, but the level of uncertainty in his life had reached a new high. The leaky townhouse was sucking up money faster than he could make it, but he couldn't pull out, not before it was fixed. He was in too deep, and he needed a big win, right about now. The condo deal was it; he knew it. He had a coveted location, impressive building plans and investors lined up. But he recognized that feeling in the pit of his belly, that slight wobble of panic that made him fear risk and try to play it safe. He couldn't let it ride him. He had to go forward, trusting the plan.

It would all work out, as long as they secured both sections, and the council didn't sit on their plans for too long. He had to just keep calm and carry on. And do something to take his mind off everything – that's where the theatre came in.

Judging by the open doors and the spotlight, Gareth was already there, most likely having a smoke by the back door. Mac jogged across the floor and hopped onto the stage. Since nobody else had arrived, he peeled off his hoodie and did a few jumps on and off the stage to warm up. Some people approached improv purely with their minds, but he loved involving his whole body, and the adrenaline boost it gave him.

He'd landed in the group by accident, after visiting with his brother once. Mac had come along for moral support, but after Izzy transitioned into film making behind the camera, Mac kept coming. Improv was his secret weapon. It had taught him to observe people, listen intently and respond to 'prompts' just like on stage. If you truly cared to read, people's secrets were written on their face. The more comfortable he became in his own skin, the more he noticed how uncomfortable others were, their attention stolen by the inner critic. If you focused on yourself, you missed so much.

He'd broken a light sweat by jumping when he heard the back door click and hopped off the stage. Gareth arrived in a cloud of cigarette smoke. Their acting coach was in his fifties, taller than average, and surprisingly nimble for someone who carried so much excess weight.

"Mac! Always the first one, eh?" Gareth slapped him on the back, his deep resonant voice amplified with a faint echo.

The front door opened, and Teana entered, followed by her friend Brooke. Teana was gorgeous. If it weren't for her blind ambition and appetite for dating anyone higher up in the show biz food chain, Mac might have been interested. Brooke, on the other hand, had a criminal record, neck tattoos, and viewed acting as one of her last remaining career options. Too bad she had no natural talent. Doing a scene with her felt like acting with a vacuum cleaner. She made a lot of noise, but in the end, just sucked.

Gareth motioned them to gather on the stage.

"Hi, Mac! How're you?" Teana flashed him a smile.

The door opened again, and the nauseating giggle of two lovers told him it was Hills and April, the couple who did everything together. Hills had been a lot more fun before he'd started bringing his girlfriend. Mac didn't begrudge anyone's happiness but hoped their co-dependent relationship would run its course.

Like a 200-kilo gazelle, Gareth lowered his frame down on the stage and patted the floor next to him. "Let's get started!"

As he said it, he glanced at the door. Mac followed his gaze, wondering if they were expecting someone new. Now and then they had a visitor, but most people never returned. He preferred a bit of turnover. Seeing the same people every week meant getting to know them, and he preferred not to be known. Despite several months of weekly practice, he'd never told any of the group members what he did for a living or where he lived. He knew that the minute they saw what he drove and where he lived, he'd no longer be one of them. Only Gareth knew his background. A successful director and acting coach, he was hardly a starving artist himself and respected his privacy.

Gareth turned to Teana. "What's on top?"

She launched into a detailed account of her flatmate's antics and her own struggles with employment at a homeware store. "No matter what I do, they only give me two hours a day. Driving there for a two-hour shift, it's just ... I almost quit this week. But I don't have anything else lined up."

Mac joined everyone else in their expressions of sympathy. Some days, he worked two hours by choice. In his world, work hours didn't equal money earned. Sometimes, he wished he could tell these people how money really worked, but he doubted any of them had the potential to succeed. People craved security and were willing to trade their time and freedom for it.

"Should we skip you, Mac?" Gareth mused.

The others were used to Mac's vague replies, but this time, he felt like adding some flavour. "I had a great week. Met this three-year-old girl who stole my heart. Not in a creepy way."

Everyone laughed, and that's when the door opened.

Before she even stepped into the light, he recognized her silhouette. Shasa.

Why was she here? How did she even know about the improv group? They didn't advertise. Watching her diminutive frame approach, he felt both violated and impressed. He'd crashed her meeting – now she was crashing his.

Gareth jumped up, extending his hand. "Welcome aboard! You must be Shasa."

"I must be." She flashed him a cute smile.

Gareth asked her to join their circle on the stage. She chose the spot furthest away from him and folded her legs under her body. In loose T-shirt and tights, she looked different, like she was dressed for the gym at YMCA.

Shasa didn't expect diamonds.

The thought snuck up on him without warning, and his insides twisted. Was he really looking at her as a woman? He leaned his elbows against his knees, stealing glances at her. He couldn't go down this road. His future and sanity depended on it. But no matter how hard he tried to focus his eyes and thoughts elsewhere, they kept returning to her, cataloguing everything. Without the dreadlocks and overload of cheap jewelry, he could see the woman underneath. Understated, yet gorgeous.

The room fell quiet, everyone studying the newcomer with palpable curiosity.

Gareth cleared his throat. “We were just finishing up our ‘what’s on top’ round. Sharing highlights from the past week. What’s been on top for you? You don’t have to go into any detail, we just want to know what kind of emotions you’ve been dealing with.”

Shasa jerked, her doe-eyes enormous. Mac almost felt bad for her.

Chapter 13

Oh, God. What was she supposed to say? Shasa blinked, hoping for some magical insight to drop into her brain from the shadowy surrounds. Was it necessary for the lighting to be this dramatic?

She'd never met any of the others, but Gareth seemed genuinely nice. Sometimes, it was easier to be honest with a group of strangers. She drew a breath, gathering her courage. "I … can't say it's been an easy week. A while ago, I was told the house we live in is going to be demolished. On Sunday, we held a meeting for people interested in cohousing, to see if we could get this project off the ground, but… it didn't go well."

She waited for Mac to interject, but he simply stared at her, so she continued recounting the trials of trying to establish a cohousing community. "I suppose it wasn't meant to be. Now I have to find another rental, and this developer will knock down our home and build his stupid condos." Her shoulder slumped in defeat.

If she made him believe they'd given up, maybe he'd lower his guard and reveal something. Shasa studied the faces around her, expecting someone to call out Mac, but nobody even glanced at him. Did they not know about his property business?

The beautiful Māori girl on Mac's left let out a frustrated growl. "What a jerk! Those guys think they can do whatever they want, eh?"

Others joined in, expressing the same sentiment, grumbling about the wealth gap, a whole generation being priced out of the property market, cursing the greedy guys who exploited the system to endlessly grow their portfolios. Shasa glanced at Mac, watching his face for any signs of discomfort. He gazed back at her, a tiny smile tugging at the corner of his mouth. Shameless.

Gareth raised his hand, halting the conversation. "Okay, let's move on."

They went around the circle and each person introduced themselves to Shasa. Two of them, Hills and April, were a couple, and a clingy one at that, leaning on each other and holding hands. The girl with a neck tattoo was Brooke, the gorgeous Māori girl Teana.

Shasa felt sorry to have missed the proper catch-up round. Lilla hadn't been too keen to part with her. She'd spent fifteen minutes bargaining with her daughter, hoping to leave without the screaming. In the end, she'd made a dash for the door while Marnie distracted her daughter with chocolate.

Gareth gathered himself off the floor. "Okay, let's see if we can get your minds off all that stuff, shall we? Everyone, please get up!"

He turned to Shasa. "Would you be more comfortable just watching? If this is your first time?"

Yes! A million times, yes!

But before she could answer, Mac cut in. "No, no! I've seen her on stage. She's not shy. She's here to do improv, and she told me she's dying to jump in." A devilish grin spread across his face.

"You two know each other?" Gareth raised a questioning eyebrow at Mac.

"We go way back. I saw her perform at the Frankton community house. She was amazing."

Shasa swallowed her objections, rising to the silent challenge in Mac's eyes. She couldn't back down.

"Happy to go first," she said, her jaw tight.

Gareth cocked his head, his gaze darting between the two of them, assessing the situation. "Okay. You go first. And it sounds like Mac volunteered to pair up with you. Let's go."

The others moved off the stage, taking seats in the front row.

Gareth explained he'd give them a prompt, and they'd have to improvise a scene, accepting each other's suggestions. "That's the most important thing to remember. Always say yes."

Shasa stared at Mac. Had she ever said yes to him before? Taking a deep breath, she squared herself to face him. Her whole body bristled, like a dead toy suddenly filled with charged batteries.

Gareth searched something on his phone, then looked up at them. "You're in the doctor's office waiting room, and someone just farted."

Mac pulled two chairs from the side of the stage, offering her a seat. Sitting down next to her, he sniffed the air and looked away, as if embarrassed for her.

Shasa straightened her back. As adrenaline flooded her veins, her mind cleared, firing ideas.

"It's called irritable bowel syndrome," she said, her tone dignified.

Mac looked genuinely shocked. "I'm ... sorry to hear that."

She frowned at him. "You're sorry to hear the sound of someone passing gas? I'd think the smell is more unpleasant."

"Oh, no! I'm here for a cancerous growth in my... um... nasal area. I can't smell a thing, but the sound of farting offends me. It reminds me of my disability."

She managed to keep a straight face, but they were interrupted by Gareth's howling laughter. "Okay, okay! Next! You are... selling shoes at a leper colony."

Shasa took off her sneaker and lifted it up to Mac. "This ground-breaking technology allows you to turn the shoe inside out to easily scrape off any flesh that's left behind when you remove the footwear."

He took the shoe from her and turned it in his hands. "That's fantastic. I've been using a spoon, and it takes me hours."

"Ugh, disgusting!" April yelled, burying her face in Hills' shirt. "Come on, Gareth. Something a bit nicer, please?"

Gareth shrugged. "Okay. You're on a date. One of you is nervous to propose. The other one wants to get a puppy. Go!"

Shasa locked eyes with Mac, her stomach in knots. She would happily joke or try to gross him out, but this was nauseating. Why couldn't Gareth just assign us roles? Why did they have to figure it out?

Before she could decide what to do, Mac dropped down on one knee and cleared his throat.

She waited, but he didn't say anything.

Eventually, she threw out her arms. "What are you doing down there?"

He turned his attention to his shoelaces. "I just need to tie these. I think my shoes are coming off."

"Is your leprosy acting up again, darling? Because on

those days when your flesh is falling off, wouldn't it be nice to have a bit of help? Someone who could fetch your slippers or bring the newspaper?"

Mac got up and turned his chair to face her, like they were sitting around a small table.

"You mean, like a butler?" he asked, cutting an imaginary steak.

"Yes! Like a butler… dog."

"You're right, I've been thinking… on those days when my flesh is falling off—" he paused and gave her a meaningful look, while the group giggled in the background "—I'd love to know there was someone in my life I could count on. I feel like everyone's leaving me. My family, my friends, my flesh… It's difficult. You're the—"

"That's exactly what I mean! Dogs are so faithful! A well-trained labradoodle would never leave your side."

"But what if it eats the bits that fall off? I was rather thinking another human… someone as principled and self-sacrificing as you could be a better companion. If you'd consider…"

He reached his hand across the imaginary table and took hers. The sensation released a fresh batch of butterflies into her stomach. She couldn't escape his gaze, and it churned her insides. He was good. She almost believed him.

'I love you,' he mouthed at her, a pleading look in his eyes.

The laughter in the background had ceased. The whole scene was ridiculous, yet something in his eyes held her captive. Maybe it was the freedom of make-believe, the commitment she'd made to going along with the story.

Who would back down first?

Shasa got up and circled the invisible table, standing right by his chair, and took his face into her hands. "I can't believe I never noticed ... you have puppy dog eyes!" She leaned in as if to study them.

"Woof!" He blinked, fanning her with the most impressive fringe of eyelashes she'd ever seen. She could actually feel the breeze on her face.

"Oh, my God. Don't do that! I can't resist ..."

He dropped down on one knee again, lifting his hands up like paws, curling them under his chin. "Will you marry me?"

"Yes!" She laughed, expecting Gareth to call 'cut' or someone else to stop them, stop the madness.

The room was silent.

Mac stood and gathered her in his arms. "I'd kiss you, but my lips may fall off. Oh, what the hell!"

He cupped her chin and pulled her into a kiss. Soft and hot, absorbing. For a split second, Shasa forgot about the group, the stage, and everything else. His thumb brushed her cheek, the kiss deepened and her fingers curled against his chest.

Time slowed down. She was engulfed by fire, white and hot—

"Thank you." Gareth's baritone brought them back to reality.

Mac let go of her and hopped off the stage. Shasa didn't catch his eyes before he disappeared into the shadow. Was he as flustered as she was? Probably not. He must have been used to this. She wanted to rush off the stage, but she didn't want to appear embarrassed, so she flashed the group a cheeky smile and curtsied. Whatever had gone down, she'd own it. Everyone applauded and Brooke whistled.

Her cheeks burning, Shasa clambered off the stage, looking for a vacant seat. The last one left was at the end of the row, next to Mac. She briefly considered going for the second row. No. She couldn't. If she was going to own it, she had to sit next to him.

As she settled in the plastic chair, Gareth cleared his throat. "Thank you, Mac and Shasa. That was... great commitment. Let's move on. How about Teana and Hills?"

Hills peeled himself off his other half and hopped on the stage. His girlfriend resettled in her seat, squirming like she'd lost a limb.

Shasa let out a long sigh, grateful to sit in the dark and watch other people embarrass themselves for a change. She could almost relax. If only she had been sitting further away from Mac. Her whole body seemed hyper-aware of him – his knee nearly touching hers, his wide shoulders encroaching into her space. She could smell his shower-fresh hair, mixed with a hint of perspiration. Had their scene caused him to break a sweat? Maybe he wasn't as aloof as she'd thought. She smiled to herself, reliving the kiss from moments ago.

It had felt so real, so delicious... She'd never thought he'd kiss like that, with such intensity. Hunger. She had to stop thinking about it.

Hills and Teana acted out a scene involving Mr. and Mrs. Santa on a desert island. It fell a bit flat, but Shasa enjoyed watching April flinch every time the other woman stepped within two feet of her boyfriend.

When they stepped off the stage, Brooke got up. "April, could you go with Brooke?" Gareth asked.

"I'm not feeling well."

She didn't sound that unwell, but Hills wrapped his arm protectively around her.

"Okay," Gareth nodded. "Who wants to go again?"

He cast an appealing look at Mac, who seemed reluctant but made his way onto the stage.

Within two minutes, Shasa understood why. Brooke was the worst actor she'd ever seen. Wooden, slow, and loud, as if she was performing her own show, completely unrelated to her acting partner. Gareth seemed to know her limitations and kept the prompts simple.

"You are two astronauts floating in space. Go!" Brooke flailed her arms and made a loud moo, sounding like a distressed cow.

"Is that space sickness?" Mac asked.

She thrust her body as if she'd been knocked by a gust of wind. "My life is flashing before my eyes like a film. I can see all the important things that ever happened to me!" Her voice echoed from the back of the theatre.

Mac looked like he was trying to suppress a laugh. "Turn off the video feed. There's a button on the side of your helmet."

Everyone giggled. Happy with the response, Brooke stopped the animal noises and broke character, waving at Teana. Then she went back to flailing her arms like she was falling from the sky.

Mac matched her spastic performance, down to the guttural sounds. "How odd that we were experiencing such strong winds here in outer space."

He was a good sport, distracting us from the horror of Brooke's acting, allowing everyone to laugh with them.

After their performance, Brooke beamed and gave him a hug. "Cheers!"

Gareth glanced at his watch. "I'm sorry, I was hoping to do another round, but we were running quite late, so I'm afraid we'll have to wrap it up. I have a dinner date."

With happy chatter, they filed out the door. Mac veered towards a Lime scooter lying in the middle of the footpath and picked it up, turning back to wave at them. His eyes scanned the group until they landed on Shasa and a smile spread across his face.

Without even thinking, she stepped closer, searching for words, any words... Her lips still tingled from the kiss, but they were complete strangers. Rivals. "That was fun," she whispered, stopping right by his scooter.

He kept smiling, subtly licking his lips. "Yeah. Thanks for coming. I hope you'll be back. I'd love to do another scene with you." His gaze dipped to her lips and Shasa's throat dried up.

She'd enjoyed herself, unexpectedly, but how could she come back? What would Elsie or Marnie think?

"Maybe." She swallowed, her body buzzing from the way he kept looking at her, knowingly, with open interest. "I have to go now."

She had no reason to keep their conversation going, as much as she wanted to. What could she achieve, anyway? She'd failed to find out anything useful about Mac or his plans with the section. Instead, she'd kissed him on stage and was now under some evil spell, unable to think straight. She was the worst spy in the history of espionage.

Her heart hammering in her chest, Shasa turned around and hurried away from the theatre, letting the cool evening air fill her lungs. Hopefully, the fifteen-minute walk to Marnie's place would clear her head.

Chapter 14

Mac had just scanned the Lime scooter when Gareth caught up to him. "Wait up! Can I have a word?"

He glanced at his phone screen. "It'll cost you thirty cents a minute."

Gareth laughed. "I'll be brief. I'm running late, anyway. About the girl you sparred with tonight. Shasa. She's got talent."

"Agreed." Mac had been thinking about it the whole time and hearing it from Gareth gave him a smack of satisfaction.

"You know I'm directing a play at Clarence Street, Roman Holiday, based on the old film. It's such a timeless classic, and it's been done as a musical before, but never as a dramatic play. The long-term plan is to take it to the new theatre they're building in the CBD. It'll be big."

Mac held his breath.

Gareth gave him a weighty look. "I want you to audition for the lead role."

"Seriously?" His nerves fired up and Mac leaned on the scooter for balance.

"Seriously."

Mac shook his head. "You know I'm in the property business. This is just a hobby."

"Bullshit." Gareth's expression didn't give an inch.

Mac loved acting far more than he cared to admit. He couldn't pass on a chance like this.

He ran his fingers through his hair. "You want me to audition?"

"I want you and her. You as Joe, Shasa as Anya. The producers are looking at established actors, but you're my dark horse. I want to prep you two. We'll practice for a couple of weeks, then organize an extra audition after hours, blow their socks off. You in?"

Gareth's enthusiasm gave him a jolt. But him and Shasa? She wasn't an actor. He was pretty sure she'd come along just to spite him, snooping on him like he'd snooped on her. Not that she'd ever find out anything. He knew how to keep his mouth shut.

He wondered if Shasa now considered them even. They'd let him sit through their slideshow, dunking biscuits in a cup of tea. He'd put Shasa on the stage. But if you joined an improv group, you had to do improv. And he had to agree with Gareth, the woman had held her own. Shasa had raw talent, a good stage voice, and a delicate, expressive face he couldn't stop staring at.

He hadn't bought her spiel about the cohousing project failing. The vendor was still undecided, which meant something was going on. He glanced at his phone. He was out four dollars.

Mac blew out a sigh. "I'm in. But I can't speak for her."

"Find out, will you, and let me know. We'd have to start rehearsing this week."

He swallowed air. "I will."

Gareth jogged towards his car and Mac hopped on the scooter, turning the handle. He could only hope the connection he'd felt with Shasa on stage was mutual. She had every reason to dislike him, but during those moments, he'd noticed something else, a heat burning under the surface. The moment he'd touched her, a surge of electricity had shot through him, forcing him to fight for balance. He hoped she'd felt even a fraction of it. He needed every advantage to win her over in this timeframe.

Chapter 15

"You did what?!" Marnie's voice echoed in her cosy kitchen, her eyes huge.

Shasa's face felt hot. "It was just a stage kiss, part of the scene. Isn't that common?"

Marnie shook her head, her earrings whipping. "I don't think so. It was an improv class, right? Don't you usually goof around and make each other laugh?"

Shasa took Lilla's banana to finish it for her. The girl was whiny and tired; she had to get her home before there was a major meltdown. "It wasn't exactly a romantic storyline," she argued, mouth full of banana. "Farts, flesh-eating bacteria... it was gross."

Lilla giggled. “Mummy said fart!”

She nodded at her daughter. “See? Comedy gold.”

Marnie narrowed her eyes. “And you got from that to kissing, how?”

Shasa took a breath, focusing on the collection of colour-coordinated mugs hanging on chrome hooks. Marnie’s place was so comforting. “I can’t remember. It just ... went like that.”

Had she steered the scene in that direction? Maybe, but he could have backed out at any moment. If she were complicit, so was he.

Marnie broke into a conspiratorial smile. “So, was he into it?”

“What? No! We were just acting. Honestly, I think he wanted to wind me up. I could tell he was annoyed I’d crashed his group.”

Marnie lowered her voice. “Is he a good kisser?”

Her face burned. Because Mac was a good kisser. So good that she’d slipped up. For an instant, she’d forgotten everything else, and responded like it was a real kiss, sneaking a taste of him. He hadn’t pulled away. In fact, he’d held her even tighter, their tongues connecting like they were pulled together by an inevitable force neither of them could resist. But she’d been the one to go beyond a stage kiss. She’d made the first move.

“I’m going to take that as a yes.” Marnie’s face turned serious. “But remember, we’re not on the same side here. I know he's hot, but he's in it to win it."

"I know." She swallowed the rest of Lilla's banana to lubricate her throat. "I don't like his type at all. I think I like acting, but that has nothing to do with him, right?"

"Right. You should do an acting class. Maybe we can organize one at the community house?"

Shasa's shoulders relaxed. "Great idea!"

That's what she needed. The night had thrown her into a whirlwind of emotions, and finally, something made sense. She liked acting, and she could pursue that on her own. It had nothing to do with Mac or his kissing skills. She lifted her daughter onto her hip and headed to the front door.

Marnie's place had such a lovely feel, so grown-up and nostalgic. The fresh tea towels and hanging baskets of fruit always made her feel like a teenager. Her own house resembled a student flat – worn-out and decorated on a budget.

"Are those curtains new?"

Marnie smiled. "They were on special. I also got new bathroom rugs and hand towels."

"What's the occasion?" She didn't expect there to be one, so Marnie's telling smile took her by surprise.

"There is a special occasion? Spill!"

Marnie fiddled with her greenstone necklace. "The writing group's meeting at my place next time, so I wanted to spruce things up."

Something didn't add up. "Anyone new in the group?"

Marnie smiled sheepishly. "You know how we haven't had any males since gay Dan left? I heard there's a new guy coming. Someone my age, Berta said. I think the ladies are setting us up, so I'm freaking out a bit."

"You've never met him?"

Marnie blushed. "I saw a photo, and ... he's dreamy! I know I'm too old to talk like this, but I can't help it."

"You're not old!"

She glanced at her friend's flowery top and white three-quarter length pants. Although no expert in mainstream fashion, she had a feeling Marnie could shave ten years off her age by changing clothes. Based on a group photo she'd seen on Facebook, her friend dressed exactly like the sixty-year-old ladies in her writing group. One day she'd find a way to bring it up, gently.

They made it onto the deck, Lilla dozing off against her shoulder.

Marnie stroked a brown curl hanging over the girl's face. "You know what I just realised? We're both single. At the same time!"

"Single mums." The term made her shiver.

"It's not that bad," Marnie assured her, turning on the porch light. "Everybody has baggage these days."

As Marnie walked them down her driveway, towards her car, they nearly bumped into the lone character emerging from the darkness. Marnie's ex-mother-in-law, Nanette.

Her chignon was partly undone, her eyes wild. "Someone's

in my garden. Someone's stealing my tomatoes."

Shasa cast a sympathetic look at her friend, mouthing 'good luck'. Marnie had the patience of a saint.

Rushing away, she heard her friend's firm and reassuring voice. "You didn't plant tomatoes this year, remember?"

Chapter 16

Elsie was buttering a sandwich for a late dinner when her phone rang. It never rang in the evening and the sound made her jump. She didn't recognise the number and hesitated for a moment before picking up.

"Elsie speaking."

"Hello! It's Earl, from the council. I'm sorry to bother you at home so late." He sounded out of breath, like he'd been running.

Elsie stretched her mouth into a smile, hoping it made her voice friendlier. "Earl! What a surprise."

"I'm just leaving work and was wondering ... I have something that might interest you, a couple of printouts.

I'm driving past your house, so I could drop them off at your door or maybe in your mailbox if it's too late?"

Elsie looked at the clock. Seven-thirty p.m. What kind of nana did he take her for? "No, I was just making a cup of tea. Text me when you're at the gate, and I'll buzz you in."

"Great. I'll be there in fifteen minutes."

Elsie put the phone down, perplexed. She'd never spoken to Earl outside the council building. Town planners didn't make house calls, so this was unorthodox. Something to do with the section, no doubt.

She picked up her phone again and brought up Shasa's number. It was still saved under 'Audrey' as she'd first thought of her. Shasa was such a strange name, and the girl looked a lot like a young Audrey Hepburn. At least she would if she'd ditch the ethnic wardrobe for a classier one. She had the figure.

Shasa picked up on the second ring. Elsie explained that Earl was coming over with some papers and asked if she and Marnie wanted to join them. "Just a quick cup of tea at my place, if it suits."

She heard the little girl talking in the background and her insides clenched. Elsie hadn't even considered the girl's bedtime.

"Sounds good. We're just leaving Marnie's. She's got her hands full with her mother-in-law but we could stop at yours on the way home. You're somewhere on the other side of the lake, right?"

Elsie gave her the address and ended the call. The phone still in her hand, she sat down in her Eames armchair. What was going on? She rarely had visitors, especially at night. Her social life had shrivelled after the divorce, and she'd been contemplating ways to improve it. Now this little get together had come together without any advance planning. Ann, her nosy neighbour, wouldn't be able to peel herself off the window when the cars started arriving.

Entering her kitchen, Elsie arranged some Afghan biscuits on a tray, along with cheese and crackers. She also filled Stina's bowl and tried to wake up the napping dog. She feared the old girl wouldn't be much fun to play with.

After a moment, her phone beeped, and she opened the gate to Earl's Hyundai. It was strange to see him here. Standing in the open doorway, she waited for him to cross the yard. He looked as hapless as ever in a cheap, wrinkled collar shirt and polyester pants. If he'd attempted to comb his fluffy hair, the effort was undone by the gentle breeze blowing from the lake. He smoothed his hair with his free hand as the other one gripped a yellow envelope.

"Come on in!" she said.

He bowed his head as he stepped in, like visiting a temple.

She led him to the lounge. "It's good to see you."

Earl took a seat on the couch next to Stina. He rested his hand on the dog and stroked her fur, relaxing a little.

Elsie sat in her armchair and indicated towards the tray of tea and biscuits on the coffee table. "Tea?"

"Thank you."

She fixed him a cup according to his preference and placed it on a coaster in front of him.

As he sipped black tea, she picked up the folder. "What's this? It must be important?"

Earl cleared his throat. "It's ... nothing. Just an old soil report I dug up. You know how I said there wasn't one? Well, this is old, but it might save you a bit of money." She'd never seen him like this, with a hint of colour on his cheeks, almost school boyish.

"That's lovely, thank you. Is that all?"

"I know it's not urgent, I'm sorry if I misled you. It's just... I was just..." He seemed to have lost his ability to speak.

Elsie waited, biting her lip. She'd heard she was intimidating. She wanted to change, but it wasn't easy. People had to work with her, show some courage. Right now, Earl had to take a breath and explain himself.

The doorbell rang.

"That must be Shasa."

Earl looked startled. "Who?"

"One of the people organising this cohousing the project. She was at the council with me, remember? When you told me you're bringing important papers, I invited her along."

Earl's face fell, but he covered it quickly with a smile. "Yes, of course."

Elsie left to get the door, wondering if she'd disappointed him. Had he been expecting to be alone with her? Was there something else in that envelope – something he wasn't happy to share with a stranger?

The tired toddler hung off Shasa's slight frame like a koala.

"Your place is so beautiful," Shasa said, adjusting the girl onto her hip.

Elsie smiled at her sincere reaction.

"Where's doggy?" Lilla asked, lifting her groggy head.

Elsie led them to the lounge to meet Earl, who was now standing, either out of courtesy or because he was keen to leave. He shuffled his feet, greeted the arrivals, and sat down in the armchair.

Shasa chose the couch Earl had vacated. Lilla curled up against the sleeping dog, falling asleep in seconds.

Elsie looked at the sleepers. "I'm sorry I called you in so late. Let's keep this brief."

She turned to Earl, expecting him to continue where he'd left off. It was easier to study him like this, with other people present. He was slim and slightly hunched with thinning hair, but his eyes were bright and youthful, like he was hiding his vitality under a layer of office dust.

Earl twisted the envelope in his hands. Instead of opening it, he got to his feet, addressing Shasa as he spoke. "I'm sorry you got brought into this. I don't have any important information, only a soil report which I easily could've emailed. The reason I came over ... I suppose I was just hoping to catch up with an old friend. I now realise I should've been open about that. I'm quite rusty. Apologies."

He turned to leave, then swivelled back to drop the envelope on the coffee table and turned again in an awkward pirouette. Elsie was so stunned she took several seconds to follow him to the door. By then, he was already in his car with the engine humming, waiting for her to open the gates. Elsie stepped outside, trying to catch his eye, but he stared ahead, knuckles white around the steering wheel. She swallowed and pressed the button on her remote, allowing him to drive away.

Shasa appeared behind her. "Oh, poor Earl," she said, her eyes full of compassion.

"Poor Earl?"

"He's obviously in love with you, and then we showed up."

Elsie shook her head in disbelief. They returned inside and sat down. Lilla slept peacefully, her hand around Stina's neck.

"We should go, too." Shasa cast her an uncertain look.

Elsie pointed at the tray. "Since you're already here will you have a cup of tea? I'd rather not be abandoned by two people on one night."

Shasa smiled, biting into a biscuit. "You must get that a lot. Lovesick men showing up with flimsy excuses?"

"Excuse me?" Elsie raised her brow.

"I just mean, you're gorgeous, wealthy. You must be fighting them off."

Elsie exhaled. "I'm really not. I think they're too scared

to try."

Earl must have been terrified but had still showed up. He hadn't reeked of booze either, like some men who approached her at the club. She had to respect that.

Shasa poured herself a cup of lemon and ginger tea and lifted it to her nose to inhale the steam. "Can I ask, how do you feel about him?"

The question made Elsie nervous. She'd never been with anyone like Earl. A few years ago, she'd have instantly dismissed him as a submissive beta male. Working as a Hamilton City town planner wasn't the career path of a winner. He'd been in the same role, sitting behind the same desk, for as long as she could remember.

"He's a fine friend," she replied. "I never realised he fancied me. I thought we just had a common enemy, my husband."

"What did your husband think about him?"

Elsie laughed. "Jeffrey wouldn't have noticed him. Earl was one of his minions. Not someone he'd consider ... competition."

She could have had an affair with Earl without Jeff suspecting a thing, she thought with amusement. Not that she'd ever considered cheating. That was Jeff's domain. She'd been too busy trying to secure her position as the first lady, the one who couldn't be replaced. And for what?

Elsie sighed, pouring herself another cup of tea. It was lovely to talk to someone other than her dog. She pulled a soft throw over her legs, relaxing into the chair. "For a long time, I thought if I lost my marriage, I'd lose everything – my place in the society, my friends. Everything was tied up with Jeffrey – his connections, his businesses. We made friends with other so-called power couples, and every social interaction was an opportunity to advance his business deals. It was… exhausting."

"And what happened? I mean, after the divorce."

"It all came true. I lost most of my friends and connections."

The only ones left were Kerry and Rita, divorcees with whom she did Zumba and had occasional drinks. And now, she had Shasa and Marnie. They were a window to a foreign world. Maybe it was because of them that she could even contemplate getting to know someone like Earl. Her world was getting a little bigger, a little more colourful.

"It's not all bad," she said, a smile bubbling under the surface. "I got half his money. Well, half of what he failed to hide. I built my own house, my own way. It's quite enjoyable. You'll see."

Shasa gazed up at ceiling. "I hope so. Even if our budget is a lot smaller."

"You'll have to be creative. The most expensive choice is not always the best. There's a lot of tacky, hideous stuff you can waste money on. I've seen it far too many times."

Shasa finished her tea and stroked Lilla's back. "I better take her home to sleep."

She picked up her daughter and carried her to her sardine can of a car, which was parked on the road. Elsie held the car door open and helped her fasten the seatbelt, trying to get the limp rag doll to sit straight enough on her booster seat. Her peaceful, sleeping face brought up the dark cloud again, but it felt more like an old friend, someone she might get used to. She gently brushed a dark curl off the girl's face.

As she closed the car door, she found Shasa behind her, a smile tugging at her lips.

"It's not my place, but I just wanted to say that I really like Earl. He seems like a thoroughly nice guy."

"Duly noted, little matchmaker." Elsie couldn't help smiling.

A thoroughly nice guy. No one had ever said that about Jeffrey. Maybe it wasn't the worst idea to get to know someone different, like Earl. Except that she'd humiliated the poor man. If she wanted to see him again, she'd have to take the first step. But what kind of step?

Chapter 17

Mac approached Shasa's house with trepidation. It was past eight o'clock. He had tried to pick a time when the little girl would be in bed, but not so late that he'd risk waking Shasa. In his experience, women were grouchy when woken up from sleep.

He left his ute at home and grabbed a scooter. Parking anywhere near his parents' house ran the risk of his mum spotting him. Shasa's banged-up Toyota blocked the driveway. He noticed a light on in the kitchen but didn't see any movement.

Mac left the scooter on the footpath and snuck through the front gate, grateful for the lack of outdoor lighting. He knocked on the door as softly as possible. After a moment, he heard footsteps.

Shasa cracked the door, peering at him over the tightly stretched security chain. “What are you doing here?”

“Hi! Is this a bad time? I have something to discuss with you.” He glanced at his parents’ house and noticed a curtain moving. “In private, please?”

She shook her head, her eyes bewildered. “I don’t think we should be talking at all.”

“It has nothing to do with real estate, I promise. And I’m desperate for the loo. You don’t want me to pee on your front lawn, do you?”

That worked. Shasa sighed and opened the door. Just in time. As he stepped inside, he heard the creaking of his parents’ front door – probably his dad going into the garage.

Once inside, he flashed Shasa an apologetic smile. “That was a lie, sorry. I don’t need to pee. But before you toss me out, can I have a quick word?”

She stared at him like she could hardly believe her eyes. “You’re ... you’re...”

“Charming?” he suggested.

She huffed, spun on her heels, and marched into the dining room. He took it as an invitation and followed her. The house was tidier than last time, although no amount of cleaning was going to make the old place shine. He liked her thoughtful touches, though—the hand-painted flowerpots and ink-dipped curtains. She used a lot of color and combined it in ways he'd never seen before, down to her own mustard yellow top and flowery pants.

He thought about going out with her, being seen together. What would Rick say?

Shasa sat down at the round dining table and nodded at the seat on the other side. "What do you want?" Her voice wobbled.

He watched for signs of desire or interest. Maybe she didn't fancy him, but she'd loved being on stage, he was sure of that.

Mac sat down and made eye contact. "Gareth's directing a play. He wants you to audition for the lead role."

She took a moment to process his words, slowly shaking her head. "I'm not an actor."

He caught the glimmer of a smile and it gave him courage. "Gareth said he'd get us a private audition after hours. We'd be the wild card or something like that."

She laughed. "It's wild alright." After a few seconds, her laugh dried up, her eyes sharpened. "Us? You said us?"

"There are two lead roles. It's a play based on an old film, Roman Holiday. Have you seen it?"

Shasa shook her head.

"Me, neither. We can watch it. I mean, you can watch it on your own, and I can watch it somewhere else."

"Because you could never sit next to me for an entire movie?" Her eyes twinkled.

Mac's spine tingled. That was his opening. "You've made

it clear you can't stand the sight of me. I was just trying to offer you an acceptable alternative."

She got up and popped into the kitchen. "Tea?" she asked, turning on the kettle.

"Do you have coffee?"

"Instant."

"God, no."

He immediately regretted his gut reaction. He should have just accepted whatever tree bark juice she was serving. He rubbed his temples, watching her back as she silently prepared a cup of tea for herself.

She returned to the table, a weary look in her eyes. "I don't have a lot of time for hobbies. I have a kid."

He nodded. "Look, if it weren't for this play, and what Gareth said about us playing so well off each other, I'd leave you alone. But you're great on stage. I suppose I was hoping we could put a pin on the other stuff and pursue this play together. No matter what happens with... you know."

"My home?" She shot him a challenging gaze.

He took a breath. "The house. The section. Your blueberries..." Her look softened, and he congratulated himself for remembering the bloody bush in the backyard. "You like acting, don't you?" He caught her eyes and saw the spark.

"I do."

"Then, do it for yourself!"

She stirred her tea. "But I'd have to do it with you.

Someone who's putting us out of our home and trying to sabotage..."

"Hey, hey! I'm not trying to sabotage anything! It's all business, nothing personal. It was pretty straightforward before you gathered your leftie troops to buy the same section and sabotage *my* plans!"

Her eyes flashed. "Leftie troops? I'm just trying to make an omelette when the eggs are already broken! There are no decent rentals. Somebody has to fight for those who aren't already on that damn property ladder and buying up half the town!"

"And you couldn't do that on any other section?"

He noticed a glimpse of shame as she stood up, releasing a deep sigh. "I need a bathroom break."

She rushed into the hallway, leaving him staring at her steaming teacup.

Chapter 18

Shasa looked into the bathroom mirror, trying to calm down. She hated this guy. She hated everything he represented. Part of her wanted him out of the house, while another part, the one that like to play with fire, insisted he stayed.

Her logical brain perked up, offering the fire-loving part of her ammunition. She could use this audition as an opportunity to find out about Mac's plans. That's what she was supposed to do. He had admitted they were messing up his business. Had he meant to say it? If she kept him talking, maybe he would reveal something else.

She splashed cold water on her face to cool down. She had to get her phone and text Elsie. She would know what to do.

Maybe it was best to keep Mac here a bit longer, to make him think she was considering the play. That way, if Elsie had any questions, she could try to find out the answers.

The idea of playing spy made her heart pound in her ears. Where was her phone, anyway? In the bedroom? She made it back to the kitchen and found Mac sitting back, thumbing his phone.

"I think I heard Lilla, I'm just going to check on her, okay?" She rushed out again, leaving him looking bemused.

He had such a gorgeous face, dark eyes, a sculpted jaw, and a delicious mouth perfectly framed by dark stubble. He dressed for success, all tidy and above board but looked as dangerous as he likely was. A shark. Someone who would eat her alive and swallow the bones. She shivered as she snuck into the bedroom, taking in the view of her sleeping daughter sprawled across the bed. Why did toddlers insist on sleeping sideways?

She picked up her phone from the nightstand and sent a group text to Elsie and Marnie.

> **Shasa:** Mac's here, wants me to audition for a play with him (weird, right?). What do I do???!!

She stood for a moment, waiting for a reply. Could she risk bringing the phone with her? On silent, she would feel the buzz if she had it in her pocket. If she had pockets. She scanned her wardrobe for options and landed on a pair of grey slacks that could hide the phone. Then she wrapped herself in a long cardigan to hide her cleavage. A double win. She looked like she was ready for bed and could keep her phone discreetly hidden under the layers.

She checked herself in the mirror, brushing her hair with her fingers. Part of her wanted to dab on perfume, but she stopped herself. Ridiculous! He would think she was hot for him.

Mac was the kind of man she had been trained to hate – a self-entitled jackass. Years of discussion on the widening wealth gap and the mad, unfair ruthlessness of the property market flooded her brain, carrying fragments of truths, statements, and sad stories. She rubbed her forehead, trying to push aside the voices. Ollie's voice, the loudest of them all, called for justice, for a revolution, for redistribution of wealth. Why was she even entertaining the idea of spending time with Mac? Why did seeing him have such an effect on her?

She stopped at the kitchen doorway and studied his profile, his lips moving slightly as he read something on his phone screen. She wanted to kiss him again, feel that mouth on hers and the hot, white heat between them. Her lady parts agreed, waking up with a tingle. It's just a physical reaction, she told herself, a cocktail of hormones and loneliness.

Still, as she stepped closer, she was grateful he couldn't read her mind.

"Is she okay?" he asked, looking up.

"Yeah, fast asleep… now."

It was true, technically. She found it hard to lie to him, especially when he looked at her with such concern. It was fake, obviously. He was just a great actor. How could she ever match his skill on stage? It wasn't the same as doing improv. She'd have to remember her lines and perform well enough for a paying audience.

"Can you tell me more about the play?" she asked, sliding into her seat.

If she showed interest and kept him talking, she could win some time.

His face lit up. "Look who's coming around! I don't know too much about the play, but if you're interested, we could meet up with Gareth, and he can explain it better. Although he said we should watch the film first because he'll be referencing that…"

"Whoa, hold on! I didn't say I'd do it." She held up her hand but nothing seemed to extinguish the hope in his eyes.

"You don't have to decide now. We can watch the film and meet with Gareth first."

The phone buzzed in her pocket. She drained her tea and got up to rinse her cup, deliberately shifting behind a corner. She fished the phone from her pocket and found two messages. Marnie's text began with a row of surprised emojis, like a tiny choir of yellow faces singing.

> **Marnie:** Oohh, he's snooping! You should do the same! Just be friendly, get him to talk. Find out how much he offered for the section!

Elsie didn't do emojis.

> **Elsie:** Ask about the number of apartments and how many are pre-sold. That information would be valuable.

Shasa replied with a thumbs-up emoji and hid the phone in her pocket. Elsie and Marnie were right, but how could she pull this off? Her nerves were vibrating, and she placed her teacup in the sink, feeling like a dirty double agent. But her friends trusted her. They were investing in her project, and that's where her allegiance had to lie.

"Okay," she said, looking him square in the eye. "Let's watch that film."

He met her stare with such excitement that she had to swallow a hot ball of guilt. She wasn't lying, though. Part of her longed to curl up on a couch next to him and inhale his scent... Okay, she didn't care about the film part. She was just lonely and horny.

"Tomorrow night?" Mac asked.

"Sure. Is it easier for you if we watch it here, after Lilla goes to bed?"

Shasa blushed. "I don't have a TV."

He glanced at the doorway giving to her living room like he didn't believe her. The corner of his mouth tugged upwards. "That's okay. I can bring my laptop?"

Her fingers brushed against her pocket, feeling the outline of her phone. If he invited her into his house, she had a much better chance of snooping around. "I can get a sitter. Marnie's usually happy. She just brings her iPad and writes here instead of at home." She kept her expression neutral, like she didn't mind either way.

"Great. You can come to my place then. I'll download the film."

"Sounds good."

A faint cry from the bedroom told her that her daughter had woken up, this time for real.

Shasa cast an apologetic look at Mac. "That's my cue. You should go before she really gets going. Save yourself."

She turned around, leaving Mac to find his own way out. At the bedroom doorway, she noticed him right at her heels. Lilla sat on the bed, wide awake. Noticing Mac, she whipped her head from side to side, stunned silent. Mac took a step closer.

"Mac!" Lilla lifted her hands for him to pick her up.

Mac looked at Shasa. "May I?"

She shrugged. "Sure."

He wasn't a stranger anymore, and Lilla didn't seem scared. If anything, she was delighted to find him in her room and wrapped her hands around his neck as he held her. She was already too heavy for Shasa to hold for longer than a couple of minutes. She usually lowered her back down as soon as possible or lay down on the bed next to her. But Mac stood and held her like she was still a baby.

Lilla relaxed her head against his shoulder, and her eyelids dipped. In a couple of minutes, she was asleep. Shasa stared at the absolute miracle unfolding before her eyes. It must have been beginner's luck, if that was a thing with children.

"Should I put her back down?" Mac whispered.

"You can try. It doesn't always—"

He was already in motion. She hurried to catch the girl, in case she woke up and started thrashing around, but Lilla remained fast asleep, happily snuggling under the blanket.

They tiptoed out of the bedroom to the front door.

Mac reached for the doorknob, then turned back. "I'm sorry. I'm not sure if I should've done that. I just thought you might need a break, that's all. It can't be easy."

"Thanks. It's not." The deep sigh that escaped Shasa's chest took her by surprise. She'd meant to put on a smile and play it down like she usually did.

We're okay. We manage.

But something about his eyes coaxed out her true feelings.

"She's cute. Looks a lot like you." His gaze lingered on her face, making her tingle all over.

Shasa feigned a yawn, which quickly turned real.

Mac took the hint and opened the door. "I'll let you get some sleep."

She stepped back to keep a safe distance. This movie-watching was going to test her self-control.

"Thank you for considering the audition," he said as he stepped onto the deck.

A gust of cool night air hit her face. "No worries."

"I'll see you tomorrow, then?"

He pulled a wallet out of his jacket pocket and unearthed a business card – the same blue one he'd given her earlier. "Here's my phone number, in case you've... misplaced the last one. Text me, and I'll text you the address."

"What time?"

"Any time that works for you. I don't have a kid, so..."

"It'll be closer to eight."

"Perfect." He took a step closer and opened his arms.

Startled by what she thought was an incoming hug, Shasa raised her hand to his shoulder. His stubble brushed against her cheek as he kissed the air, then retreated down the steps. His warm breath lingered in her ear as she watched him disappear into the darkness. She'd been so close to sliding her fingers through his thick mane and pulling him in for another kiss. Dangerously close.

Chapter 19

Shasa inched forward in the ice cream queue, holding Lilla's hand as the little girl swung in the air between her and Marnie. They were at Hamilton Gardens, along with hundreds of people who had come to see a new themed garden. The midday sun was still scorching hot.

"You have a date tonight?" Marnie asked, casting Shasa a meaningful look.

"No! Not a date," Shasa protested. "Just research for the play."

"But you're going to his place?"

"I thought that'd be good if I'm supposed to snoop around. Not sure I'll find anything, though. He knows we're after the same section. He'll be careful."

Marnie shrugged. "You never know what might be useful."

"How was writing group? I mean, how was the new guy?" Shasa asked.

"He didn't show up. I think he got weirded out by all the meddling. The ladies are a bit intense." She rolled her eyes.

Shasa raised her brow. "How about you approach someone or make yourself available? I wouldn't leave it to those old ladies."

Marnie shook her head, smiling. "I'm not impulsive like you."

"You write stories with perfect, chiseled guys... but you won't actually date one in real life?"

Marnie dipped her head, hiding behind a cloud of curls. "I pair those guys with gorgeous women, not someone like me."

"You are beautiful, you know that, right?" Shasa let go of Lilla's hand and hugged her friend.

Lilla joined in, hugging Marnie's legs. Marnie was touchy about her weight, while Shasa was jealous of her curves.

"Thanks," Marnie whispered, wiping her eyes. "I needed that."

Once Lilla got her ice cream, they wandered through the gates towards the new Surrealist Garden, their meeting spot with Elsie.

The gardens were Hamilton's pride and joy, built over what used to be the town's rubbish dump. Before Lilla was born, Shasa had loved coming in late at night and sitting in the Renaissance garden. When Ollie had dreamed of saving whales in the Pacific Ocean, she'd dreamed of climbing narrow cobblestone streets in Tuscany. She hadn't shared those dreams with Ollie. Tourist trips burdened the planet with a massive carbon footprint.

Lilla spotted Elsie's old dachshund and ran to give her a hug. Elsie waved at them, looking stylish in wrinkle-free linen and a wide-brimmed hat. They exchanged hellos and took a quick tour of the new garden. Apart from a couple of oversized items, it held nothing of interest. They tracked back towards the tropical garden.

"I received early drawings from the architect. I'll send them your way," Elsie said. "We're working hard to stay under budget, but it's important that you're happy with it."

Marnie waved her hand. "I'm not fussy. All those new builds look the same to me, to be honest."

"That's so true!" Shasa echoed. "They must order all the kitchens from the same manufacturer or something. White cabinets and that grey lino with fake wood grain. I'm fine with it, though."

Elsie gave them an odd look. "White and grey is the standard palette for rentals, but there are other options out there. Would you like me to find out what we can afford?"

Shasa looked at her like she was her fairy godmother. "Yes, please!"

They made it to the round atrium with a water fountain.

She pointed at the long, hedge-lined walkway. "Can we go to the Renaissance one, please?"

At the vine-covered doorway, Elsie suddenly stopped in her tracks. "Oh, no," she whispered.

An older Caucasian man in a formal jacket, surrounded by a group of Asians, raised his hand in greeting. Straightening her back, Elsie crossed the cobblestone path and stopped a few feet away from him. Shasa and Marnie followed a few steps behind.

The silver fox smiled. "Elsie! Good to see you."

"You too, Jeff." She glanced at his companions.

"This is Elsie ... Joyce, my old business partner," he told the group, who smiled and did slight bows. "Mr Chu and his associates just arrived from Beijing. I'm showing them around Hamilton."

Elsie gestured at Marnie and Shasa. "Meet Marnie, Shasa, and Lilla," she said. "They're working on a cohousing community I'm advising on."

Jeff's face looked blank. "A what?"

"A cohousing community," Marnie repeated louder, like the man was hard of hearing.

Elsie suppressed a smile.

Jeff recovered from his surprise and greeted them. "G'day. I'm Jeffrey Alders."

Elsie's ex-husband. That made sense. The air bristled with tension.

Shasa shook his hand. "We're so lucky to have Elsie

onboard, she has a wealth of knowledge."

Elsie shuffled her feet, clearly eager to move on.

Jeff tilted his head. "Cohousing? Like a commune? Yurts? Sounds ... exciting." His smile reminded Shasa of Al Pacino playing the devil.

She glared at him. "No, it's just an apartment building with shared gardens."

Mr. Chu and his associates wandered towards the balcony; cameras pointed at the fountain. Lilla ran after them, disappearing down the stairs to the orange grove. Shasa was about to chase after her, but Marnie signaled her to stay and ran to fetch the girl.

Jeffrey folded his arms, studying Elsie. "I see you've found a nice charity project. You should have done that years ago."

Elsie tried to match his stare. "Instead of butting into your business?"

Shasa shifted an inch closer, to show support.

Jeff huffed. "For twenty years, you complained about being lonely and disconnected. Still, you wouldn't get involved with anything. I had to drag you to every charity event and fundraiser."

Elsie's jaw ticked. "This isn't a charity, just a fun project with new friends."

Jeff's eyebrows sailed up. "So, you're not funding this... comm... housing?"

Elsie rubbed her neck. Jeff's gaze flicked between her and Shasa, trying to make sense of it all.

Shasa spoke without thinking, desperate to alleviate the rising tension. “Elsie is investing! We’re so grateful. We couldn’t do this without her!”

Jeff’s eyebrows inched even higher. “Investing? Is that right? That’s gracious of you, Elsie. You’re right, it’s nothing like those charity projects you thought were fake. It’s nice to see that you’re cultivating *real* friendships now.”

Elsie visibly shuddered. “Goodbye, Jeffrey.”

She motioned to Shasa, and they strode to the balcony, past the Chu group, and down to the orange grove, joining Marnie and Lilla at the far exit. Elsie powered up the leafy path, and they struggled to match her pace. In front of the gift shop, she stopped. Shasa caught up with her first.

Elsie looked mortified. “I’m sorry you had to see that.”

Shasa offered a sympathetic smile. “Are you okay?” Worry churned in her stomach. She could feel their dream slipping away, along with this woman. Was there anything she could do?

“I’m fine.” Elsie turned on her heels and headed towards the carpark.

Marnie caught up with Shasa. “What’s going on?”

“Her ex-husband got to her.”

“Got to her? How?”

“I’m worried she’s going to rethink her involvement in our project.” Shasa’s breath caught in her throat.

Marnie’s eyes widened. “Are you sure? Maybe she’s just reeling from the encounter and needs some time to cool off?

Ex-husbands can push your buttons."

Shasa shook her head, her face hot. "That jerk... he said 'oh, you've found yourself a new charity project' or something, and she looked mortified. She was embarrassed of us. And I made it worse, talking about her involvement."

Marnie secured Lilla on her hip and used her free hand to rub Shasa's shoulder. "I think you're reading too much into this."

"But it's true!" Shasa insisted, fighting tears. "We need her, but she doesn't need us. It's not collaboration, it is charity!"

"So what? There's nothing wrong with charity."

"She's not into charity projects, her ex-husband said that. So, if she realises that's what this is, she'll drop us. We'll be finished."

Marnie stared into the distance, biting her bottom lip. "Money's not the only thing we need from each other."

Shasa picked at a thread hanging from the edge of her shirt. "I should cancel the movie night."

Marnie shot Shasa a furious look. "No! You need to do everything you can to find out about this guy! With your help, we can make this a good investment for Elsie. She told us your street is one of the best in town. Good investments aren't charity. I know it looks bad right now, but Elsie hasn't told us she's out. Until then, we'll keep going, right? Let's not self-sabotage. Life's hard enough as it is."

Shasa took a deep breath and tried to smile, even if her

eyes were welling up. "You're wise beyond your years, you know that?"

Marnie placed a hand on her chest, adopting a look of exaggerated graciousness. "I know."

They strolled towards the carpark, letting Lilla dart around the path before them. Marnie linked arms with Shasa. "We'll sort this out, I promise. Just focus on your date tonight. Be charming. Don't ... you know ... channel Ollie, okay?"

"Channel Ollie?" Shasa's eyes rounded.

"You know what I mean. Don't be judgmental. You need this guy to let his guard down and trust you. He's clearly into you, so that's a good start."

Shasa sighed. There were several inaccuracies that she should have corrected. It wasn't a date. Mac wasn't into her. She'd initiated the stage kiss. She was the one with wobbly knees around him, and it scared her. To get him to let his guard down, she'd have to lower hers even further, and she was already in the danger zone. She leaned on Marnie's shoulder, inhaling the familiar scent of mango body butter, taking comfort in the steadiness of her gait. She had to keep her eyes on the prize. Her own home. No more landlords. No more uncertainty. It was worth it.

Chapter 20

At seven p.m. that night, Lilla worked on a bowl of Weetbix, her pyjama sleeve soaking in the milk. Shasa rummaged through her pantry for snacks and tea. Her fingers fumbled from nerves.

Marnie placed her iPad on the table and sat down. "Stop. I can find my own snacks. I know where you keep stuff."

Shasa glanced at her daughter. "Just put her to bed when she starts nodding, okay?"

"We're fine. Go get ready." Marnie waved her away and she rushed out to take a shower.

Ten minutes later, Shasa stood in the bedroom in her underwear, staring into the mirror. She had no idea how to dress. It wasn't a date, but was she supposed to look nice? The address Mac had texted her was in the wealthy part of town. In her usual clothes, she'd stick out like a particularly sore thumb. Would it affect her chances of connecting with him, spying on him or whatever she was meant to be doing?

The questions were pointless given the limited choice in her wardrobe. After some deliberation, she decided on a pair of tights and a casual cotton wrap dress with pockets, which highlighted her small waist and showed a little cleavage. Not something she should have been concerned about, just a happy accident. She went light on jewelry and exchanged her ensemble of colorful bracelets for two simple ones.

Lilla let her go with minimal drama. She was getting used to Marnie as a babysitter. A huge relief. Marnie sometimes sat for her during the day to let Shasa go shopping or take a break, but she hadn't been out at night in two years. Not since Ollie had left. A few minutes later, she was on the road, trying to calm down by listening to mindless chatter on the local radio. Driving by herself at night brought on a strange feeling, like she'd just run away from her daughter. The sun was low, and the horizon glowed a hazy peach.

As she turned onto Mac's street, she took in the enormous houses. Each design was more complicated than the last, featuring angled windows and multi-faceted roofs. They sprawled across small sections, leaving hardly any space in between. Mac's house was a tall and dark specimen of stone and cedar paneling. She parked in the driveway, her car dwarfed by his truck.

The yard was lit by several spotlights, revealing a landscaped garden of tiles, pebbles, and tufts of grass that looked almost too neat to be real. The pebbles were perfectly round, and the black tiles glinted in the evening light.

Shasa didn't have a proper handbag and decided to leave her canvas bag in the car. She slipped her phone into her dress pocket in case Marnie called, or she found something she needed to photograph. The thought terrified her.

She approached the house, her nerves vibrating. Before she could choose between knocking and texting, Mac opened the door. Barefoot, in a pair of worn jeans and a T-shirt, he looked too informal for the setting. He seemed to have two wardrobe choices – that million-dollar suit or the overly casual tees and jeans. She preferred him casual. It made him less intimidating, and she found it easier to forget their differences and focus on other things – like the contour of his chest under the thin fabric. Nope. Don't go there.

She raised her gaze to his face. "I like your house."

His cocked his head, studying her face, his mouth twitching. "No, you don't."

Shasa's cheeks burned. "I mean I appreciate its... it looks expensive."

To her relief, Mac dropped the subject. Giving her a cheeky smile, he led her across the marbled floor, past a high-tech kitchen of charcoal and cherry wood, to a toddler-death-trap staircase leading to the second floor.

At the foot of the stairs, he paused. "TV's upstairs, but would you like a drink first? Coffee? Should we grab some snacks?"

She shrugged, looking at the spotless kitchen. She couldn't see any traces of food or even a fridge. It must have been disguised as one of the cabinets. "I don't know. Whatever you're having is fine with me. Except alcohol, since I'm driving."

Also, she needed to stay sharp. Mac circled the huge kitchen island and opened a drawer. "I have tea. Regular, or... irregular?"

He beckoned her closer. She peered at the colourful rows of tea packets, all wrapped in plastic. "I thought you didn't even drink tea?"

A faint pink appeared on Mac's cheeks. "No, but I thought you might."

It was enough tea to last her half a year.

"You went shopping for me? I mean ... you bought these for me?" She gawked at the selection, then stared at him for so long he practically squirmed under her gaze.

"What's the big deal? I knew you were coming over, and I thought you might not like coffee or beer."

He turned to fill the jug and turn it on, probably to hide from Shasa's questioning eyes. She couldn't get over the gesture. It didn't make any sense. She browsed the packets, noting the expensive brands she never bought. "And how many years did you think I'd stay over?"

Mac handed her an empty teacup, his cheeks even redder than they'd been before. "Ha ha. I just wanted to give you a choice. I didn't know what you liked."

She held onto the chunky, ceramic teacup, dumbfounded. "If you visited me... would you expect me to get every brand of coffee and beer for you, just in case?"

"No. I expect you to pick a tea you like and put the bag in your cup," he grumbled.

She pulled out a packet of something called 'Relax' – appropriate, she needed to chill. It came in a triangular tea bag that held entire leaves and flowers, like potpourri. They waited for the jug to boil, a heavy silence hanging between them. For lack of anything else to do, she strolled around the kitchen island, surveying the shiny finish on every surface. There were no fingerprints.

"Do you wear gloves?" she asked.

"What?"

"It's so shiny and spotless." She blinked, wondering what stupid thing would next escape her mouth. She clearly couldn't help herself.

"I moved in two months ago. I don't use this kitchen a lot."

"Why? Whose kitchen do you use?"

Mac laughed. "I eat out or... I used to hang out at my girlfriend's place, but not anymore."

He turned his back to her, taking a bottle of beer from a tall cupboard that was hiding the fridge. She wondered if he was implying they'd broken up. Maybe the girlfriend's place was unavailable for another reason.

"We got a lot of takeout before Christmas, too," she confessed. "Things were so busy. I always felt bad. It's so unhealthy."

Mac looked up, surprised. "Unhealthy? What about Japanese, or the vegan place downtown? It's full of veggies."

What world did this guy live in? "Um... those meals are pretty pricey. The only Asian we do is the chicken fried rice from the corner shop. It's under ten dollars and there're enough leftovers for the next day."

She could tell Mac was trying to hide his disgust. "That's a good deal."

Her eyes wandered around the kitchen. What a waste of square footage.

Mac followed her gaze. "I know, I hardly need a kitchen like this, but it's hard to sell a house without one, so I told the builders to install it, anyway."

Her lips curled at the joke. As she relaxed, she realised she felt jealous – not just of his amazing kitchen, but of the way he made fun of it. She could joke about her lack of money with friends, but not here, surrounded by all this marble. It would sound like a pity-party. She had to find some common ground and stop channelling Ollie. Marnie was right. She did that, almost on instinct.

The jug boiled and Mac made her the cup of tea, handing it over with a smile. She inhaled the rich aroma, hoping the relaxing qualities transferred with the smell. Waiting for Mac to pour himself a glass of beer, she wandered over to the lounge which sprawled into another sitting area. How many living areas did one guy need? The house was furnished, but not in a homely way. It looked like it had been staged for sale.

She glanced over her shoulder, wondering if Mac was okay with her exploring.

"Go ahead!" He grinned at her. "There are more rooms I don't use in that direction." He gestured at an arched doorway, and she moved forward, intrigued.

Having a tour of the house with his permission didn't qualify as spying, but she was curious. She'd never seen anyone her age living like this. Some of her friends had newer rentals with shiny white walls and chrome appliances. Compared to her old villa, they looked fancy in a sterile cookie cutter way. Mac's house was something different altogether, with every detail upgraded from the standard rental look, from the complex skirting boards to soft oatmeal walls and feature lights that hung at just the right height. It didn't have the artistic flair of Elsie's house, but it looked similarly expensive, like an upmarket hotel.

She inwardly groaned at the thought of their first encounter, at her pigsty of a home. Had Mac been disgusted? Did he pity her? She stepped into a third living area with quadruple doors opening to the back garden and a large deck outside.

Mac joined her, holding a glass of beer. "It looks better in daylight. I haven't had a chance to install the outdoor lights yet."

"But you do have lights." She pointed at the two spotlights illuminating the deck.

"I mean garden lights."

"Why? Do you garden at night?"

He laughed. "No. It just looks better with lights. More... festive."

"Doesn't it use a lot of electricity?" She bit her lip. Again, the words had floated out before she could stop them. Why couldn't she let this go?

"You can get powerful solar ones these days. They have batteries, so they charge during the day and then burn all night."

"Wow. That sounds amazing." She smiled, pleased that her voice held some genuine enthusiasm. "Those must be expensive?"

"No, I reckon I can get the whole lot done for a couple of grand."

She held her breath. That was more than she'd spent on her car. She stared into the black garden. "But you'll be asleep." She winced. She couldn't help these thoughts. She couldn't lock them in, either.

Mac shrugged. "Before I go to sleep, I might have people over and we might be sitting outside on the deck."

"And you want to see the garden?" It was meant to be a

simple statement but came out like a question.

He knitted his brow. "Why is this such an issue for you?"

Why, indeed?

Heat crawled up Shasa's neck, burning her cheeks. "I don't know. I suppose it's the idea of someone spending thousands on lighting up their garden, when there are people living in garages who can't afford heating or shoes for their kids."

She sighed in exasperation. Everywhere she looked, she saw evidence of the giant chasm between them. How was she supposed to get closer to him, to build trust? They didn't even speak the same language. With every word, she dug a deeper hole for herself.

"You know what?" Mac's sharp tone gave her a start. His eyes bore into hers with a fierceness that made her shiver. "You've seen my parents' house. I didn't grow up rich, but I got tired of being poor. I got tired of the attitude, this idea that I was meant to give it all away as soon as something landed on my lap. That I wasn't allowed to hold on to wealth, whatever that means. I wasn't allowed to invest. That's how my parents stayed poor, and that's why they struggle to feed all those kids every week. They give everything away, so now they have nothing left to give."

"It's not nothing. They feed the kids!" She couldn't help raising her voice.

"It's nothing compared to building houses for the homeless."

"Who's building houses for the homeless?"

Mac clamped his mouth shut, looking out the window. What was he on about? She sensed he'd said more than he'd intended, but she couldn't let it go.

"Are you building houses for the homeless?"

Mac glanced at her, his jaw twitching. "That's the plan. Well, not exactly homeless, but I want to help people on low income into homeownership. I just need to build capital first. If I give everything away too early, it won't be enough to make a difference. It's not something I advertise, but I've set up a trust and I'm working on it."

She stared at her bare toes, shocked by his admission. Bloody Ollie. He'd poisoned her against everyone who didn't represent his own brand of charity and goodwill.

"I'm sorry," she whispered. "I thought you were just in it for yourself."

"Yeah, well. Looks can be deceiving." Mac studied her, his expression guarded, voice barely audible. "But you're right. I have nothing to show for myself, yet."

"But you have a plan." Her face burned with shame.

They stood in silence, staring at the dark backyard.

When Mac spoke, his voice was soft and heavy. "Sometimes, I worry I won't have the strength to carry out the plan, that I get greedy and decide to keep it all."

Seeing the pain behind his eyes made her chest squeeze. She shifted closer. "You've told me now. I'll hold you accountable. You know how annoying I am. I can't let anything go." She smiled, her voice filled with remorse.

"Good." He held her gaze for a moment. "And you're not annoying at all."

"I'm not?" Her voice was nearly inaudible.

"No, Shasa. You're a strange creature."

His voice was so tender she shivered from head to toe. She caught a whiff of his scent and held still, trying to breathe it all in. "That could be good or bad, I suppose."

"It's good, trust me."

His mouth curling into a reassuring smile, he reached out to the collar of her dress and picked up something between his thumb and forefinger.

It looked like a flake of Weetbix, transferred from Lilla as she'd hugged her goodbye. Shasa stared at it, her face hot. The slight touch left her body humming. "Weetbix," she said.

"Yum," he said, popping it into his mouth.

She watched in stunned silence as he washed it down with a swig of beer and flashed her a smile.

"Did you skip breakfast or something?"

"I may have."

"Do you want to check the back of my dress? There might be some more." She turned around.

"Okay, let me see. Yeah, there's a bit of toast, thanks. And some bacon."

Delicious shivers shot through her in waves as his fingers trailed down her back, pretending to pick up imaginary items. Oh, how she craved that touch. She turned back to face him, peering into her own cleavage. "I probably have some more crumbs down here. Wouldn't be the first time."

She felt her pulse under her collarbone as his gaze descended to her chest.

"I would love to dive in, but I'm afraid of overloading on carbs."

Shasa chuckled, and her blush deepened as she spotted another Weetbix crumb just inside her bra. Oh, dear God. She was hopeless. She watched Mac swallow as she fished out the crumb. She was about the toss it when he grabbed her wrist and swiped the second crumb into his mouth. "Let's not waste food, right?"

Her heartbeat pounded in her ears, warmth spreading everywhere. What was he doing?

Change the subject.

She turned to look out the glass doors, clearing her throat. "I'm sure the lights will look great."

"It's a good investment."

"Like the huge kitchen that you don't use?"

"Yeah." His playful smirk both relaxed her and made her giddy. She sensed the rift between them closing, which scared her more than any argument.

"Should we start the film?" Mac straightened his back.

She followed him through the house and up the floating staircase, leaving some distance between them.

The upstairs space was cosier, with a fluffy rug and two over-stuffed couches facing the largest TV she'd ever seen. "And I was worried you didn't have a TV big enough to do justice to a fifties black and white film!"

He rolled his eyes. "Very funny."

She sat down on the couch directly facing the TV, placing her teacup on the coffee table.

Mac remained standing, holding his half-finished beer. "Do you want popcorn? I forgot to bring it."

She shrugged. Eating popcorn in a room this tidy felt sacrilegious, but Mac hurried back downstairs. She took several seconds to recognize the opportunity. He'd left her unsupervised. She was here to spy, but his earlier admission and all the chest-touching had thrown her off and she felt torn.

So what if he was planning on helping others with his money? It didn't mean they couldn't pursue the cohousing community. Mac could make his money a thousand different ways, while they had one shot. Shasa took a breath, trying to focus. She couldn't afford to be derailed.

One door led away from the room. Through the half-open doorway, she caught a sliver of a perfectly made bed with a plush charcoal spread. Soft on her feet, she moved across the thick carpet – also charcoal – into the bedroom. This guy was a big fan of charcoal.

The bed looked like a king, or a super king, ridiculously big for one person. Maybe he had regular visitors. Part of her wished he did. Knowing someone had a girlfriend or casual relationships was always a turnoff, and she needed something to reign in the stirrings in her belly.

The sound of the water running downstairs told her Mac was still in the kitchen. She tiptoed across the room to the sole spot of disarray she could see, a pile of papers on his dresser. To her disappointment, it was a play. Not Roman Holiday, but Closer. She flicked through the pages and found a scene covered in yellow highlighter. He must have been practicing lines.

"Please, check out my bedroom. Would you like to peruse my sock drawer as well?"

Shasa jumped, whipping around so fast her head felt dizzy. She took a deep breath, waiting for her heart rate to settle. Thankfully, she could hear a smile in his voice and tried to match his cheeky grin. "Well, you did check out my dirty laundry, so..."

Mac marched past her and pulled open a drawer full of balled up pairs of socks. So neat and tidy. "There. Inspect away."

"Where are the odd ones?" she asked.

He stared at her like she had a screw loose. "Why would I keep the odd socks?"

"In case they get separated in the wash and the lost one turns up later. Then he'll be like 'where's my mate?'" She mimed, acting like a lost little sock.

Mac stared at her with baffled amusement. "Then I'll just throw out another sock. What's the big deal?"

"You'll end up with a pair of perfectly good socks in your rubbish bin!"

Mac cocked his head, his eyes glinting with glee. "What do *you* do with the odd ones?"

Shasa swallowed, fighting her embarrassment. "You can make sock puppets, pin cushions, stress balls... Almost everything we throw out can be recycled into something useful."

She thought about her odd sock collection, which was much larger than the one in her actual sock drawer – dozens of socks forever waiting for their mate, or a new life as something else. Would she ever have time to craft stress balls? The task itself felt so stressful that it almost defeated the purpose.

"What a coincidence! I make mine into stress balls, too. Look." Mac took one of his balled-up pairs of socks and squeezed it in his hands.

"Ha ha," she said drily. She should have left the room, but her eyes had fixated on the tendons and veins on that sock-squeezing arm. "Make fun of me all you want; I just hate waste."

He gazed out the window, his voice soft. "My ex-girlfriend was the exact opposite. She'd throw out pairs of socks if she thought they didn't match my wardrobe. I lost so many towels and sheets and coffee mugs to that woman."

"Seriously?" Shasa swallowed, her mouth dry. So, he was single.

"Are you going to tell me what you're really doing in my bedroom?" The low rumble of his voice vibrated through her and she lifted her eyes to his face, her heart thumping against her ribcage.

Did he know?

She swallowed. "Nothing. Just having a nosy. I don't get to visit houses like this. I'm just trying to... soak up the experience." She waved her arms, going for bright enthusiasm.

Mac's eyes narrowed and a subtle smile hovered on his lips. A challenge. "Then you should definitely test the bed."

Her heartbeat amped up even more and her confident smile was not that confident anymore. "Why? Is it like a special one?" Her voice cracked a little.

He sucked in his lips, that tiny smile still creasing the corners of his eyes. "Well, it's a bedroom. There aren't that many experiences available in here." His gaze dipped down to her cleavage. "And for some reason, I can't stop thinking about Weetbix."

She huffed a laugh, her neck burning. "You're an ass."

"What? I'm just looking out for you."

"Are you, now?"

"Yes! You're here to soak up the experience. If you don't try the bed, you'll never know the full extent of what my house can offer."

"Is that what you tell all your visitors?"

"Only the cute ones."

A muscle on his forearm ticked and for a moment, she thought he might pick her up and throw her on the bed. And for a moment, she wished he would. That probing, teasing gaze was warming up her insides and messing with her head. She wanted his hands on her. She needed them.

"Come one. I dare you." He gestured at the bed, raising his brow.

She lifted her chin, holding his gaze. "Make me."

As soon as she said it, she dashed for the door, and for a split second, she thought she'd made it. But as she reached the doorway, his arms hooked around her waist, lifting her off the ground. She fought back, legs kicking the air, her body pulsing with heat. She put up such a good fight he didn't manage to heave her on the bed. Instead, they fell together, sideways, his arm still around her.

The mattress received them like a cloud, softer than anything she'd ever felt. But it wasn't the mattress her body focused on. It was that strong arm pressing against her stomach, stealing her breath. How long had it been? Liquid warmth rushed down her belly, emptying her mind of coherent thought. For a moment, they lay still, locked in the odd embrace.

Reluctantly, like waking up from a dream, she wiggled out of his grip, sitting up. "It's a nice bed," she said diplomatically, bouncing up and down. Mac's eyes followed her, a little hooded and soft. Dreamy.

Why was he being so weird? Or was it her? She'd practically thrown herself at him. She filled her lungs and clambered off the bed. After a beat, Mac followed.

Passing his dresser, she lifted the script. "Are you doing another play?"

She had to change the subject. Get back to normal.

Mac appeared by her side, peering over her shoulder. "That's just for my scene group. We practise scenes from movies and act them out." His breath made her neck tingle.

Shasa turned around, adding a bit of distance between them. "How many acting groups are you in?"

Mac smiled. "Just those two, at the moment."

She turned the script in her hands and noticed some handwritten notes on the other side. Before she had a chance to read a word, he grabbed it from her and slid it in the top drawer. It landed on a pile of other papers. Why hadn't she looked in the drawer? If she'd gone straight to it, she might have been able to check if there was anything relevant.

Feigning disinterest, she turned to the bedroom window. The street sloped down towards the town. The endless carpet of domestic, suburban lights looked cosy, like a scene from a picture book.

"I like this view."

Mac joined her at the window, again stepping so close that her body took notice. "Me too. That's why I bought the section."

"You built this house?" Her voice climbed to a higher register.

"I designed it. Builders built it."

"You know what I mean."

"This was my first one with the builders I now work with. I thought, if they got this right, I could trust them with the bigger developments."

She nodded, unable to think of anything to say. He clearly knew a lot more about building houses than her. What was she doing here? This whole thing was a bad idea.

"Shall we?" He gestured at the door, and she followed him back into the lounge.

She let him guide her to the couch directly opposite the TV and tried to ignore the fact that he sat right next to her, edging closer to show her his phone screen. "I downloaded this file. I'll just cast it on the TV screen. Let's hope it works."

She wasn't sure why she had to see the file name in his download folder, but she leaned in, inhaling his shower fresh scent, replaying the feel of his arm around her. Mac tapped on his phone, and the opening credits appeared, grainy on the massive screen.

Shasa couldn't remember the last time she'd watched a black and white film. She didn't have time for movies, other than the Frozen ones. Days were long and exhausting. By the time Lilla fell asleep, she hardly wanted to stay up for another two hours.

Tonight, she wasn't sleepy. Every fibre in her body stood to attention, whirring from her proximity to Mac. He'd brought up a bowl of popcorn, cheese and crackers and two bottles of beer. She wanted to eat but felt too highly strung to digest food. She hugged herself, hoping for her insides to settle.

With her brain processing a flurry of conflicting emotions, she struggled to shift her attention onto the movie. Fortunately, the storyline was easy to follow. A few minutes into the movie, Mac sprawled back on the couch. She leant forward, creating just enough distance between them that she could concentrate. Despite the slow fifties style filmmaking, she gradually found herself drawn into the story of Princess Anya craving the anonymity of a commoner, touring Rome, and falling in love with a reporter called Joe.

"Did they use the phrase 'regular Joe' in the fifties?" she asked. "Is that why the character's name is Joe?"

She turned to Mac, who jerked like he'd just woken up. "Huh?"

"I mean, she's a princess, and he's the regular Joe. It seems deliberate."

Mac shrugged. "Sure, why not?" He had a guilty look on his face.

She narrowed her eyes. "Were you asleep?"

A hint of a smile played on his lips. "No." He reached for his phone and paused the film. "I may have lost track of it. Can you fill me in?"

"Seriously? The beginning was slow, but it was just starting to get interesting."

He twisted his mouth. "Sorry. I'm not usually this distracted."

The air was vibrated between them. Barely breathing, she

risked a glance at his crotch. His jeans weren't that tight, but she could see his hard-on, tightly lodged in the left leg. So, she wasn't the only one. It was almost a relief, if it weren't for the way her body reacted to the observation, sending signals from one erogenous zone to the other, like a game of inner laser tag.

She focused her eyes on the screen, heat sweeping up her neck, burning her ears. The film was paused on a close-up of Audrey Hepburn, her giant eyes looking up at Joe. So innocent.

Mac's voice was gruff. "Okay. Full disclosure. I'm distracted by you."

Chapter 21

Shasa looked over her shoulder, her whole body captured by that pair of dark eyes.

"I can't stop thinking about you. And that dress..." Mac sat up, closing the distance between them.

She barely heard his words. They were overshadowed by the hunger she saw in him. Raw, desperate need that reflected her own, speaking a language that transcended words. She inhaled a lungful of his scent and held her breath. His gaze dipped to her lips, full of aching need, and her body responded before her brain could catch up. Hiking up the skirt of her dress, she whipped around and threw her leg over his lap to straddle him.

For a split second, she feared he would push her away, but his hands gripped her hips, firm and inescapable, and as she leaned in, he met her halfway, his mouth crashing on hers like she'd offered oxygen to a drowning man. Tasting him brought back the memory of their stage kiss, the one that wasn't supposed to be real. This one was. She felt him hard against her crotch, further melting whatever was left of her resolve, or better judgment.

She explored his mouth like she'd paid a thousand dollars for a dessert. The price was too high, but it was better than anything she'd ever had.

Mac slid his hands down to her bottom and his tongue connected with hers, sending a powerful surge through her body. She gripped his T-shirt, letting her other hand trail down his chest. Every inch of him felt hot and hard. Her underwear was already soaked, probably staining his jeans. Why hadn't she gone with jeans? It was like she'd planned this – arriving here alone at night, in a dress that opened like a bathrobe. Which he'd already figured out, pulling on the string that held it together, exposing her bra. This was further than she'd planned, even in the dark corners of her mind. The bra was discoloured and had a noticeable rip.

Intense embarrassment cut through her arousal. She wedged one hand between them and used the other to wrap the dress back in place, gasping for breath.

Mac released her, his eyes like two wildly clanging warning bells. "Wow."

"Yeah. Wow." She used the moment of clarity to roll off his lap, back on the couch, back to safety. "I'm sorry," she panted. "I can't be around you. I don't know why... I'm just... I'm so, so stupid."

"No, I'm stupid." His voice was thick.

She exhaled like a deflating balloon, closing her eyes. "I should go."

"Why?" He rubbed his forehead with his fingertips.

"Are you okay?" she asked.

Her throbbing arousal turned into a dull ache as she thought of the implications of this colossal mistake. On a whim, she slapped her own cheek to sober up.

"That's a good idea." He laughed, copying her move. "I might also need a cold shower." He flashed her a pained smile. "Honestly, I don't behave this way. I never do this."

"You never kiss girls who willingly climb into your lap and throw themselves at you?" Shasa winced.

"I mean, I don't invite friends over under some pretense of watching a movie for research, and, you know..."

"Me, neither! I never do any of this. Not since Ollie left. And that was two years ago." That was far more information than she'd intended to divulge, and her stomach lurched.

"Two years? Seriously?" He looked stunned.

"I mean, I didn't know he wasn't coming back, until recently. I had my suspicions, but..."

Shut up, woman.

What was wrong with her? She was here on espionage,

not to pour out her sad life story to this guy who was out to destroy her dreams and rip out her blueberry bush.

"I'm sorry. Two years is a long time." His voice was soft.

Something about his eyes tugged at her heart, and it frightened her more than anything else happening in her body.

"Yeah. I guess it explains me... jumping you." She tried to laugh, but it sounded more like a cry.

Mac shifted, rubbing his chin. "That's not the whole truth." He turned towards her and waited for her to look him in the eye. "Look. There's something between us. Whatever it is... it's physical. Maybe we just emit the right pheromones or something. I feel it when I get close to you. And you feel it, too?"

Shasa nodded. "It's like my body has a mind of its own. It's scary."

He looked away, deep in thought. "Maybe that's why we have great chemistry on stage."

It made sense. Like a magic ingredient.

"So, what do we do?" Her voice cracked.

Mac straightened his spine. "We'll use it."

"Use it?"

The primal part of her hoped he was talking about pinning her against the couch. But of course, he wasn't. They couldn't.

"It'll take a lot of willpower, but we need to just keep our hands off each other, except when acting. Channel that chemistry into the performance."

She gave him a slow nod. "Because if we do something..."

"We might lose the tension," he finished for her. "And things will get complicated."

She sighed. Complicated was an understatement. She had to agree, even as her lady parts protested, carrying angry signs and megaphones.

"Sounds like a plan," she said, trying to lubricate her throat with a bit of saliva. There wasn't any. All the moisture in her body had moved south a while ago. "So, we finish the movie?"

"Sitting far apart." He got up, gesturing at the other couch.

"Yes."

"And you cover that dress with... um... I'll bring something."

"Then you have to cover..." She looked at him, standing there with his hands tucked into his jeans pockets, lips pulled into that annoying, irresistible smirk. "Everything. Including your eyes."

"But I'm supposed to watch a movie." He flashed her that gorgeous smile.

"And change your voice to something grating and high-pitched, please. Or do you have one of those vocoder thingies that you press against your throat, and it makes you sound like a machine? That'd be good."

He chuckled. "So, you like my voice?"

She blushed, realising what she'd just confessed to. Oh,

well. She couldn't pretend she wasn't turned on by him. As much as she also hated him. It was too confusing to even think about. One thing she knew for sure was that she'd regret sleeping with him. And now she knew she had to work a lot harder to avoid that mistake. Being honest with what was going on with her stubborn, sex-deprived body was a good start.

"Yes, I like your voice. And your jaw, and your eyes. And your forearms, and that muscle above your collarbone. Cover it up, please." Her gaze brushed over his crotch, cataloguing one more thing that attracted her. She could still detect the shape of it and had to tear her eyes away.

Mac nodded. "I'll just change into a sack or something. I'll see what I can find."

The bedroom door clicked as he closed it behind him. Shasa got up and crossed the room, pressing her forehead against the cool window. Her body still throbbed, hot and bothered, but her mind reeled, utterly mortified.

The view from the lounge was even more impressive than the one from the bedroom, stretching out further. Hamilton had never looked so big. Shasa stared into the distance, trying to focus on the house she could have, the blueberry bush, the safe playground for Lilla. Their plan was more important than her stupid libido. But what if Elsie pulled out? Their project would die. In that case, why wasn't she in the bedroom with Mac?

She could hardly stop thinking about that kiss. She may

have initiated it, again, but this time he'd responded in a way that left no room for ambiguity. He liked her. No, he was physically attracted to her. She would do well to remember the difference.

What a night.

Shasa threw herself back on the couch and groaned. A few minutes later, Mac returned in his pyjamas. They were bright red and had emojis all over them. Smiley faces, thumbs up... even the poop.

"Where did you get those?" she asked, doubling over with laughter.

"My brother. He thinks it's funny."

"No shit!" She hiccupped.

"Shit, indeed." Mac raised his brows, pointing at one of the poop emojis.

"Here's your new dress." He threw her a rolled-up blanket, then cranked up the air con.

As she covered herself with the soft charcoal throw, Mac took the other couch, turned on the movie, and uncapped a beer. She stared at the other one. Maybe she could have half of it and drive, but she couldn't risk lowering her inhibitions any further. Still, her mouth felt like sandpaper.

"Can you just pause for a minute? I'll get a glass of water." She peeled off the blanket and turned to the stairs, but he pointed at the two empty glasses on the coffee table.

"There's a tap in the master bath, for your convenience." He nodded at his bedroom.

"I do like convenience."

It was only when she passed the dresser that she remembered the papers in the top drawer. She couldn't linger, but maybe, if she was lightning quick... The drawer slid open without a sound. She found the script, turned it over, and scanned the page. The handwriting was messy, but she could tell it had nothing to do with the section. No numbers or property notes. It looked like a pitch for a movie. She caught words 'one-eyed girl,' 'circus,' and 'murder.'

She slid the papers back in the drawer and hurried to fill her water glass. When she stepped back into the lounge, she found Mac watching rugby, the TV on mute. Had he been listening in on her? "Sorry, just checking the score."

She sat down. "That's okay."

"So, did you snoop around my dresser?" he asked, his tone even, eyes firmly on the game.

"Yeah." If she lied, he wouldn't believe her, anyway. "One-eyed girl?"

Mac smiled. "It was just a movie idea. A stupid idea."

"How do you know?" She downed her glass of water.

"Most ideas are. It doesn't matter. You can't even copyright an idea. Execution's the hard part."

She studied Mac's relaxed frame, spreading across the couch in those ridiculous pyjamas. He'd expected her to snoop and wasn't concerned about it. Did it mean he'd cleaned up anything confidential before she arrived? She felt stupid, but also oddly relaxed in his company. Especially now that couches, blankets, and pyjamas stood in the way of physical connection.

She curled up on the couch, starting to feel comfortable. "You should write it, see if it works."

He shook his head. "My brother's the filmmaker, not me. He's obsessed with that stuff. Every time I'm with him, I start jotting down stupid ideas like it's contagious."

She could tell from his expression how much he loved his brother and she tried to ignore the warm glow in her chest. "That sounds like fun."

"Yeah, he's pretty entertaining. And he never has money. You'd like him." Mac's eyes sparkled with mischief.

Shasa glared at him. "I don't glorify poverty. I don't wish it for anyone. It doesn't make you a better person or anything. In fact, it makes you worse. Just like extreme wealth."

"Extreme?"

"I'm not talking about you!"

"Good. Because I think if you ever visit the royal palace or some sheik's summer cottage, you'll run out of superlatives."

She scoffed, which turned into a chuckle. "I get it. Your house is totally average. Which makes my house a dump."

Mac didn't laugh. His voice was tender. "No argument. I don't know how you do it."

"Do what?"

"How you live in that house all year round, with a child. I don't even like to think about it." He looked at her with such concern her insides twisted.

She tried to replace her confusing feelings with anger. "I don't let her get cold! I just heat up one room at a time, and that's where we live."

"Like the lounge?" He frowned.

"No, the lounge is too big to heat. The bedroom works better."

"You eat in the bedroom?"

"Only for those couple of months when it gets really cold." She looked away, sick with embarrassment. What she'd thought of as normal was shocking to him. Was she endangering her child? "I make sure she's warm," she insisted. "She always has her beanie on, even in bed. I know it's not ideal, but I'm doing the best I can." Her voice faltered, eyes stinging.

Mac sat up. "Please don't think I'm judging you. I'm not. I just have my pet peeves… these disgusting things that are normalized in New Zealand. My parents wash black mould off the ceiling every spring like it's no big deal. It shouldn't grow there in the first place!"

She heard the passion in his voice, and it surged through her. "So, you want to demolish their house?"

"I can't wait to!"

"And where are they going to live?"

"I can put them up in one of my rentals for a few months, and then they can move into one of the new townhouses."

She nodded. He had a plan. She had a plan. Their plans weren't compatible. Was there any way they could build the cohousing community on another section, somewhere else? Maybe in time they could, even without Elsie. She could keep saving and hope for the best.

"So, you have rentals?" She asked, holding her breath.

She'd brushed off his offer before, but if Elsie was out, she couldn't be too proud to ask for help. With the cohousing plans in motion, she hadn't done any house hunting. She hadn't submitted a single application. It was careless. Risky.

Mac's gaze lingered on her, the concern still clouding his eyes. "I have a couple of apartments vacating in town. Nothing with a backyard, unfortunately. But I'll ask around, see if anyone knows anything. It'll be a bit more than you pay now, though."

"I know."

She'd never find another deal like that. They'd have to skimp even more, skip any longer car trips, and stop buying takeaways altogether. Beans on toast was always cheaper.

"Should we finish this?" Mac nodded at the TV, now displaying game scores.

He turned the movie back on, and they sank into their respective couches. Shasa was happy to focus on something outside her own reality. Going back to the fifties was perfect. The movie was full of royal references, from fancy mouldings to protocols. It had nothing to do with them, yet she couldn't help seeing parallels. They were like Anya and Joe, only reversed.

With 'The End' hovering on the screen, Mac turned to her.

"What do you think?"

"It's old but fun. Feels timeless."

"I think Gareth's planning to modernise it a bit."

She hoped he wouldn't modernise the physical side of things. The old film was mild on touching. Still, they'd have to close the distance in the rehearsals, and it worried her. They couldn't play their parts dressed in blankets and pyjamas.

Best not to think about it, Shasa decided, stretching her arms. "Thank you for a ... lovely evening. I better get home."

She got up. Without the blanket, she felt exposed, and hurried down the stairs. She heard Mac's footsteps behind her but didn't turn to face him until she was safely outside the front door. The night had cooled, making her shiver. Next time, she'd go for jeans and the ugliest cardigan known to mankind. If there was a next time. And if there was, it couldn't be like this – the two of them alone in his house.

She allowed herself one last look at the man who made her so wobbly. What was it about him? And what was he thinking?

"I'm sorry," Shasa whispered. "I behaved horribly."

"No, you didn't."

"I did," she insisted. "Not just, you know, but also before. I don't have any friends who live like this, I don't know how to be around you. It's Ollie. He blames the rich for everything, and we used to talk about it so much that my mind goes there. I'm sorry."

Mac lifted his brow. "Rich? I have some assets, but I also have a lot of debt. Can we blame the actual billionaires? The one percent, or the point one percent?"

She laughed. "That's fair. Let's blame them."

Mac took a step closer. "Now that the apologies are taken care of, I just wanted to say I enjoyed hanging out with you."

"Really?"

"Really." His eyes glistened as he stepped closer. He whispered, "I know we decided it was a bad idea, but..."

She shivered, both from the cold and the sensation of his fingers tracing her cheeks, brushing strands of hair behind her ears, holding her captive. His hot breath mixed with hers. She couldn't fight it. She didn't even want to. When his lips touched hers, she nearly lost her balance. He tasted of malt and salt all the seductive things she shouldn't have been tasting. His hands travelled down, tracing her sides like he was trying to both sculpt her shape, and keep her warm. She never wanted it to end, but it had to.

He pulled back, his gaze full of mischief. "There. Just a wee peck on the cheek."

"Totally." She coughed, her face burning hot.

He smiled and closed his mouth on hers again, firing up her body before she'd had a chance to cool down. Encouraged by his eagerness, she dragged her fingers down his chest, all the way down to the waistband of his pyjamas. He was so solid. So hot.

Finally, he let her go and flashed a sheepish smile. "I think

I missed your cheek again."

"I may have turned my head the wrong way." Her voice was shamelessly breathy. "Sorry about that."

"No problem."

She took a step back, like retreating from a cliff's edge. "Bye, Mac!" Not looking back, she ran to her car.

Oh, God. What had she got herself into?

Chapter 22

Elsie took her usual table at Gothenburg, one of the nicer restaurants on the riverbank. The familiarity of the setting usually soothed her, but this afternoon it couldn't settle her nerves. She'd asked Marnie to meet her here, without Shasa. Marnie was the easier option, the one without childcare issues, the older of the two, who also dressed more conservatively. They wouldn't look so mismatched sitting at the same table. Not something Elsie should have worried about, but a lot of her old friends frequented the restaurant.

She had to start with easy and work her way to difficult. This was uncharted territory.

Running into Jeff had raised difficult questions. Was

she capable of building real friendships? What did Shasa and Marnie think of her? Was she an investor, or an acquaintance? She was too old to ignore these things; it was time to clear the air and shape the life she wanted to live.

Last night, sitting on her balcony, drinking another solitary glass of wine, Elsie had decided she wasn't happy with the status quo. The divorce had left her with an empty life, but she didn't have to accept it. Come to think of it, she didn't have to accept any of Jeff's values or opinions. If Jeff thought she had nothing in common with Shasa and Marnie, she didn't have to agree with him. The more she'd thought about it, the clearer it became. By the time she dropped her head on the pillow, she'd decided to start with Marnie, and see if she could make a friend. How did single people make friends at her age?

Elsie watched as the waiter filled her water glass. She could have picked a different meeting place, but it was hard to break habits. She'd spent years avoiding the less affluent parts of town and never ate at malls.

The lush greenery behind the ceiling-height windows shook in the wind, creating a tropical vibe. Elsie had always loved this spot, right by the sturdy glass that shielded her from the elements but allowed her to see everything, like being outside without any of the discomforts. Behind the branches, she caught a glimpse of the Waikato River, deep green and churning.

"Hi!" Marnie's chirpy voice gave Elsie a start.

"Hello! Please have a seat."

Marnie sat down, wrapping her cardigan around herself. "It's chilly in here!"

"They have good air conditioning. Would you like to order?" Elsie slid the leather-covered menu across the table.

Marnie perused it with a slight frown.

"It's on me, obviously," Elsie added.

"Oh, it's okay. I'm not that hungry."

"Try the scones."

Marnie shrugged, closing the menu. "Tea and scones sound great."

Elsie beckoned the waiter and ordered for them.

As he left, Marnie broke into an anxious smile. "I'm so glad you called. Shasa told me about the encounter with your ex-husband. It must have been awful. I haven't seen mine in months, and I prefer it that way. I'm over him, but... Time goes by and I start thinking that I've changed. He doesn't know the new me, right? Wrong! He finds a weak spot in two minutes."

Elsie sighed. "Sounds familiar. I thought Jeff was extraordinary in that way."

Marnie shook her head with a pained smile. "No, it's standard ex-husband stuff. Still sucks though."

Elsie returned the smile. She'd have never worded it quite like that, but she wholeheartedly agreed. Maybe it was best to be frank. "I called you because it got me thinking and I... I want us to be friends."

Marnie's mouth hung open.

"I know it takes time to build real friendships, and I'm sure this is out of the blue for you, but I'm old. I'm divorced. I'm tired of playing games. I'm tired of the social climbing and using relationships for whatever gain. I know I got onboard your cohousing project as an advisor, and I'm happy to advise. I'm even happy to invest. But I'd rather be friends." Elsie's heart pounded against her chest. Was she going to give herself a heart attack? She'd never been this forward in her life.

She studied Marnie's face, which slowly split into a wide smile.

The waiter arrived with their tea and scones, taking a while to arrange everything. "Thank you, that's all good," she told him, waving him off.

The waiter left with the menus, and Marnie spoke. "I like not playing games. And there's no social climbing with me, I guarantee it. Knowing me won't open any doors."

"Good."

Marnie's expression shifted. "So, you want to be friends with me, or both Shasa and me?"

"Both of you, of course! I just thought I'd start with you, with Shasa being busy with her daughter and Mac..." She paused, looking for clues about what Marnie thought of the property developer.

"I know. She's been quite busy lately. I almost wonder..." Marnie focussed on splitting and buttering her scone.

"What?"

Marnie's gaze went out the window. "Shasa's been alone for so long, waiting for that useless man, Ollie. I think she's quite lonely. I know I am. Being alone does things to you. You might find yourself attracted to someone even if it's against your best interest."

"I was wondering about the same thing," Elsie confessed. "I'd hate for her to get hurt."

Marnie turned back to her, eyes blazing. "Hundred percent! That's why I've been so worried. I know we told her to spy on him, but what if?"

"If she's under his influence, she might accidentally reveal something to him, rather than the other way around. Especially if that's his end game."

Marnie's eyes widened with concern. "He's a bit of a player, isn't he?"

Elsie fiddled with her serviette. "From what I hear."

"Okay. Look. I agree with you, there's a risk. But I don't want to tell her to not date him or whatever if that's what she wants to do. I don't believe it ever works. Some mistakes we just have to make. And maybe that guy's like a palate cleanser. He's so different from Ollie."

"A palate cleanser?" Elsie suppressed a smile, wondering if the ladies in her Zumba class knew these terms. She'd clearly been living under a rock.

Marnie took a long sip of her tea, rolling her eyes from behind the cup's golden rim. "Nothing wrong with cleansing

Ollie out of her life, though. Anyone who puts the planet before his own child gets a pass in my books."

Elsie gave her a measured look. "If you're worried about Shasa accidentally revealing something, there's an easy solution."

"What?"

"Well, how much does she need to know about the build, the numbers? I mean, eventually she's going to have to sign the purchase agreement and get a mortgage, but we could keep the details vague while we're formalising the plan. I get the idea she's not into budgeting, anyway."

"She's not a numbers person. She hates doing the community house accounts so much that she volunteered to clean the gutters to get out of it." Marnie pulled a face. "She signs anything I put in front of her."

"That's not wise."

"She trusts me."

"We don't want to abuse her trust. We shouldn't really discuss her behind her back in the first place. I'm sorry—

Marnie shook her head. "No, but like you said, we don't want her to get hurt. And if this guy's playing her, then he's playing us. If he succeeds, we all lose out, including Shasa."

Elsie nodded, warmth filling her chest. The sun had broken out from behind the clouds and cast its warm glow on the opposite side of the river.

What a perfect afternoon tea moment.

She dropped her butter knife on the plate and cast a

meaningful look at her new friend. “We’ll make sure that doesn’t happen.”

Chapter 23

"Are you sure?" Mac asked, trying to keep his tone casual.

Rick him an odd look. "I mean, I'd have to check my files but I don't think I have anything like that. I only have a couple of those older properties anyway, and they're with long-term tenants. Why? I thought you already had a short-term rental for your parents for when you're building?"

He leaned back in his armchair at their usual café. Gusty wind was blasting outdoors, forcing them to go for indoor seating. Even with the occasional sun, it smelled like autumn.

Mac chose his words carefully. "I do have an option, but it's not the best fit. I was just wondering if you had anything else. Anything with a decent backyard or a space for a garden."

"How much gardening can they possibly do in five or six months? It's just a temporary arrangement."

Mac's stomach tightened. He'd eventually have to come clean about the fact that the rental wasn't for his parents. "I don't know. It's enough time to grow some lettuce, right?" He shrugged like he didn't care either way.

He was desperate to find Shasa and Lilla a new home, but didn't want Rick to suspect there was anything going on between them. There wasn't. That's what they'd decided. So, he had nothing to tell.

Keep telling yourself that.

He'd texted her the same night, when he could still smell her perfume, when the feel of her lips still lingered on his. And they'd kept texting.

That ongoing conversation had become his lifeline.

Rick perused his phone. "There's one house in Flagstaff, but it's out of that price range."

"How much? Maybe I can cover the difference."

"This one's seven hundred per week. But it's brand new."

Mac swallowed. It was twice as much as Shasa's current rent. Could he do it? More importantly, how could he do it?

He leaned in, lowering his voice. "They'd be too proud to let me pay, but if you told them the rent was four hundred and I covered you for the rest?"

Rick's frown looked slightly suspicious. "If you insist." He lowered his coffee cup on the table, matching Mac's tone. "I mean, they're the perfect tenants. An older couple. No pets, no kids, no parties, right?"

"They haven't partied since their own wedding." Mac kept his tone light, but a sick feeling welled under the surface. "You don't actually exclude tenants who have kids, right?"

"Why? Is your mum having another baby?"

Mac laughed along. "Not that I know of. But you know they like to feed the neighbours. There are kids everywhere."

Rick exhaled. "Look. I trust your parents, but given the choice, I will always pick the tenant with no kids. Every fucking time."

"Seriously?"

"Kids are worse than some dogs. You should see the damage I've had to deal with."

Mac nodded. It made sense, but he couldn't help the sick feeling. Was this what Shasa was up against? She'd never be offered the nice, new rental because she had a kid? He'd never chosen childless tenants over child-free ones, but only because he mostly owned smaller apartments that families didn't apply for.

"I'll keep that in mind," he said gingerly. "Can you just hold that house for me? I'll check with them and let you know. Oh, and send me some photos, okay?"

He'd send them to Shasa and see what she thought.

"Sure, no problem." Rick picked up his briefcase. "And Marama street is under control?"

"Yes! Just getting the contracts drawn up. All good." He waved his hand at Rick, who disappeared out the door.

Finally. He picked up his phone and his heart leapt at a new message.

Shasa: We bought some used yoga mats for the community house. I picked them up from Rototuna and drove past your house.

Mac: You should have stopped by for all the tea. No one else is going to drink it.

Shasa: So I'd come for one cup and leave with a giant gift bag for of tea? That sounds tempting.

Mac: I'd ration you. Two packets per visit, so you'd keep coming back.

Shasa: What are you, a drug dealer?

Mac: A responsible one. I don't want you to overdose on chamomile.

Shasa: That is a concern.

Mac: I want you hooked for life. A good drug dealer won't let a client overdose. They'd lose the income.

Shasa: I love how you choose to deal tea, of all drugs.

Mac: I'm a new age drug dealer. We do tea, mild shrooms and yoga mats.

Shasa: I clearly went to the wrong house for yoga mats. I could have got them with shrooms! What kind?

Mac: I don't actually know anything about shrooms. Or other drugs. Sorry to mislead you.

Shasa: I've never done drugs either, just messing with you.

Mac: Phew. You had me for a moment there. I mean, I thought you alternative types all grew some cannabis in the backyard.

Shasa: Blueberries, man. I grow blueberries. It's hard to maintain a drug habit as a single parent.

Mac: So you don't get high during naptime?

Shasa: No. I try to get a cup of tea, but sometimes can't even manage that. When stupid real estate agents turn up at the door and wake up my kid.

Mac: Yeah, I hate when that happens. Jerks.

Shasa: Even the good-looking ones, unfortunately.

Mac: The good-looking ones are the worst.

Shasa: Hate them so much. Especially the ones with brown eyes and incredible eyelashes. They make me sick.

Mac couldn't wipe the goofy smile off his face. They'd kept the conversation light, carefully avoiding hot topics like housing, but every conversation revealed a little more about the woman he was quickly becoming obsessed with.

They had no reason to meet, not until the next rehearsal, which was tomorrow. A couple of days ago, Mac had began counting the days, becoming gradually more and more wired as the rehearsal night drew closer.

He abandoned his half-eaten sandwich and got up, too unsettled to eat. Striding down the windy Victoria street, he wondered how he could ever keep his hands off Shasa. Every exchange built up the connection between them, making it harder and harder to imagine a life without her, even if he never got to touch her again. He craved her comments and delighted in her sharp wit. Her mind worked so differently, yet he found her thoroughly captivating. Like a foreigner who spoke the same language.

Mac recognised the danger.

Even though they hadn't met since the movie night, he enjoyed her voice too much. If she fell silent for two hours, he became agitated, sometimes bombing her with a string of messages. Every time he had an interesting thought, or even a not-so-interesting one, he had the urge to share it with Shasa. She was the first and only one on his mind.

Reaching his ute, Mac dug up his phone again.

Mac: Ready for the rehearsal tomorrow? Remember to wear a sack.

Shasa: If you wear the poop pyjamas. Poopjamas, I mean.

Mac sighed, sliding behind the wheel of his ute, reluctantly putting away the phone. Could their relationship remain like this? A weird, intense friendship, with a bit of flirting? Okay. A lot of flirting. Neither of them had mentioned the make-out session, but it bubbled under the surface, an explosive force they both pretended to control.

Standing at his doorstep that night, he'd been a breath away from pulling her back inside his house and taking her on the couch. She'd wanted it. He wanted it. He could have just kept kissing her, not giving either of them the opportunity to talk, to tap into any kind of reasoning. He could have just pressed on to see if she'd stop him. It was a bad idea, but did he truly care anymore? Every part of him craved more of her. Seeing her again, he already knew he'd take anything she was willing to give.

Chapter 24

Shasa dropped her bursting canvas bag on the floor and joined Marnie at her favourite Hamilton East cafe. Marnie had left work early to visit their mortgage advisor and had invited Shasa and Elsie for a 'cohousing catchup' afterwards.

The tiny café was full of recycled items and dried flowers. Best of all, it had a playroom that kept Lilla happy. Oh, the bliss of child-free teatime.

Shasa set her phone on silent, hiding it in her pocket. She could still feel the buzz, should Mac message her. Their intense texting had filled her mind, making her distracted. But seeing Marnie in person, she felt ashamed. She'd been flirting with the enemy, nonstop, and hadn't found out anything useful. Even with all the banter between them, Mac was playing for the opposing team. As much as she enjoyed his attention, she had to remember her loyalties.

Marnie blew out a sigh. "What a week! I'm so glad it's Thursday already."

Shasa took a long sip of her tea, wincing as it burned her throat. Thursday. Tonight, she would see him again. The thought turned her insides to jelly.

"I picked up something on the way." Marnie winked as she laid a stack of paint samples on the table.

"Paint samples!" Shasa grabbed the pile and flipped through it.

She'd spent a lot of time on Pinterest, saving ideas for her dream home. It wasn't the healthiest activity for someone on a tight budget, but it was the only way she could avoid thinking about Mac, at least for a moment. If she kept her eyes on the prize, she could have a forever home for her and her daughter. It was worth every sacrifice. Even better, she was doing it with a friend - or as Marnie now insisted - friends.

The door rattled and Elsie stepped in, her cream pant suit so pristine Shasa instinctively checked their vacant chair for ketchup stains.

She couldn't quite understand why Elsie wanted to befriend them, or even what she meant by it. Yet, she appreciated that Elsie hadn't pulled the plug on their project. If she needed a friend, Shasa would be one.

As Elsie sat down, a young waiter with a bushy beard and a beanie approached them with two scones.

Once he left, Elsie scooted closer and lowered her voice. "Your landlord approached me today. He's ready to hear our offer. I assured him he'd have it by the end of the week and that it would be worth his while. If we can't find out what Mac's offering, we'll just have to take a guess. The seller won't tell me anything. I think he's using blind bidding to check if Mac's giving him a good deal."

"Well... I'm meeting Mac again tonight," Shasa said, her face burning. "Maybe I can find out something."

Marnie's eyebrows shot up. "Tonight? Is it getting serious?"

Elsie's eyes sharpened. "Are you two... dating?"

"No, no!" Shasa's heart pounded. "I told you about the play. I agreed to audition, and now we have a rehearsal with the director."

Her phone buzzed, sending a vibration up her thigh, waking up a cloud of butterflies. Could her friends see the terrible crush she was harbouring on her face?

Elsie nodded, studying Shasa thoughtfully. "Be careful. He's a clever man. You might think you're spying on him, but he could be doing the same."

"I know." Shasa hid behind her teacup, her ears hot.

She peered into the playroom to check on Lilla. The girl was filling a miniature oven with stuffed animals, talking to herself.

"How much can we offer for the section?" Shasa asked.

Marnie and Elsie exchanged an odd look.

"What?" she demanded.

After a dreadfully long moment, Marnie spoke. "Maybe you shouldn't look at the numbers just yet. You're hanging out with this guy who's trying to find out our plans. I trust you, but I know how easy it is to let something slip. If you don't know the details, you can't possibly reveal anything. Even if he drugged you, and—"

"He's not going to drug me!" Shasa buried her burning face in her hands.

This was humiliating, but Marnie had a point. She didn't trust herself around Mac. She was under some horrible spell and would take her friends down with her.

She hung her head. "I'm terrible with numbers anyway, I shouldn't be discussing them with anyone."

"How's it going with Mac?" Elsie asked softly, sipping her coffee. "Are you gaining his trust?"

Shasa stirred her tea. "I'm... getting to know him." Worried about her face giving her away, she got up to check on Lilla.

Hiding in the playroom, she checked her phone.

Mac: I'm trying on poopjamas but it's sweltering out there. Permission to go for something lighter?

Shasa: Hem them shorter if you must, but I need the poop. You must NOT show up attractive. I can't take it.

Mac: Fine. I'll try to get less attractive. But just know that there's nothing you can do to achieve the same. It doesn't work. I've already seen too much, and my imagination will just fill in the blanks, Shasa.

Shasa: Imagine whatever you like but remember what we agreed!

Mac: I'm trying to, but some of the memories from that night are fading... while others are getting more vivid.

Shasa sighed, fighting the delicious pull in her stomach those words conjured. She had the exact same problem and talking to Mac made things worse. His texts filled her with excitement but standing in the café where she was meeting with her friends, they felt wrong. Pocketing her phone, she returned to the table with her daughter in tow. Lilla climbed onto her lap, tackling the remains of her scone.

Elsie smiled at them. "If we're done with the cohousing items for now, I could use some advice."

"From *us*?" Shasa blurted.

"What kind of advice?" Marnie asked, more appropriately.

"Shasa, you may remember a gentleman caller I had the other night?"

"The council guy! Earl?"

Elsie's cheek twitched, like a wayward smile was trying to break through. She liked Earl! With everything else going on, Shasa had forgotten about her visit to Elsie's house.

Elsie recounted the night's events for Marnie's benefit,

her cheeks getting rosier as she spoke. "Now I don't know what to do. I don't like how things ended, but how do I fix it? The one idea I've had so far is to make a similar surprise visit to his house. I've had his address for years, since I always send a Christmas card..."

Marnie and Shasa shook their heads in unison.

"Don't just turn up," Marnie said. "You said he works at the council. How do you think he lives?"

Elsie shrugged. "I don't know. But he invited himself over, so I thought if I do the same, make a fool of myself, that'll balance things between us."

Shasa grimaced. "When your house isn't that nice, surprise visits can be humiliating. At least call ahead and give him time to get ready. Better yet, offer to meet somewhere neutral, like a restaurant."

Elsie raised her brow. "I hadn't thought of that. You're right. I'll call and ask him out for dinner."

"Or coffee?" Marnie added. "That way he doesn't have to dress up."

"Right." Elsie slid her fingers under her gold necklace like it was strangling her. "This is not my area. I haven't been out on a date in decades."

"Don't think of it as a date," Marnie suggested. "Just two friends catching up."

Elsie stared out the window, deep in thought. "Okay. I can do that."

Shasa could barely imagine what it would be like to be

single at Elsie's age. She'd been out of the game for five years, two of them in this limbo of long-distance abstinence. If she had to get back out there, she'd be just as lost. She wanted to share her experiences, but she couldn't talk about dating without mentioning Mac. And how could she talk to them about Mac?

Lilla fidgeted in Shasa's lap. Noticing the restless girl, Marnie gathered the paint samples. "Good meeting, girls! So, Shasa will spy on Mac, Elsie will patch things up with Earl, and I—"

"Babysit Lilla?" Shasa cast her a pleading look. "Remember, I need a babysitter tonight, for the rehearsal?"

Marnie's hand flew over her mouth. "Oh, no! I can't! I know I said I'm free all week, but Tom called yesterday. He's coming home and wants to take me to this gallery that's showing one of his paintings. I'm so sorry!" Marnie's firstborn had started college and was rarely home.

Shasa's heart fell. "No, I'm sorry. I should have double-checked. Seeing your son is way more important!" She'd have to cancel on Mac. Her whole body ached at the thought, even if part of her was relieved.

Marnie squeezed Shasa's arm. "Could you get a babysitter through an agency?"

Shasa hugged Lilla, who'd coated herself in scone crumbs and was trying to climb on the table. She'd never used a babysitting service. How would her daughter react to a random stranger?

"I'll take her," Elsie said. "Just bring her over with some extra clothes and whatever she needs."

Shasa's mouth dropped open. "Are you sure?"

Was she just being polite? Lilla could be a lot to handle. What if Elsie decided she didn't want anything to do with them after the babysitting gig?

Elsie offered a reassuring smile. "I'm sure."

With questions running through her mind, Shasa turned to Lilla. "Would you like to play with the doggy tonight?"

"Yesss!"

"Sold." Shasa turned to Elsie and lowered her voice. "Can you please put any priceless artwork and stuff like that behind locked doors? I won't be able to cover the cost should anything happen."

She waved her hand dismissively. "I have great insurance."

After they settled on the details, Elsie waved them goodbye and disappeared out the door.

Marnie got up and scooped Lilla in her arms. "Are you okay with this?" she asked Shasa.

"Lilla has been to Elsie's house. She loves the dog."

"What about you?"

Shasa took a deep breath, trying to erase the image of Mac her brain conjured in vivid detail. Would she be okay?

Chapter 25

Elsie took another look at her living room, trying to see it through a child's eyes. Was there anything interesting? She had no toys. All she had was an old, tired dog, napping on the couch. Why had she signed up for this? She had no experience with children, at least no recent experience. She'd looked after her sister's child a few times before his untimely death over twenty years ago. After that, Bridie had left her husband, the unwitting driver of the car, and moved overseas. These days, she was happily settled in Sydney with a long-term partner and a cat. With no other kids in the family, it had been easy to keep the little people at arm's length.

Elsie strolled into the kitchen and lined up the age-appropriate snacks she'd bought on her way home. When she heard the doorbell, she quickly closed her laptop. Shasa didn't need to see her searching 'foods three-year-olds like'.

Shasa stood at the door holding Lilla's hand, using her other arm to manoeuvre a huge rectangular pack Elsie guessed was the travel cot.

Elsie held the door for them. "Come on in."

"Where's doggy?" Lilla asked, looking up at her.

Elsie pointed to the living room, and the girl sprinted away, her socks slipping and sliding on the polished wood floor. A unicorn backpack hung off her shoulders, stuffed so full that the unicorn looked bloated.

"Don't run, walk!" Shasa called after her.

Elsie noted that Shasa wasn't wearing her usual ensemble of flowing fabric and excessive jewellery. Her outfit was rather revealing – denim shorts and a light knit over a tank top. Elsie understood the shorts – the night was exceptionally balmy for early March – but she wondered if Shasa was changing her style for Mac. She didn't want to ask, since the girl had been so touchy about it in the cafe. Developing feelings for someone you shouldn't was confusing and embarrassing. Elsie could certainly see why women fell for Mac, who seemed to possess a movie star style charisma. No wonder he was acting in this play.

"Would you like a cup of tea before you go?"

Shasa shook her head. "No, sorry, I'm running a bit late,

and I don't want to draw out the goodbyes. And it's easier with Lilla if I just go."

She carried the travel cot to the living room and, to Elsie's relief, set it up in the corner. Lilla had found her spot on the couch next to the dog. Poor Stina already had three pink hair clips hanging off her fur and a little girl with a hairbrush working on her tail. Luckily, the dog was mellow.

Elsie saw Shasa to the door.

"We'll be fine," Elsie reassured her, or maybe herself.

As soon as the door clicked, Lilla appeared by her side, panic in her eyes. "Where's Mummy?"

"She'll be back soon. Let's go back to doggy."

"Mummy!" Lilla reached for the doorknob, desperately trying to turn it.

Elsie moved in to stop her from getting out, the terrifying screams sending shrills down her spine. Two-seconds in, and this was already a disaster. At least Shasa wouldn't hear anything through the solid door.

The girl hung off the doorknob, tears running down her face. Elsie knew she needed help, but who could she call? She dashed back to her laptop to search for solutions, browsing useless articles she had no time to read. The wailing at the front door grew louder.

As her panic amounted, the answer eventually emerged. Earl! He had children and grandchildren. He'd know what to do. Before she could talk herself out of it, Elsie dialled.

While she waited for Earl to pick up, Lilla opened the

front door. Elsie ran ahead of her to check the front gate was closed. All good. Having made it out of the house, the girl seemed calmer, her sobs subsiding as she explored the garden. It was still light, but long shadows stretched across the lawn.

Earl's 'hello' sounded like a question.

"Hi, Earl," Elsie said. "I'm so sorry to call you like this, but I could use your help. I'm looking after Shasa's little one. She's three, and she got very upset when her mum left. I honestly don't know why I said I could do this. I don't have kids in my family, and I'm completely out of my depth."

She was cut off by Lilla's harrowing scream. It seemed the girl had figured out her mum wasn't hiding in the garden.

Elsie raised her voice to compete with the cries. "So, if you have any tips on how to settle her, what to do... I'd be extremely grateful!"

"She sounds quite upset. How about I come over with some toys, and we tackle this together? I keep some things in my house for the grandkids."

"That would be wonderful!"

They ended the call with Earl promising to get to her as soon as possible.

Elsie slipped the phone in her pocket and looked for Lilla. It was suddenly quiet. The girl had vanished. After double checking the garden, Elsie returned to the house, her heart pounding. The front door was still open. Had she gone back inside?

Elsie hurried to the living room and there she was, back on the couch, hugging the dog.

Lilla's eyes burned with accusation. "Mummy's gone."

"Yes, she's gone. She'll be back later. We can play with the dog. And have snacks."

By the time Earl arrived, Elsie had managed to give Lilla one grape.

"She won't accept any food," Elsie said, grateful for Earl's presence.

He gave her a comforting smile. "Maybe she's not hungry?" The plastic crate under his arm looked heavy, full of worn out, mismatched toys. "Trust me, this stuff is kryptonite," he said, dropping it on the living room floor.

"Lilla?" he called the girl. "Would you like to have a look at these toys?"

Lilla glance up from the couch, her cheeks still wet with tears.

"It's okay if you don't. I know another girl who might like them, I'll just take them to her instead."

Lilla perked up and slid herself off the couch. "I can take the toys."

"Good girl. I'll leave them here, then."

She started digging through the box like her life depended on it, pulling out one-legged dolls and other unidentifiable objects.

Earl joined Elsie on the couch. "She'll calm down soon."

"Thank you so much!"

Earl seemed less nervous than the last time. He sat back on the couch and sighed. "The young ones are straightforward. Their brains get stuck on something, and you just have to help them to switch gears. Most of the time you can simply distract them."

Lilla held up a stuffed unicorn and smiled. "I found unicorn!"

Elsie stared at Earl with newfound appreciation. "I can't believe how quickly you calmed her down!"

She'd always liked Earl. He'd been nice, helpful, and loyal. But she'd never thought of him as someone who came to her rescue, someone who took charge of the situation.

"Let's all get something to eat," she suggested, getting to her feet.

Lilla followed them into the dining room, her eyes lighting with curiosity. Elsie set all the snacks she'd bought on the table and made a cup of tea for herself and Earl. When she returned from the kitchen with the cups, she found Lilla at the table, helping herself to a handful of grapes.

The corner of Earl's mouth tugged upwards. "I think she's hungry now."

Elsie joined them at the table, dipping a rice cracker in hummus. She knew Lilla had eaten an early dinner, so she'd filled bowls with strawberries, grapes, crackers, cheese, bread and various dips. After getting home, she'd stared at the selection in despair, wondering if any of it was child friendly.

"I should've bought those kiddy biscuits, or yoghurt, or cereal."

Earl laughed. "You're overthinking this." He had a nice laugh, one that beckoned her to join in.

"How many grandkids do you have?" Her voice came out more relaxed than she'd expected. The topic of children had been off the table for such a long time, she'd assumed herself incapable of discussing like this. With lightness.

"Four," Earl answered, popping a grape in his mouth. "The youngest was just born. Little Ayla."

"Congratulations! What a lovely name!"

He nodded. "You have to be grateful these days if it's a proper name, don't you? Not a colour, or a food, or something else they thought to repurpose."

"Oh my God, you're right! Like Blue, or Cinnamon, or... Princess."

Earl smiled, his gaze lingering on her face like he was waiting for the right moment. "I was wondering," he said, shifting in his seat. "Could you tell me more about the cohousing community? Is it all sold out?"

Elsie raised her brow in surprise. "Are you interested?"

"I just sold my unit in Whitiora, close to all those motels. It was handy for work, but it got a bit too restless there for my liking."

Elsie shuddered, thinking of the area. "Yes, two out of four units are still available. And Marama Street is lovely. It's close to here."

If Earl bought into the community, he'd be on the opposite side of the small lake. She hoped he was interested in the connection, rather than just a place to live. A strange buzz vibrated in her stomach, like butterflies waking up after thirty years of hibernation. She couldn't remember the last time she'd felt this way, sitting next to a man.

Earl's voice was serious. "I understand it's not a regular housing development. I looked up some links about cohousing. I rather like the basic principles, such as sharing the outdoor areas."

"It's good for grandkids!" Elsie agreed. "And this is a small-scale community with no frills. We're not building a common house or anything like that, just four units. The girls would be delighted to have you."

"I'd love to talk to them about it in better circumstances." Earl cleared his throat. "Last time, I left quite abruptly. I'm sorry about that. It was..."

"It's all good. A misunderstanding. I'm sorry, too. I was quite tone deaf myself. I haven't dated in decades. It's been quiet since the divorce." She let out a sigh, relieved to be speaking candidly. All the politeness was getting on her nerves.

Lilla reached for the last grape in the bowl, her eyes searching for the next best thing on offer. Strawberries.

Earl turned his chair to face Elsie. "I find that hard to believe. You're absolutely stunning." Earl's face turned red with the bold statement, but he didn't turn away. He held his head up high, the light in his eyes burning more brightly than before.

Elsie experienced a sudden jolt. Maybe he wasn't such a teddy bear. Maybe she'd misjudged him. A man didn't need to be a self-important jerk to have presence, or courage.

"I know you're out of my league, as they say, but I feel very lucky to be here." Earl smiled, taking her hand.

He leaned in and she caught a whiff of mint and aftershave. His eyes looked bluer than before.

On a whim, she closed the short distance, placing a kiss on his cheek. It was hardly more than a friendly peck, but she'd never done anything so playful. Giddy laughter escaped her mouth.

Earl's eyes darkened. He lifted her chin with his fingers, eyes dipping to her lips as he waited. Her laughter fizzled out and nerve endings sizzled. Was she ready to kiss him for real? Elsie drew a breath and closed the remaining distance. He kissed her softly, holding her chin with unshaking hand. She could feel him holding back, as if giving her a small taste of the passion that hid under the surface. But it was more than enough to convince her the man knew what he was doing. His eyes stayed on her as he pulled back, smiling.

"Yuck!" Lilla yelled, smiling with a mouth full of strawberry, bright red juice running down her chin.

"Right back at you, buddy," Earl chuckled, handing her a napkin. "I like Auntie Elsie, I hope you're okay with that?"

Lilla shrugged. "I guess."

Elsie couldn't help laughing at her suspicious, wide-eyed expression. For the first time in twenty years, she felt lucky to be Auntie Elsie.

Chapter 26

The single spotlight cast a perfect, bright circle on the stage floor. Mac did some deep breathing, trying to prepare himself for the rehearsal. Last weekend's events played in his mind like a film reel. Shasa. Was she coming? Would he see her again?

Mac blew out a deep breath. How had he ended up lusting after the one woman he desperately needed to stay away from? After their movie date, he'd called Rick and pleaded for his friend to set him up with someone. He'd clearly been single for too long and needed to focus his sexual energy on someone else. Anyone. Anyone who wasn't trying to sabotage his most important business deal yet.

But all of that felt pointless now. Once they'd started texting, he didn't want to meet anyone else. No one else existed. Even if he never got to touch her again.

The door creaked open.

Shasa. She arrived in a tank top and denim shorts, bringing his thoughts to a grinding halt as she crossed the floor, her hips gently swaying, bare legs glowing in the low light. Bloody never-ending summer season.

He glanced at Gareth and saw him exit through the backstage, holding a buzzing phone. Oh, no. He wasn't meant to be left alone with Shasa. No. He'd fantasized about this far too many times, and those fantasies never ended up with him sticking to their agreement. His willpower hung by a thread, relying heavily on having third wheels or meeting in public places.

She halted a few steps away, an unsure smile on her lips.

He shook his head, waving a finger at her outfit. "What the hell is this? We agreed on a sack, remember?"

She pulled a face. "It's one hundred degrees out there! And Gareth said we should wear something we're comfortable to move in. Sacks are really cumbersome. I tried." She moved closer, imitating his finger-waving. "Besides, you're not doing your part." Her finger landed on his T-shirt-covered chest, waking up his body like she'd hit a big red button.

He steadied his feet, willing for Gareth's phone call to end. "I don't have anything else. It's T-shirts and jeans, or a suit."

"What about those pyjamas?" She bit the fullest part of

her bottom lip.

"In public?"

"It's Hamilton! Go shopping in Nawton and you'll see pyjamas in public every night!"

"I don't go shopping in Nawton."

"Of course, you don't. That's why I said 'go'." She flashed a cheeky grin.

"I'll go if you come with me." He couldn't stop the words slipping out. A part of him, a part he had no control over, was ready to hang onto any opportunity to spend time with her. Even in Nawton.

"I can take you around my favorite op shops, too."

"Oh, God." He shook his head and she chuckled.

"I mean it! I volunteer to be your personal guide, just to see you sweat."

"Come on! I wore my cousin's second-hand clothes through my entire childhood. My mum still buys everything used. I'm not the snob you think I am."

Her voice was quiet. "I don't think you're a snob. Not anymore."

"What do you think?"

She leaned in and whispered. "I think you're a jerk." It sounded soft and sensual, like a term of endearment.

"I am."

"Self-entitled, greedy knob." Another breathy whisper.

"Absolutely."

Her gaze dipped to his lips. Even in the dark, he could tell she was blushing, and it shot him full of need. Her finger traced down his chest, a fingernail leaving behind it a trail of tingles.

They stood for a moment, breathing in the darkness that allowed them to misbehave, waiting for a cue, something to stop them. Could he risk a taste of her?

She was so close he could smell her warm vanilla scent. He could almost taste her, taste the willingness that had burned in her eyes on Saturday night, evidenced by the stain on his jeans she'd left behind. Her scent had lingered in the air, intoxicating. He'd met willing women before, but no one had ever climbed him like that. She was so delicate, yet wild and foreign and fearless… someone he'd never truly understand. It drove him wild.

"You need to take a step back," he warned, inhaling her, willing his hands to stay by his sides. "Because you're right. I am greedy. And what I want is standing right in front of me."

His hands twitched. He'd give himself a medal later, for all this willpower. Superhuman willpower.

"Does this happen to you a lot?"

"What?" He blinked.

The spotlight reflected off her eyes. "This chemistry, I mean. With someone who's all wrong. I hate that I can't turn it off. Look at me touching you." She winced, lifting her finger off his chest.

He held his breath for a moment, missing that finger, until the truth broke out as a gruff whisper. "No. I've never felt like this. I don't know what to do."

"You don't want to be attracted to me," she concluded, her voice soft. "I get it."

"No! I mean... no." He brushed a strand of stubborn hair behind her ear. "It's complicated. Every time you text me, I get this surge of... energy. I live for those moments. I wanted to call you so many times this week. Because I seriously couldn't stop thinking about Saturday night and just seeing your written words was not enough. I can't get you out of my mind."

She nodded, pain behind her eyes. "I know. You've made me completely addicted to your texts and this... attention. You. I'm hooked, Mac. And it's all your fault!"

A flurry of conflicting emotions swept across her face and she shoved him, too softly to create any distance between them.

He caught her shoulders, pulling her tightly against his chest. "It is. I'm sorry. I couldn't stop. I can't stay away from you," he whispered into her hair. "Blame me. I deserve that. But I can't let go of you, Shasa."

"I don't want you to. But it's going to mess up everything and we can't—"

"Can't what?" He pulled back to peer at her face, noticing the moisture gathered in the corner of her eye. He caught it with his thumb, tracing down her face, brushing her lip.

The more he stared at her, the longer they spent in this bubble, in the dark theatre, the less he cared about anything else. It was like the world and its realities had momentarily vanished, leaving only him, her, and the desire he could hardly fight. What sizzled between them and crackled in the air held him completely spellbound.

"Shasa. We've already crossed the line. Did the world end?"

She huffed. "Yes. But that's okay. Let it burn."

The way she exhaled the words made him crave her so much his body ached.

His hands settled on her waist like they had independent decision-making capabilities and his mouth landed on her parted lips with force he could barely contain, muffling the soft moan that escaped her. She tasted even better than he remembered. Sugar and spice. Fireworks, as soon as their tongues collided.

He pulled her flush against him, feeling her soft warmth against his aching hard-on. He'd been hard for this woman for a week. Who was he kidding? There was no willpower left. Nothing but need.

Shasa shifted against his hard cock and whispered, "It's good we're not alone tonight. I couldn't trust myself."

"Me neither," he rasped, diving back for her mouth.

And that's when the door opened.

Chapter 27

"Evening," Gareth bellowed.

Shasa launched herself off Mac at the exact moment he released her, resulting in an uncoupling that was far too theatrical, even in a theatre. But it was dark, and they were far from the spotlight. Their feet clattered on the hardwood floor, and her heart pounded in her throat.

Before she could form a coherent thought, Mac grabbed her hand and spun her around on the floor like they were dancing.

Gareth narrowed his eyes. "What are you doing?"

Mac let go of Shasa with a bright smile. "We were just acting out that scene where they're going upstairs, holding hands, and Audrey walks past the staircase. He spins her around and guides her up the steps. We were trying to figure out if there's a way to do that without stairs on stage. It's such good comedy."

Gareth nodded. "I see you watched the film. Great! I'm not sure we'll have stairs. If we can figure out a way to use them for more than one joke, it might make sense."

Shasa stared at Mac, astonished at how effortlessly he could think on his feet. He didn't even sound nervous. Gareth's gaze shifted from Mac to her. She smiled, not trusting herself to speak. She'd never be able to match his breezy tone.

If Gareth suspected anything, he didn't show it. He asked them to join him on the stage and kicked off a series of warm-up exercises. All the jumping, flexing, and stretching made Shasa feel like she was at the gym, although it was more fun than a workout. Moving her body in a dimly lit space felt liberating, like swimming at night.

"Theatre is physical," Gareth explained. "You need stamina, flexibility, endurance."

Shasa flinched, trying to stretch her mouth open like a lion then squinting like a mouse. Her facial muscles ached. She walked everywhere and sometimes took part in exercise classes at the community house, but she didn't train every muscle group. She survived. After a couple of minutes of trying to touch their noses with their tongues, Gareth stopped them. "Okay, that's enough warm-up for now."

"Thank God!" She shook from relief and laughter.

Watching Mac stretch his tongue, she could hardly concentrate on anything else.

Gareth handed them two scripts and showed them the scene. "I have one highlighter. Did either of you bring a pen? Let's do a cold read, and you can mark your own lines any way you want. This is the scene we decided to use for the auditions. Not the whole scene, just the first two pages."

Shasa began reading, casting her mind back to the princess waking up in Joe's bed, not remembering how she got there.

Gareth's booming voice filled her ears. "I love this scene. Joe now knows she's a princess. The stakes are higher. She wakes up slowly. In her half-asleep state, she reveals how much she enjoyed her nightly escapade, thinking it was a dream. Then, she fully wakes up and tries to process what happened, but she doesn't react like a commoner. She's trained to act gracefully in any situation."

She swallowed, thinking of how she'd acted in Mac's house. Graceful was not it.

Gareth turned to Mac. "Joe's put everything on the line here. He's gambled his money, his career. It all hinges on her. He needs a story from the princess. He needs to keep her in his apartment, to stay with her long enough to get the photographer there to take those pictures. But he's also enamored by her sweet innocence and beauty. He's never met anyone like Anya."

She glanced at Mac. He stared at the script, frozen and

glassy-eyed. She could tell he wasn't reading it.

Gareth went on, his deep voice making her feel like she was listening to the radio. "What's important here is that they're both deceiving each other. Joe conceals the fact that he's a reporter. Princess Ann introduces herself as Anya, thinking she can hide her identity from him. Each of them thinks they're fooling the other, and that's where the tension lies."

Shasa felt hot. This movie, or play, wasn't about them. For starters, she wasn't a princess. Marnie had told her that in her short hairdo, she looked a lot like Audrey Hepburn, but that's where the similarities ended.

Prompted by Gareth, they read through the scene, trying to memorize the lines. The stage adaptation was a bit different from the movie, but the beats were essentially the same.

Next, they moved on to acting the scene. Shasa dutifully laid herself down on the stage, relishing the sensations of the cold floor against her back. It grounded her. Acting was an escape – being someone else, someone without the internal conflict that made her a wobbly mess, especially around Mac.

She'd kissed him again, knowing in the back of her mind Gareth was about to step in any moment. If she kept going like this, chasing the high of his touch, drinking in his attention, where would they end up?

Gareth poked her with a rolled-up yoga mat. "Put that

under you, it'll be more comfortable."

She did, laying down on the slightly sticky mat. Mac hovered at the edge of the spotlight, giving her a bit of space.

"Now, allow yourself to go into the story. You're a real princess. The real deal. That's all you've ever known."

She nodded, her eyes closed. Whatever she thought about the monarchy, whatever Ollie thought about it, there was no way of doing this without going all in. She drew from her own experience, waking up, remembering something tantalizing had happened the night before, enjoying the memory before her conscious brain kicked in.

"I'll feed you the lines this time," Gareth said. "Let's just run through it once."

They did. She was surprised by how easy it was to stay in character, even with someone speaking words in her ear, words she had to first process, then repeat as her own.

Mac didn't seem to need the script or a stage whisperer. He played off her reactions, radiating a mixture of fascination and nerves that perfectly fit the scene. He wasn't doing Gregory Peck. There was more angst, a different masculine energy that reminded her of James Franco. Unpredictable, cheeky, dangerous. They ran the scene twice.

"Let's go through it once more," Gareth suggested. "Try something different, whatever you want. Forget the lines, use your own words. Have fun."

She laid back on the mat, her nerves sizzling in the most delicious way. She'd just follow Mac's lead; he was so much better at this. She stretched her arms over her head, imagining herself waking up after that Saturday night, reliving the craziest thing she'd ever done.

"I had the craziest dream," she said, sighing. "A gorgeous, hot guy took me into his house. I was someone else, someone fearless... I didn't act properly. I was naughty..." She cracked her eyelids and peered through her lashes at the blurry darkness.

Mac was right there, hovering above her like he was about to eat her, but somehow held himself back. "Is that right?" he asked, his voice low and gravelly. "Tell me, what did you do?"

That woke her up. Her mouth dropped open, and she scrambled up, hugging herself. "What did I do?" she asked, her heart pounding. "What happened?"

He sat back, his eyes soft. "Nothing you should be ashamed of. And something I'll always remember." His voice was achingly wistful, making Shasa's chest squeeze.

It was just a scene. Make-believe. But his words soothed her like balm, like he was trying to reach her through this alternate reality. She attempted to compose herself. Be a royal. But she'd played the role differently, her words dripping with real worry and regret, her voice catching in her throat. "Thank you for saying that, but I must forget. I don't know how, but I must."

"Thank you," Gareth said quietly. "I think I need to rewrite this scene."

Cold sweat prickled on Shasa's neck. "Did we... do it wrong?"

Gareth broke into a smile. "No! No! You guys are fantastic. You brought so much more to it that it made me think. We can do more with the emotions at play here. Less cute, more real. The shame, the arousal... the regret. It's not the fifties anymore, we can take this story to the next level. Joe's character could be a bit more dangerous, less of a gentleman."

The spotlight glinted off Mac's eyes. "I'm okay with that."

Oh, no.

"And Shasa, your character could have more pent-up desire, ferocity. She's been in a prison of sorts and hasn't been able to live life on her terms. Now, she's going after what she wants."

More ferocity? Shasa was already scared of what welled under the surface. She was out of her depth, yet part of her wanted to drown.

She weaved her hands together to stop them from shaking. "Sure."

Standing up, she rolled up the yoga mat and returned it to Gareth. They made plans to meet up in three days. Gareth rubbed his hands together. "Thank you, guys! You've given me a lot to work with. I'll bring the updated script, so don't worry about learning the lines for now. Just work on your intentions, inner dialogue, all that. In fact, maybe go out tonight, grab some dinner, get to know each other. You must be able to trust each other implicitly since you may be asked to do a bit of improv, too."

"Will you join us?" Shasa asked, her throat dry.

"No. I need to get home. We have a babysitter booked, and we're going to see a cabaret." They hopped off the stage and headed towards the front door.

Mac turned to Shasa. "That's a good idea. Let's grab some dinner?"

As they reached the door, Gareth stopped at the alarm control panel on the wall. He punched in a code. "Just be careful not to get involved." His voice was matter of fact, like he'd told them to avoid carbs late at night, but the digital screen flashed the words 'ALARM ON' and Shasa felt it in her bones.

Mac shot her a warning look and turned to Gareth with a level expression. "Of course not."

They stepped on the street, and Gareth hurried towards the carpark. The sun was setting, casting its last rays on the riverside trees.

"Where's your car?" Mac asked.

Shasa shook her head like her hair was on fire. "Oh, no. We're not going out."

"Why not? Do you have to go home? Who's babysitting? Marnie?"

"No, Elsie. It's not that. We just can't."

Thinking of Lilla and Elsie, Shasa pulled out her phone to check her messages. Elsie had sent a photo of Lilla, asleep in a travel cot, with a caption. 'Happy and asleep. Stay as long as you need to.' She showed it to Mac.

He stared at the screen in amazement. "Elsie Alders is looking after your daughter. Whad'ya know."

"Yeah, she's great."

"So, you have no excuse." Smiling his permafrost-melting smile. "Let me just buy you dinner, as a friend. I haven't seen you for like two weeks."

Her heart did a back flip, but Shasa steeled her face. "It's been six days. And I think we just proved why we shouldn't meet in private at all."

Following her gaze, Mac glanced over his shoulder at the theatre. "Oh, that. It doesn't count. Anything that happens in the theatre is make-believe. Didn't you know that?"

Shasa rolled her eyes so theatrically it hurt. Mac took her hand, his eyes pleading. "Come on! Just a simple dinner between friends. No funny business."

Oh, how she wished it were that easy.

Mac carried on. "We'll be in a restaurant. A public place. It's not like I'm taking you to a secluded spot by the river."

She glanced in the direction of the river. It would have taken them five minutes to cross the street and descend the steps. There'd be nobody around. The short stretch of sand would still be warm from the long day in the sun.

Mac's breath tickled her face. "What do you say?"

She whipped around and headed towards town. Getting away from the bridge, the river, and the warm sand would be job number one.

"I get to choose the restaurant!" she called over her shoulder.

Chapter 28

Shasa took in the visual overload of the Mexican restaurant. She'd counted on it being busy and not too intimate, with shared tables and zero privacy. But the waiter showed them to a private corner table. At least there weren't any candles or a particularly romantic soundtrack.

Although she wasn't sure romance was the problem. What was between them felt primal, uncontrollable. Would it go away if they broke contact? Would it eventually fizzle out? How much would it hurt?

"So, what did you want to chat about?" Shasa asked, trying to keep her voice business-like.

Mac held her eyes for a moment, as if trying to decide

something. “Can we order first? I’m starving.”

“Sure.” She shrugged. She was hungry too.

They ordered fajitas and ginger beer.

“What do you think of Roman Holiday?” she asked as the drinks arrived. “It’s a bit of a chick flick, right?”

Mac sat back in his chair, looking out the window with a faint smile. “It’s a fairy-tale, but there’s something real at the heart of it.”

She wanted to frame that moment, the way the evening light hit the side of his face and that faraway look in his eyes. Layers and layers she’d never get tired of uncovering.

“That film fascinates me,” she confessed. “The secrets they’re keeping, how they’re both playing the game, and both think they’re winning.”

“I think he wants to save her.” Mac turned to look at her, his brown eyes glistening.

“I thought he wanted to make money out of her, sell her … story?”

“It starts that way. Then he falls for her and it changes. But it’s not just about winning her over. If it were, it’d be a happy ending of sorts. She kisses him, so there’s your happily ever after. I mean, it’s the fifties, they’re not going to give you a night of passion. But that’s not what he wants. He wants to save her. And he doesn’t get to.”

Shasa’s stomach hollowed out. “So, it’s an unhappy ending?”

“I suppose.” He leaned back, taking a sip of his drink.

"Just like us," she said quietly.

He sighed. They both knew it.

"I don't know what the future holds, but this moment is perfect." He lifted his glass at her, his smile a little sad.

Her phone chimed, and she pulled it out of her canvas bag. It was a text from Marnie.

Marnie: Hope it's going well? We believe in you!

She turned the phone on silent and hid it in her bag.

"Everything okay?" Mac asked.

"Yeah. Just an update from Elsie. Lilla is doing well." The lie tasted awful in her mouth.

The end was around the corner. She could feel it like a winter chill in the air. They'd been pretending nothing else existed, ignoring the ticking time bomb waiting for them down the road. One way or another, they were going to get hurt. What would she be left with? Memories of those brief moments? Sexual frustration?

"You think if the film was made in this decade, they'd spend a night together?" she asked.

"Totally. That kiss in the taxi, at the end. It's like a metaphor." He winked at her.

She licked her lips. "A metaphor for sex?"

"Yeah. The director originally wanted to show Gregory Peck pounding Audrey Hepburn against some royal carving somewhere, but they had to downgrade it to that godawful snog in the taxi."

She laughed. "It was an awful kiss! It looked like mouth-to-mouth."

"Back then, they had a three-second rule for on-screen kisses. Anything longer would've been indecent."

"Are you sure? I think I've seen kisses longer than that in old films."

"You need proof?" He picked up his phone, ready to google it.

She waved her hand. "No. But if that's the rule, we may have broken it a couple of times."

"What? No! With those innocent pecks on the cheek?"

They locked eyes for a moment, and she sucked in her bottom lip, thinking of the kiss. She was teasing him, testing his resolve. It was mean and ill-advised, since she hardly had any of it herself.

Mac took another gulp of his ginger beer and got up. "Excuse me."

She watched him disappear through the bathroom door. She pressed her cold drink against her blazing hot cheek, trying to gain some level of composure.

Warm, tingly, and distracted, she nearly missed her opportunity. Mac's phone. He'd left it on the table. She picked it up, trying to act natural. Her forefinger touched the screen, and it lit up. No passcode? He must have bypassed it with his thumb when he'd picked it up earlier.

Her heart beating like a drum in an echo chamber, she

opened Mac's email inbox, searching for something related to the section.

Within a few seconds, she spotted her landlord's name and opened an email chain, jumping to the beginning. There it was. No attachment or legal papers. He'd typed his offer in the body of the email. In the next email, her landlord accepted it. Just like that.

Cold sweat prickled on her back. This was her opportunity. Not giving herself a chance to back out, she took a photo of the email on Mac's screen and sent it to her group chat with Marnie and Elsie.

As soon as it was done, she dropped Mac's phone like it was burning her hand. What had she done? But there was no time to think. She hit the home button and placed the phone back exactly where it had been, hoping Mac would stay away long enough for the screen saver to activate. Was there a way to turn it on manually? She drank her ginger beer, watching the phone like she was expecting it to catch on fire.

The fajitas arrived, the approaching waiter making her jump. Past the steaming tray he set on the table, she saw that the phone lock screen had turned on. She was in the clear. The biggest giveaway would now be her face. If she truly had some natural acting talent, she needed it now. All of it.

The bathroom door opened, and Mac joined her at the table, hungrily eyeing the food. "This looks good!"

He offered her half of everything, far more than she could handle.

He was so good to her. Too good. But he had several houses, she reminded herself. Losing this one deal would only hurt his pride. She tried to focus on her plate. She had to relax her body enough to accept food.

"Shasa?"

She looked up, her gut squeezing at the sincere look in his eyes. "Yes?"

"I... um... I have something on my phone I wanted to show you."

Shasa swallowed, willing the bite she'd swallowed to keep going down, not up. "What do you mean?"

Mac tapped on his phone, whipping it around to show her a photo. A huge brick house that looked brand new. Freshly cut grass so neat it must have been photoshopped.

"One of your houses?"

"Not mine, but I can get this for you if you're interested."

Shasa produced a sound that was more of a scoff than a laugh. "We can't afford anything like that!"

"It's four hundred a week."

She rolled her eyes. "No, it's not! Unless it's a flatshare or a brothel where I'm expected to work fifty hours a week."

His mouth tugged. "Neither of those. It's just a rental house in Flagstaff."

She shook her head. "Flagstaff is expensive. Four hundred... what's the catch?"

He looked uncomfortable. What was he hiding?

"Okay. If you must know, I would cover part of the rent and keep some stuff in the garage."

"Do you need a garage?"

He looked away, then back at her. "Shasa. I just want to help. I want to make sure you and Lilla are okay. I can't stand the idea—"

"We're not your responsibility. Trust me." The lump in her throat swollen to the point she could hardly speak.

The way he cared about her was too sweet for words. It made her ache all over. But she couldn't let him do down this road. She'd made her choice.

Mac's voice was dark. "Okay. You don't have to say anything if you don't want to, but what happened with Lilla's father? Is he around?"

The question took her by surprise. She hadn't thought about Ollie in days. Was that right? He'd called her two days ago, but she'd simply fetched Lilla, then stayed out of the room and ended the call when he tried to talk to her. There was no space for Ollie in her thoughts. After all the heartbreak and time she'd wasted obsessing over him, she'd turned a corner, like a drug user replacing one substance with another. Mac was her new obsession, one that kept her company late at night and during quiet moments at work.

"He's not around," she said, poking her fajitas with a fork. It smelled so good, but her intestines were closed for business. Only nerves were at work, misfiring on all cylinders. "He's been away for two years now and just decided to extend his contract on the ship."

"Is he in the navy?"

She burst out in laughter. Ollie, the lifetime pacifist, who couldn't wear leather shoes. "No. He works for Greenpeace. Saving whales, working on oil spills, that kind of thing."

Mac smiled. "That makes more sense."

"When I found out he wasn't coming home, I cut off my dreadlocks. That's why my hair's like this. The hairdresser tried to fix it, but it was too much of a challenge. I have to wait until it grows out." She pointed at her uneven pixie cut, her hand shaky.

"I like your hair." His eyes studied her, head tilted. "You look just like Audrey Hepburn. Except hotter."

She nearly choked on the tiny piece of chicken she'd managed to put in her mouth. She smiled, trying to shrug off the compliment.

Mac's eyebrows drew together. "What doesn't make sense is why he'd choose to stay away from you and his own daughter?" His voice was thick with compassion.

Shasa shivered. She could make it through the waves of physical desire, like waves of nausea. You just had to stop and wait, get some fresh air. But she couldn't have him say things like that, especially after what she'd done. She had to shut this down.

"It's his dream. He's saving the planet. In the grand scheme of things..." The words got stuck in her throat, unable to get past the fresh lump.

No. No. NO. She was not going to cry. Not here. Not over Ollie. She took a deep breath and counted to five. It almost worked. She was nearly over the hump when he rested his hand on hers, releasing a gush of warmth that shot straight into her heart.

His voice was heavy and solid. "There is no grand scheme of things that matters more than you. Not in this context."

Nothing could stop the tears from falling.

"Let's go." He placed a hundred-dollar note on the table and helped her up from her chair.

She grabbed her bag and let him guide her out the door, into the cool night air. His arm around her, she felt safe. If they were two different people, in a different town, at a different time, they could be happy together. So happy, like Audrey Hepburn had said at the end of the film. So happy.

Was there a way, somehow, for this to work? No. She'd made sure of that, abusing his trust.

They walked quietly down the road, back towards the theatre. He didn't take his arm off her shoulder, and she didn't want him to. Maybe this night was all they'd ever get. She wanted to soak it all in, to never forget what it felt to be this desired. To be this seen. She smiled up at him, her lashes heavy like pine needles after rain.

"So happy," she said, quoting the film.

"So happy," he said, imitating Audrey's accent.

Part of her wanted to leave everything behind, take him

by the hand and flee. If they could shed all the baggage. Her job, her plans, his business... But how could that ever work?

"Let's go to the river," she said, half expecting him to say no.

"Okay."

They strolled down the road onto a side street leading down to the river. Without streetlamps, they had to feel their way down the footpath, the leaves rustling against their clothes as they descended through the bush and onto the sand. In the dark, the water looked solid, a piece of black marble. The sand still felt warm, and the beach was deserted, just like she had imagined. Dangerously deserted. They were so close, so private. She couldn't resist finding out more about him.

"Why are you so different from your parents?" she asked as he sat down next to her. "I mean, Marnie could hardly believe you're related. They sound so..."

"Self-sacrificing? Not materialistic?" His voice held a sarcastic edge.

Shasa wrinkled her nose, looking for a word that sounded more neutral. Maybe there wasn't one. "Yeah. They sound like they're not concerned about getting ahead."

"Like me?" he finished darkly.

"But deep down, I feel like you're not that different. Like you... try to be, but something else is coming through. Most people hide their greedy side and present this caring, selfless image to the world. You do the opposite."

Mac laughed, a short and sad sound that disappeared into the night. "You're right. I was brought up to be good. Better to be a good man than a great man. That's one of my dad's favourite sayings. But it always bothered me that we were scraping by, that they could barely look after themselves. If you want to do good, you need resources. Poverty isn't the goal, right? But my parents always acted like it was. My brother, Izzy, he's taken that to heart. He lives on nothing, in this rundown house in Bader. He has the skills, the creativity... Sure, he's had some tough experiences along the way, but he could make some money if he wanted to. If he ever left that basement. I feel like I'm the only one in the family who's able to build some wealth. If I don't, we're all just passing this defeatist attitude to the next generation."

Shasa nodded. "Yeah, I get that. It accumulates. The gap between the haves and have-nots is just getting bigger. I worry about Lilla."

He slipped his hand over hers, squeezing it lightly. "She'll be okay."

He said it with such conviction and gravity, like he'd decided to make it his personal goal. And he couldn't. She'd lose him, and it would hurt so much she didn't want to think about it at all.

Her throat tightened. "I hope so. I don't want her to grow up moving from one horrible rental to another. It's so restless and disrupting. Unhealthy, too."

"I know. I grew up like that, until my parents finally

bought. But they stopped at that one house and had no money for repairs. So it wasn't that different. A bit more settled, maybe, because we were no longer moving every year. But plenty of mould and chest infections."

She sighed, her heart squeezing for that little boy – young Mac who dreamt of something better. She could see it now, and it all made sense. "My parents moved around, too, and they never bought a house in New Zealand. Then they divorced and both moved away—"

"Away, where?"

"South Africa and Finland."

"Wow. That's far! But you stayed here?"

"I was already nineteen and studying. I've lived here all my life. What was I supposed to do? I didn't want to take sides in the divorce either."

Mac blew out a heavy sigh. "Yeah, I would have done the same. But it sounds rough, to suddenly be left on your own."

The empathy in his voice brought the tightness back to her throat. She couldn't remember the last time someone had acknowledged the loss. No one had died, so people usually moved past it, shrugging it away. But it had shaped her life and who she was. The fact that he saw it, saw her...

She could hardly move, afraid to break the spell. They sat in silence for a moment, listening to the rumble of the river.

"What's your favourite place in Hamilton?" she asked. It was the safest topic she could think of.

He threw his arm over her shoulder. "Here, with you."

His raw, honest voice shot straight to her heart, and a warm shiver ran through her. She should have wriggled away from his embrace, but she didn't want to. They were in the dark, like in the theatre. It didn't count. "No, seriously, what's your favourite?"

Mac's fingers traced her bare arm. "Maybe the gardens late at night or early morning when there're no tourists."

"Which one?"

"The Italian one, no contest."

She drew in a sharp breath, her heart beating faster. "No contest. In springtime, at dusk."

Maybe they'd crossed paths in the Renaissance garden in the past without even noticing. She'd notice him from now on, though, for the rest of her life. Earlier that night, she'd sensed his presence from across the theatre floor before she could even see him.

"It's just physical, right? Pheromones?" Her voice wobbled.

Heavy silence fell between them, filled by a soft whoosh of wind that carried the smell of wet earth.

Mac drew his arm off Shasa's shoulder, his voice rough. "Honestly ... I don't think sleeping with you would get you out of my system. Not anymore."

Her breath caught in her throat. "Me, neither. I toyed with that idea, but I could never have sex with no strings attached. Not without getting hurt. I'm not teflon."

"If you want to be a good actor, you have to be vulnerable."

"Are you?"

She could hardly see him but felt his body shift against her as his voice dropped. "What makes you think I'm not?"

She shrugged. "Money. Power. It shields people."

His low voice rumbled like the river. "Shasa. I'm falling for you. I'm as vulnerable as they come."

Her head swam. She wanted to stay there forever, staring at the black river, talking to him, breathing in his scent. But his words carried more weight than she could handle. Was that why he'd left his phone on the table? Because he trusted her, loved her? What had she done?

She got up, her heart in her throat. "I should go. I have to pick up Lilla."

He followed her up the path, along the side street, towards the city lights. When they reached the theatre, she turned towards the parking lot. Her car was there, next to his huge, shiny pickup truck. What did he need a pickup truck for? She heard his keys, and the double beep as he unlocked the doors.

Time to go. His hand was still on her shoulder, the only thing that kept her from falling. Yet she knew she'd already fallen.

"I don't want you to go," she whispered. "I know we're wrong for each other, two people in the wrong place, at the wrong time. It's all wrong, but..."

"I know. Me too."

"I—"

He took her face into his hands and kissed her so deeply and tenderly she couldn't feel the ground under her feet. His hands settled on her waist and she pressed herself against him, desperate to close the distance, to keep him there. They broke the three-second rule, ten-second-rule, and likely some modern rules on Netflix, until he pulled away.

Mac's voice was gruff. "I know what I promised, and I'm sorry. I'll stop here and let you go."

She felt a sharp twist in her gut. After what she'd done with his phone, she needed him to take her against that shiny ute, to slap her, punish her. Anything. He was supposed to be the bad guy, not her.

Mac brushed the side of her face, his touch unbearably gentle, his eyes soft and searching. "Good night, Shasa." Then he got into his pickup and drove away.

She stood in the empty parking lot, letting the warmth of his hands and mouth fade off her skin, until the last trace of it was replaced by the cool night air.

Her phone pinged, and she opened it to find two enthusiastic messages from Marnie and Elsie. Exclamation marks and party emojis. What a success! The price was lower than Elsie had expected. They could easily outbid him.

It's go time!!! Marnie's text shouted on her screen.

She typed a reply, informing Elsie she'd pick up her daughter in ten minutes. Then she sank into her car, her eyes blurring with fresh tears. If tonight was such a success, why did she feel like she'd lost everything?

Minutes later, she parked in front of Elsie's house, wiped her eyes and breathed deeply until she felt a bit better, then approached the door. It was opened by Earl.

Shasa took a step back, blinking in confusion.

"Hi Shasa," he said. "Didn't mean to scare you. Elsie asked me to help with babysitting."

"Oh. Was Lilla a lot of trouble?"

Elsie appeared by his side, smiling sweetly. "She was perfect."

They seemed so cosy together, Elsie's eyes shimmering with joy. "Earl's also interested in the cohousing community."

"I need to discuss it with you and Marnie, obviously," Earl injected. "But the timing is perfect for me. I've been saving to buy another place and rent out my old apartment."

Shasa smiled, trying to push her own mood aside. "That's wonderful."

If she didn't focus on Mac, it was great news. This was exactly what they wanted – lovely people joining our community.

Elsie pulled her inside the house, ushering her towards the kitchen. "It's quite late, and Lilla is fast asleep. Would you like to have a cup of tea and spend the night in the guest room? It might be easier. We already moved her cot there, so it'll be right by your bed."

Shasa couldn't come up with any objections. "That sounds perfect."

Earl picked up his jacket. "I'll leave you to it, then. Good night!"

Elsie rushed after him to the front door. Despite her inner turmoil, their burgeoning relationship made Shasa smile. She sat down at the dining table, browsing the half-empty snack bowls. She hadn't managed to eat much earlier. They'd left behind most of the meal Mac had overpaid for. What a waste.

With her stomach gradually settling, she cleaned out the remaining crackers and hummus. Elsie stayed away, probably talking to Earl at the door, like two teenagers unable to say goodbye. It was so sweet. Not all tangled and wrong like her and Mac.

She got up and tiptoed around the house to find the guest room. It turned out to be a huge room in its own wing, with its own lounge and ensuite. Lilla slept peacefully in her cot, her cheeks rosy under the night light's soft glow. The room felt like a country inn. Exhaustion taking over, Shasa lay on the bed, letting her body sink into the plush quilt. She wanted a new home. A safe and comfortable home. But she wanted Mac, too. One way or another, her heart would be broken.

Chapter 29

Mac pulled into his driveway, his heart beating like a drum. He'd hit the gym for a late-night workout and listened to a dreadfully slow meditation podcast the whole way home, but nothing could calm him down. Nothing could reinstate him to any kind of normal.

It wasn't just physical, either. He had known it the moment he wrapped his arm around her, out on the street, in public. He wasn't ashamed to be seen with her. And it wasn't because she was wearing mainstream clothes for once. He wouldn't have cared if she'd been in a rainbow-colored tribal dress. She was amazing. Brave, selfless, and fierce. He couldn't have cared less about her clothes or political views. He cared too much about her.

The street looked deserted, like it always did – an expensive ghost town. He tried to see his house through Shasa's eyes. What did she think of it, of him? They had chemistry, but could he offer her more? A life together? Could she be happy with him? Would her child be happy with him around?

Heaving his gym bag on his shoulder, he approached his house, his head throbbing with all the unanswered questions. Before he reached the door, his phone rang.

"It's your lucky day!" Rick sounded a little tipsy. "I have a date for you next Saturday, and she's hot!" Loud dance music nearly drowned out his voice. Nightclub music.

"Geez, thanks. You shouldn't have."

"Shut up. You were practically begging me. I'll send you the details via text. And another thing..."

"What?" All he wanted was to end the phone call and crawl into bed. And text Shasa.

"The Marama Street seller. Is he still onboard? He said he was expecting another offer. We need to be more proactive here. Offer more. Now."

"He said he'd let me know if he gets another offer, and we can negotiate."

"No! If the other offer's a lot higher, he'll think you won't be able to match it, and he'll sign the papers. We already told him we were giving him our best price. He doesn't know we're lowballing. He's not that bright."

Rick was right. Mac felt like kicking himself. He'd been distracted and complacent, thinking Shasa's group would never get organized enough to compete with him. They were just poking him, happy with themselves if they felt like they could annoy him, show him he wasn't untouchable. Which he definitely wasn't. He was an idiot.

Rick's voice blasted through his phone, agreeing with his inner dialogue. "Don't be an idiot! The other section needs to be in the bag, too. Get your parents to sign on the dotted line, okay?"

"Okay."

He'd go over this weekend for Sunday lunch and sort it out. Since Shasa's house was right next door, he could pop in to see her as well. He had to talk to her, pour out his heart and see if it was possible. He had to try. What really stood in the way?

A couple of million dollars' worth of real estate, his logical brain replied in a distant voice. So what, he argued. There had to be a way to work that out. Even if it meant he should… lose? He swallowed at the thought. Why was he even entertaining the idea? What the hell was happening to him? He couldn't lose. There was no plan B.

He kicked open the front door and dropped his gym bag in the empty hallway, noting the distinct absence of life. His house smelled like a… building. That's what it felt like, too.

He traipsed into the kitchen, yanked open the drawer full

of tea and stared at it. Would she ever be back here to drink another cup? Every part of his body missed her, but she'd shot down his plans with the Flagstaff rental. Shasa would never accept his help, not like that. What happened when they bought the sections and bulldozed her house? What would she think of him after that? It was one thing to talk about abstract plans, but she'd have to move away, with her kid. Where would she go?

Here, his heart told him. She could come here. At least temporarily. But how could he even present that idea to her without sounding like a condescending ass? They'd only known each other for a couple of weeks. Was there any way he could get her onboard without scaring her away?

Mac had no answers, but one thing was for certain. He needed more time with her, to give whatever was growing between them a chance to take hold. Maybe then the answer would come.

How could he get more time with her? She had a child. They didn't have another theatre rehearsal until next week. He couldn't wait that long. He had to make this weekend count. Leaning on the kitchen island, Mac buried his face in his hands. What could he do? Where could he take her? Was there a magical place where the real life and its mess couldn't reach them?

Of course! The idea hit him with such clarity he almost laughed out loud. How had he missed it?

Chapter 30

Lilla woke early on Saturday morning. Shasa trailed her to the kitchen and gave her a banana, hoping to postpone breakfast. She'd slept poorly, again. Ever since her date with Mac (or whatever it was), she'd felt out of sorts, almost like she was sick but not quite, her gut churning and dreams too vivid.

After getting back to Elsie's house, she'd contemplated cutting herself off and not texting him. It felt wrong to turn to him for comfort when she'd spied on him like that. Her decision had lasted until the next morning when she'd found her phone full of messages, fresh words of affection she drank up like some sort of elixir, saving the best ones deep in her memory. Their bubble would burst. Words would dry up, and she'd need those memories.

> **Mac:** I know I kissed you, but I was holding back so hard. You have no idea. Sitting next to you by the river, in the dark... I'm giving myself a trophy for not touching you.

Those words still burned inside her.

Leaning on the kitchen counter, Shasa checked her phone. No word from Mac, yet, but it wasn't even six a.m. She scrolled back to the earlier conversation. She could detect a change in his tone, from funny and flirty to intense. There were so many questions.

> **Mac:** What's your favourite breakfast food?
>
> **Mac:** What's on your playlist?
>
> **Mac:** What's Lilla's favourite food? Anything she hates?

Pancakes, she'd replied. Soul. Chocolate. Eggplant. She'd just wanted to keep the conversation going. Even if they'd never have breakfast together.

When she exhausted the text messages, her mind returned to that moment on the riverside, with Mac's arm around her, replaying the words he'd dropped in her lap like hot coals.

I'm falling for you.

The crazy thing was, she believed him. Something in her responded to those words like they were her own. It made sense, in that removed-from-reality kind of way everything about her and Mac did. She felt what he felt – that hot, unsettling sensation that drew them together again and again, damn the consequences. She wanted that. The sick feeling swirling in her stomach only lifted for a moment when she relived that moment. His touch and those words. He'd stolen her peace of mind.

Why had she picked up his phone and read his email? Did she really want this new house so badly? Was it worth it?

Elsie had contacted her landlord straight away, but they hadn't heard back. Would her friends keep her in the loop? Surely, she'd proven her trustworthiness. Would someone who was in love with Mac act the way she had?

Shasa lowered herself on the couch, watching Lilla dance around the lounge with her banana. Her daughter didn't seem even a little tired. No more sleep, then. Shasa burrowed into the couch, hiding under a woollen throw.

"Pancakes?" she asked her daughter without even lifting her head. Lilla nodded vigorously. She stuffed the rest of the banana in her mouth and reached out a sticky hand to pull Shasa up. She resisted, collapsing back on the couch.

"One minute," she whined.

A knock on the door jolted her, forcing her upright. Who was bothering them at this ungodly hour? She staggered to the door.

Her stomach flipped at the sight of Mac, standing at her doorstep in a hoodie and jeans.

"I'm sorry, I tried, but I couldn't stay away." He had a dark stubble and a wild bedhead, which he raked into an even messier shape by dragging his fingers through it.

The way he looked at her made her ache. Hope. Questions. No one had ever looked at her like that. Lovesick and nervous, yet... excited. Unable to handle his gaze, she stared down at her striped night socks. She hadn't even brushed her teeth and fought the urge to dive into his arms.

"I didn't want you to stay away," she whispered. She wanted to touch him so badly her arms twitched.

His hands dropped down to his sides, and he hooked his thumbs into his jeans' pockets as if to keep them from straying. "I tried to stay away. I really tried, at least until all the building stuff is done and dealt with. It makes sense. But you've done something to me. I can't..." The frustration in his voice surged through her.

"Mac."

She had no words. Nothing to make it better, only worse. But she had to close the distance. She took a tiny step forward, and his arms snapped around her like they were two connecting pieces of Lego, perfectly fastened. Here, she was safe. She was okay. He was the temporary cure to her sickness, even if she knew she was falling into a deeper hole.

She had to tell him. "We're making an offer on this section. I'm sorry." Her wobbly voice was muffled by his hoodie.

She expected him to pull away, but he didn't. "That's okay. It's just an offer. Can we put that aside for this morning? I have something I want to show you. You and Lilla."

Shasa shivered. He didn't know what she'd done. He didn't know their offer was higher, perfectly calculated to beat his.

She lifted her chin to meet Mac's gaze. "But what if we get it?"

His expression was dark. "If we get into a bidding war, and you win… I don't know. To tell you the truth, I've got a lot riding on this. If you win, I'll have to sell up."

"Sell up? Everything?" Her stomach wound into a tight knot.

"I'm in a bit of a tight spot. I've made some bad investments. One particularly awful leaky townhouse is sucking me dry. If I can't get it fixed, I'll have to sell that at a loss… and that's a hit I can't take." He cast her a pained look.

She took a step back, and his hands fell away from her hips. "But… you have so many houses! You're rich."

"I'm going to be completely honest with you, so you understand. The market is turning. The banks are tightening their lending criteria. They've started liquidating high-risk assets and time is running out. I'm in the red. I desperately need some cashflow, which is why I must build these condos and get those deposits in. Otherwise, I wouldn't get in the way of your cohousing project. I adore that idea." He paused for a moment, his eyes searching for hers. "And I adore you." His mouth curved, eyes still sad and imploring.

She couldn't swallow. With the cantaloupe-sized lump in her throat, she could hardly breathe. She felt Lilla's arms around her legs, then Mac's fingers under her chin, guiding her to make eye contact. "I'm so sorry about the cohousing thing. I'll help you guys find another piece of land, I promise. Can we please put that aside for now? I have a surprise for you..."

"Surprise?" Lilla chirped.

Mac turned to pick her up, his voice filled with excitement. "Yes! A big surprise, you'll love it! Let's get you dressed and in the car. Have you eaten? We can pick up some breakfast on the way."

Shasa followed them into the house. Lilla showed Mac into their bedroom and began pulling clothing options from her dresser. Mac examined the selection of unicorn shirts and skirts. Together, they landed on a light yellow one, paired with a pink ballerina skirt and green tights. Mac nodded appreciatively as Lilla laid the outfit down on the floor. "Gorgeous."

Her head spinning, she stepped in to help Lilla get changed. She glanced down at her own pyjama pants and the T-shirt she'd slept in. Maybe it was best to just focus on the next three minutes and not think about the rest of her life.

Mac stepped out of the bedroom.

"I have water bottles in the car," he called from the hallway, "so you don't have to pack anything. But take a jumper, okay?"

A jumper? Where were they going? And how much more complicated would everything get if she followed him there?

Put it aside. That's what he'd asked her to do. Lilla's eyes sparkled like it was Christmas morning. She couldn't take this away from her.

Shasa scoured her bedroom for anything clean enough to wear, landing on red parachute pants, olive green top and a chunky cardigan. There. She was dressed like a Christmas tree, to match the theme.

Mac had parked in their driveway. She'd never seen his ute there, right behind her own. It didn't fit, but it made her feel safe. She wanted his ute, him, everything about him in her life. And she'd already blown it.

She grabbed Lilla's booster seat from her own car and slid into the backseat of Mac's truck. "I'll ride in the backseat with her if that's okay." Lilla didn't need her there, but she felt like hiding from him until she managed to shove the whirlwind of emotions somewhere deep enough. If it indeed was possible.

Mac met her eyes in the rearview mirror. "All good."

He drove them away from the lake, straight through the town centre and over the bridge. She expected him to head to one of the East side playgrounds, but they passed each one, heading North.

After a few minutes, he pulled over at a roadside cafe and turned to them. "I'll get us coffee and maybe a couple of pastries. What do you want?"

"Sounds good. Flat white, please."

She rarely drank coffee, but this morning was not business

as usual. She unearthed her trusty reusable cup from the bottom of her bag and handed it to Mac. "It's a bit dirty, but you can ask them to give it a rinse."

He stared at it. "You brought your own cup?"

She shrugged. "It's always in my bag."

Mac looked like he was about to say something but changed his mind. He turned to Lilla. "And for you, Miss?"

"Chocolate!" Lilla ordered.

Shasa shook her head. "Bring her a muffin or something."

Mac gave a brief nod and disappeared inside the building. The giant backboard outside the door advertised a coffee and muffin combo deal. A few minutes later, he returned with several brown paper bags and two coffees, one in a takeaway cup, the other in her green ceramic one.

"Here you go, Miss." Mac handed Lilla one of the paper bags.

Shasa tried to grab the bag. "Not in the truck. She'll make a mess."

"Then I'll get it cleaned. Chill."

Mac steered back on the road. She wondered if they were going to his house, but he drove past his own suburb and turned onto a country road.

Five minutes later, they arrived at a sprawling lifestyle property. And there it was – a hot-air balloon, tethered to the front lawn. Lilla squealed, clambered out of the truck, and ran towards it. Shasa followed at her heels. The balloon had the classic lightbulb shape with pink and white stripes like a piece of candy.

She turned to a beaming Mac. "Where are we? Whose is it?"

He gestured at an old man who appeared from behind the basket and climbed in. "This is Hank, the pilot. The house belongs to my friend Rick. He sponsors the balloon festival."

Hank waved to them. "Morning, Mac!"

Mac introduced them, and Hank smiled, releasing a towering flame into the balloon. "The weather's perfect and we're ready to go. Just waiting for Felicity. The kiddos are up, and she's dealing with them."

Shasa looked around. "Ready to go where?"

Mac pointed at the sky. "For a balloon ride. If you're okay with that. Lilla's a bit young, but we'll do a tethered ride with the kids first."

"It means we lift off to about fifty meters up and then come back down," Hank explained. "After that, she can ride in the chase vehicle with Felicity. Kids love that."

Shasa looked at Mac. "So, you and I go for a real balloon ride?"

"If you want to?" He raised a hopeful brow.

Before she could form a reply, a lithe blonde woman approached them with two kids in tow. The girl was maybe a year older than Lilla, the boy a bit younger.

She grinned. "Mac! I've never seen you up this early! Rick's still out like a light. He just turned over in bed and mumbled something."

Mac laughed. "I promised we wouldn't wake him!"

Lilla approached the other kids, reserved but curious.

Felicity stepped closer to Shasa, exuding relaxed confidence. "She'll love chasing the balloon. My kids think that's the best part. They can't see much when they're in the basket, anyway."

"Right." Shasa tried to relax. Mac had organized this amazing experience. Whatever was going on with her, or between them, she couldn't ruin this for her daughter, who appeared by her side, practically shaking from excitement.

She hung her entire weight off Shasa's arm. "Can we go up in the balloon, Mum? Please?"

Mac caught her eye. "Are you okay? I know I sprung this on you."

"I'm fine," she lied. "I'm sure Lilla will love the ride, even with the strings attached."

Mac pulled her in for a side hug and placed a light kiss on her hair. "They're called tethers. But yeah, some things are better with strings attached," he whispered.

She squeezed her eyes shut for a second and filed away his words, too heavy with meaning. She could cry over them later.

Mac gave a signal to Hank, who gathered the kids and helped them into the basket. After double-checking the tethers and lines, he hopped onboard with them, explaining something about the physics of hot air balloon, which surely went over the heads of his young audience.

"Mummy!" Lilla called from the basket.

"Mummy can get in, too," Hank hollered. "There's room for one more adult."

Shasa cast a questioning look at Mac.

"Go!" he urged. "She'll enjoy it more if you're with her."

It was almost a relief to get away from him. He was too sweet to her, too lovely, too serious about them. He didn't know she'd already destroyed everything. Climbing into the basket, she wondered if there was any way she could get Elsie and Marnie to pull the offer and reconsider the building site. They'd think she was nuts, but that was a small price to pay.

Anxiety turned her stomach. She couldn't do anything about it now. Her phone was in the truck, and she was about to go up in the air with three excitable kids.

"I actually needed another adult here," Hank confessed, "to keep the kids from climbing."

"Feet flat on the floor, Ryan!" He told the blond boy, who tried to pull himself up the side of the basket. "Use the peeping hole."

The kids took turns looking through the peephole as Hank turned on the propane burners, and with a loud whoosh, they lifted off the ground.

"Mac is tiny!" Lilla exclaimed, peering through the hole. "House is tiny."

From high up in the air, everything looked small. For a moment, Shasa felt weightless, like she could see her tangled, complicated life from a God perspective. So small and inconsequential. The green fields spread out as far as the eye could see, dotted by occasional houses. So many lives, so many dwellings. Her life couldn't be tied up to one building project. She had to get hold of Marnie and beg her to change the plans. She had to try.

Tiny Mac on the ground waved at her, and she waved back. He was good to her. He was good to her daughter. She looked at the tethers attaching the balloon to the ground. Was there anything like that between them? Would anything stop them from floating apart?

Hank explained to the kids how they'd return to the ground and then follow the balloon with Felicity's car. "You have to keep your eyes on the balloon the whole time."

His reassuring voice calmed her. Everything would be okay. She wasn't scared of heights or flying, but the thought of spending an hour in the basket with Mac made her shiver. Thank God Hank would be with them. The silver-haired pilot carefully guided the balloon down to the ground and helped the children out, staying in the basket with her.

Felicity gathered the kids, handing each a helium balloon. "Okay, it's time!" she announced.

Her kids immediately let go of their balloons, watching them float up to the sky.

"What are they doing?" Shasa asked.

Felicity smiled. "Prepping you for the flight. This way you see the wind direction. Better than the weather forecast.

Plus, it's fun for the kids."

The two balloons rose higher and higher in the sky, but Lilla held onto hers.

"Let it go, Lil. You get to see where the wind takes it," Shasa coached her, trying to reach her daughter over the side of the basket.

The girl was too far and too stubborn, locking the string in her white-knuckled grip. She'd never had a helium balloon before.

Mac approached Felicity. "Let her keep it. Two in the sky is enough for us."

Felicity turned to the kids and pointed at a huge black people mover parked in front of the house.

"Are you ready to chase the balloon?"

Lilla shouted 'yes' with the others.

Shasa sighed from relief and waved. "Mummy will see you a bit later!"

Lilla waved back. "Don't worry Mummy, we're going to catch you!"

As Felicity steered the kids towards the car, she called over her shoulder to Shasa, "Don't worry, we took your girl's booster seat from Mac's truck!"

Next thing Shasa knew, Hank hopped out of the basket, and Mac climbed in, grasping the lever Hank had been holding above their heads.

"Where's Hank going?" she blinked rapidly.

"To drive my truck, to pick up the balloon. It doesn't fit

into the other car with all the kids."

"What? We can't ride without a pilot!"

Mac chuckled. "There's a pilot right behind you."

"You? You know how to fly this thing? Seriously?" Her voice came out high and squeaky.

"Would you like to see my licence? Hank trained me."

She turned to see where Hank had gone and found him standing outside of the basket, a couple of steps away.

He smiled. "It's true. He's qualified. Not as brilliant as me, but qualified."

Mac glared at him, then turned to her. "I'm just as good. My ego's just less inflated."

Hank rolled his eyes. "You're good to go here," he said, unhooking the last tether from the basket's side.

He hurried to the truck, and Mac pulled the handle on the burner. She was expecting the loud whoosh this time, but it still startled her. They lifted off the ground.

Chapter 31

Shasa held her breath, drinking in the scenery. She'd never seen anything like it. The ground had turned into a quilt of green fields, sprinkled with roofs. The sun still lay low on the horizon, giving the landscape a golden glow. Unlike the view from a plane window, this felt closer, more real, as if she could almost touch the tops of the trees.

Mac pulled the lever again, and the whooshing flame lifted them higher. He wrapped his free hand around her waist, pulling her closer.

"Shasa," he whispered. "Finally."

She shivered despite the cardigan he'd made her wear. "Shouldn't you keep steering, or driving, or whatever you're doing."

"The wind's driving us now." He stroked her back, and she buried her head into his hoodie, breathing in the scent of soap and coffee.

"Why do you even like me?" she asked, her voice wavering.

"Who says I like you?"

"You did, like half an hour ago."

"Right. I guess the cat's out of the bag, then." She could hear the smile in his voice, along with the gravity. "And for the record, you have no idea how *much* I like you."

She wrapped her hands around his waist and held still. How could he make her feel so grounded when they were literally floating in the air?

"What if it's not enough?" she whispered, turning to face him. "What if all this stuff between us..."

Mac's fingers landed on her mouth. "We agreed to put it aside, remember? Besides, we don't know what will happen with the section. It's all up in the air."

"Up in the air," she chuckled, scanning their surroundings, grateful for the stupid pun that stopped her from hurtling further into desperation. "Okay. Tell me something else. Distract me."

Mac peered into the horizon. "It looks like the weather's holding. We are right on course. If we're lucky, we won't accidentally land in someone's backyard."

"Has that happened to you?"

"Once."

Shasa peeked over the basket's edge. They were close enough to see kids moving in one of the backyards, jumping into a pool. That would be an unfortunate landing spot.

"How did you become a balloon pilot?"

Mac looked away. "It was Rick, actually. He wanted to sponsor the festival, and I thought it was cooler to fly the balloons than just pay for them. He told me if I got a license, he'd sponsor me. I don't think he expected me to follow through. It was way more work than I'd thought, hours of flying. And pretty expensive."

"So, you did it on a dare?"

"Makes me sound mature, doesn't it? Honestly, once I did my first flight, I fell in love with it. I would have kept going either way."

The green fields bathed in the early morning sun, every tree and house casting a long, sweeping shadow like a scattering of tiny sundials. "I can see why."

Mac kept his hand on the lever and his eyes on the horizon. Despite his relaxed tone, Shasa suspected piloting the balloon was a full-time job – one she didn't want to distract him from. Part of her desperately wanted to kiss him, but the buzz of adrenaline kept her in check, her arms locked around his waist. She rested her head on his chest.

"Can we just stay here forever?"

"I looked into getting enough propane to last a lifetime, but... you know, logistics."

She chuckled, her cheek digging into the soft cotton of

his hoodie.

He held still, like holding his breath. "Ask me what I did today," he said.

"What did you do today?"

"I bought enough chocolates to fill another drawer. One right next to the tea. And then I bought all these pancake mixes."

Shasa's heart jumped into her throat. "What? Why?"

"Because I want you with me. Both of you."

No. He couldn't bring this to her now when it was too late. She imagined waking up next to him, in his big, beautiful house. Making a mess in his pristine kitchen. Getting a gate for those horrible stairs. She didn't care about the house, but the dream of them together made her chest so tight she could barely breathe.

"Mac," she whispered. "I hope we don't get the section. I hope we lose."

His arm tightened around her shoulder and tears sprung out of her eyes, as if she was filled with them to the point of overflow. She sent a wish out to the universe, that their plans would fall through, despite her spying. Maybe, just maybe, they would lose the section and she could have this dream. The dream where she wasn't alone, without him.

She had to hold onto something.

They travelled in silence, watching the sun climb higher in the sky, warming their skin. Heading out of town, the houses became few and far between, with endless fields and occasional forests stretching ahead.

"Thank you for bringing me here." Shasa breathed deeply, trying to memorise every second, every scene. "I'll never forget this." She slid her hands under the hem of his hoodie. She noticed her anxiety had settled. Maybe she could trust the balloon, trust him. "If I kiss you, will you crash the balloon?"

"Let's find out."

His playful tone relaxed her, and she melted against him, tilting her head until their lips connected. His mouth felt hot in the cool breeze, eager and hungry. His tongue found hers, sending a surge of fire through her, like the propane burner right above them. He used one hand to grip her waist, then both hands, sliding them down to secure her against him. She felt him through the layers of clothing, hard for her, and delicious heat pooled down between her thighs. She wanted him to rip off her clothes and lift her against a wall. She wanted all the things she couldn't have, and her mind ran away with them.

Not that it made any difference. They were floating across the sky, with nothing but a bag of hot air keeping them from crashing down. 'Horny idiots killed in a balloon crash' the headline would read.

Shasa pulled away, breathless and frustrated. Her body craved so much more, but she knew she would only end up with that terrible, hollow ache.

"You couldn't have another hobby to share with me? Like

testing hotel beds?" she asked, trying to laugh.

He winced, adjusting the crotch of his jeans. "I'm seriously reconsidering every decision that led to this moment."

She sighed. "I have no idea why I'm so hot for you, Mac. I wish I wasn't."

"So, you only want me for my body?" His tone was playful, but she could hear the hurt underneath.

She thought about it. She'd been so hung up on them being wrong for each other that she'd been scared to learn who he really was. Because she wasn't just physically drawn to him. She liked him. She even... No. She couldn't let herself go there. She didn't deserve to go there.

"I'm sorry. It's not true. I know why I'm hot for you, and it's not just chemistry. It's not just physical. You're a great guy, Mac, and I like you—"

"Don't say 'as a friend'. I'll crash this balloon."

She gave a shaky laugh, pressing her burning face against his hoodie. "No! Please don't crash us. I'm totally in love with you." She made sure to draw out the words, to exaggerate, but she still felt the truth underneath, and it stung her right in the middle.

"Okay, you may live." He pulled the lever to lift them a bit higher. "Because I can see through your sarcasm."

Her gut twisted. "I just wish things were different."

"I don't even wish that. I'd rather..." He paused, searching her face.

Her heart skipped a beat. "What?"

"I'd rather go for it. I haven't felt this way about anyone in a long time. Maybe ever. I wake up, and you're my first thought, Shasa. You're my only thought. When will I get to see you, or even hear a word from you... That's all I think about. And when I'm finally with you, the world stops spinning and starts making sense. I don't want to question it anymore. I want to take a chance on us. If you're in?"

"Take a chance?" She had to draw a breath, or she'd faint.

"I'm talking about us, together. Shasa, you already live in my head. I want you in my house. Lilla, too."

As he said it, he glanced over his shoulder and grasped the lever, pulling hard. They were suddenly a lot closer to the ground, floating towards the treetops.

"Are we going to crash?" she yelped, her insides already in freefall.

"No. We just need to get over this hill and land on the other side."

She left him to work on the equipment. To her relief, they rose above the trees. She could see a large, level field in the distance. As they got closer, Mac let out air to lower them down. It seemed the wind was taking them too far to the left.

"Are we going to miss it?"

They were close to the treetops again. Strangely, being this close to the ground was scarier than floating far above.

"We won't hit the middle, but if we go down fast enough, we should be in."

"And if not?"

Mac glanced down, eyebrows knitted. "We'll make it. It might be a bumpy landing, though. Hold onto the basket."

Shivering, Shasa grasped the edge of the wicker basket. It felt too light and hollow, something that shouldn't have been able to hold them in the first place. She didn't want to ask what happened if they hit the trees.

Mac's question lingered in the air, but she couldn't focus on it. At least not enough to give him an answer. Was she in? Her whole body screamed 'yes'. Her heart shouted 'yes'. But her conscience told her 'no'. She'd betrayed him, and she'd been too scared to admit it.

She'd fix it. She'd find a way to fix it.

The ground got closer and closer, the solid green of the field turning into a detailed image featuring tufts of long grass and occasional rocks. Just before the edge of the forest, they touched the ground, bumping against it twice before landing for good. The basket fell on its side, piling her on top of Mac. For a moment, they remained in place, panting, then simultaneously burst into hysterical laughter.

Shasa lifted her head off Mac's chest. "We made it!"

"You sound surprised."

"I am!" Her shaky laugh turned into shivers, and she pressed her head against his chest.

They were partially shaded by the toppled basket, with the balloon fabric hanging over them like a makeshift tent, making everything glow pink. She didn't want to move. She wasn't ready.

Mac wrapped his arms around her. She felt his muscles tighten as he reached to kiss the top of her head. "Stay with me, Shasa. We'll make it work. Just stay with me, please."

That rough whisper stirred her insides. "I want to," she whispered. "But I can't. It's too messy. Can we just wait until the property deals are all done and talk about it then?"

He sighed, his eyes dark. "If that's what you want."

She felt his hardness against her crotch. Poor Mac. She'd break his heart and leave him with nothing. In that moment, she didn't even care about her own pain. She only cared about him.

She listened to the sounds around them. No trucks or cars. The others must not have found them yet. "Where are we? Are there even roads to here?"

"I saw one dirt road that gets close. But they might take a while to find us." His eyes flicked to the side, and a little smile hovered on his lips.

"You think we have some time?" She placed a brief kiss on his mouth and slipped her hand in between them, opening the button of his jeans.

His pupils grew, and his eyes turned glassy. "What are you doing?"

"I'm giving you something."

She shifted sideways and battled with his zipper to free his hard-on. It pushed against his boxer shorts, hot and demanding. Bigger than Ollie's, she thought, slightly embarrassed that she was sizing him up. But she couldn't help noticing, and her lower belly hummed at the thought. She wanted him so much, but she couldn't. She didn't deserve this man.

He tried to get up. "This is not how—"

"You don't like this?" She inserted enough hurt in her voice to make him pause, and it gave her a moment to act.

She peeled down his underwear and grabbed his cock, stroking it up and down. His breathless groan sent more signals down to her core, almost like she was touching herself.

He shifted under her; his voice strained. "I love it. Of course, I love it. It's you. But not like this. I didn't imagine..."

She could feel the time running out and wanted to give him everything. Everything she possibly could.

"I've imagined this," she whispered, her stomach giddy with nerves, her voice betraying her embarrassment. "I've imagined so many things, Mac. You have no idea."

He wrestled himself up to sitting, pushing her off him. "Shasa. You own my mind. You control my cock. But you could never imagine something I haven't already fantasized about many times over."

She could feel her own pulse in her ears. Her face was on fire. She wanted him. She wanted to truly lose herself to him, but she couldn't. Not here. "You don't have a condom, do you?"

He shook his head, frowning. Just what she thought. She forced her own desire into submission.

"Let me do this." She pushed him back on his back.

He groaned. "Only if you let me—"

"Don't worry, you'll get your turn." It was a lie, but she would have said anything to make him relax and just take it. She had to.

This was her last chance to leave him with a memory that wasn't sad or conflicted. A moment of pure pleasure, even if it was just for him. She pulled away his underwear and captured him in her mouth. No more arguments. She heard his heavy breathing as he tensed under her touch, pushing against her. So hard.

"Jesus! Shasa..." His fingers groped at her hair, his voice breathless and laboured. "I won't last."

Good, she thought. They didn't have a lot of time. The others would be here any minute. She sucked him in as deep as she could, pumping her fist around the base of his shaft, listening to the sounds he made, shallow breaths that turned into desperate groans, whispers of her name.

She tried to ignore the hot throbbing between her thighs. This wasn't for her.

"Shasa. Oh my God." His fingers clasped around her hair, shooting a delicious sensation down to her spine. A punishment, but not the kind she deserved. She wanted the pain, but it wasn't supposed to feel like this. This was too good.

The pink balloon fabric flapped in the wind, shielding them from the world, enclosing them in its cocoon. She glanced up, committing it all to memory. The last time she'd touch him. Really touch him. The man she'd betrayed.

Chapter 32

Mac tensed his muscles. He had to stop her. This was not what he'd wanted their first time to be like. This wasn't right. But she was a woman on a mission, turning his mind blank like an overexposed photo, with no information left to salvage.

He gathered the last of his wits, reaching for her again. "Shasa. Come here. Let me touch you. Let me see you." His hand groped at air, then landed on her head again.

She crawled up to him for a moment, placing a kiss on his lips, her hand still on his cock. As she pulled back, he saw the desire in her eyes, the hot gusts of breath landing on his chin.

"If it helps, I'm so hot for you right now. Feel me." She took his hand and guided it under the waistband of her pants.

As his fingers met her wet folds, he sucked in a breath and almost lost it. "God, Shasa. You're killing me."

He circled his fingers on her swollen flesh, and she moaned. Another rub. Another moan. For a moment, her eyelids fluttered, and she moved in sync with his hand, breathing heavily. He slipped two fingers inside, trying to focus on his breathing to hold himself back. She was so wet for him.

"Later," she said, trying to remove his hand. "Let me take care of you first."

"No." He rolled them over so that he lay on top of her, his hard-on tucked between her legs.

His whole body burned for this woman. "All I want is to see you come."

He slipped his hand back between her legs, feeling the wetness through layers of clothing. She gasped, bucking against his palm. "That wouldn't take much," she confessed.

"I want to taste you, Shasa."

Her gaze landed at the slice of grassy field peeking between the pink nylon and the basket, her eyes flashing with fear. They could be found out at any moment. But he was too far gone, and he needed to take her with him. He pulled down her pants and touched her wet underwear. Soft, feather-light circles until her gasps intensified, and she pushed herself against him, panting. He increased the pressure, pushed the underwear aside and hooked his fingers inside her, moving in sync with her hips. Her gasps turned into moans, and his cock ached. He wouldn't last. If she kept going like this, he'd lose it. He'd come all over her pants.

As if sensing his situation, Shasa fought back on top. "My turn," she panted, lowering down to his crotch.

She then sucked him in again, stealing every thought he'd painfully arranged in verbal format, every promise he'd made to himself about taking care of her first.

"But... promise me..." He fought for words, but they escaped, chased by the overwhelming sensation of her hot, wet mouth. "Promise me we do it right. I'll get to give you..."

Her other hand cupped his balls, and he felt them drawing up, the unstoppable force of his orgasm building. He was a lost cause. She never gave him a chance, tightening her hold, with her tongue circling the tip of his cock before her mouth owned him again and again.

A blinding pleasure seared through him, his entire body pulsing as an uncontrollable sound erupted from his mouth, and he filled hers with his release. She kept her mouth on him until the crashing wave of pleasure settled into gentle pulsing.

As his consciousness returned, he tried to reach for her, with one thought pounding in his brain. "Shasa. It's your turn. Let me—"

"Later." She gave him a sad smile before disappearing into

the folds of pink nylon shielding them from the world.

He buttoned his jeans and followed her, his legs almost giving in as he stood up in bright daylight.

The balloon had flattened along the grass. There was nobody else around.

"The chasers aren't here yet," she said, gesturing towards the landscape, her face filled with relief. "Thank God. That could have been awkward."

He pulled her against his chest, his body still bursting with endorphins, desperate to share that pleasure with her. "Let's go back in there, and I'll take care of you, okay?" He kissed the top of her head, inhaling her sweet scent.

She gave him such a tight hug he nearly lost his footing. "Oh, Mac. I'll miss you so much."

An engine roar penetrated his thoughts. Felicity's black people mover appeared from the other side of the field, driving along the rudimentary country road. His truck appeared right behind it.

Mac cursed under his breath. "This isn't over," he hissed into her ear before she peeled herself off him and ran towards them, waving her arms.

He followed a few steps behind, his heart in his throat. He couldn't shake the terrifying thought that this was the last time he'd see her.

Felicity parked next to the balloon, and the kids poured out, their eyes shining with glee.

"I saw you the whole time, Mummy! We never lost you!"

Lilla yelled, wrapping her arms around Shasa's legs.

She lifted her up on her hip. "Excellent chasing!"

His heart squeezed at the sight of them, his arms itching to wrap around them. Protect them. Never let them go. But did he have the right? The way she'd touched him had given him so much hope, but she hadn't told him what he needed to hear. He had no claim on her, even if she now owned every part of him.

He took a deep breath and smiled at Lilla, giving her a high-five. "Well done!"

Felicity beamed, gathering her offspring into a hug. "We had a lot of fun, didn't we?"

Hank nodded at the balloon basket. "Bumpy landing?"

He gave him an indignant glare. "Smooth as."

Hank raised his brows, turning to Shasa, who shook her head.

"I knew it!" Hank howled with laughter, and Mac gave him a good natured smile.

He didn't care what Hank thought of him. He only cared about Shasa, and he wouldn't let her slip away.

Chapter 33

Shasa glanced at Mac, trying to ignore the aching pulse still lingering between her thighs. She deserved it and felt marginally better for the superhuman strength she'd exhibited in stopping him. Or, had her sickening guilt given her that burst of willpower? Either way, this was for the best, she told herself. She'd given him something. A parting gift. Obviously, her vagina had declared war on her brain, preparing to launch missiles, but it didn't matter. She'd deal with them both later.

Hank stepped into her line of sight, offering Shasa her handbag. "Your bag was ringing, so I thought I'd bring it to you."

"Thank you." She fished her phone from underneath snacks, hairpins, and supermarket receipts. It showed three missed calls and a message from Marnie.

Her heart thumping in her chest, she opened it.

> **Marnie:** You're going to love this! The seller accepted our offer!!! Just doing the paperwork with Elsie. Call me as soon as you can! Xox

Nausea hit her like a tidal wave. So, that was it – the final blow of death. She'd betrayed him and blown him and here was her thirty pieces of silver.

Her eyes searched for Mac. She needed to see him. Somehow, even as she stood in the deep hole she'd dug for herself, she still wanted him. Desperately. And as soon as she locked into his warm gaze, the sloshing inside her settled. She returned his smile, tears rising to her eyes. She couldn't even try to hide them.

Would this be the last time she ever saw him? Standing there in his charcoal hoodie, scratching his stubble, a faint echo of a smile still on his lips. She wasn't ready for this. She needed more time.

"You ready to go?" Felicity pointed at the car, her cheery voice clashing with her inner one.

"Yeah," she managed through her straw of a windpipe.

She had to keep these tears down for a little longer. Maybe it was best she didn't travel with Mac.

Shasa helped Lilla into the car and joined her on the backseat, desperate to hide from prying eyes and questions. Squished between the kids, her head bumping against Lilla's helium balloon, she didn't have to hold herself together with so much effort. The kids chattered about their balloon experiences, oblivious to the pain behind her smile.

Outside the window, Mac helped Hank load the balloon onto his pickup truck, casting glances in their direction.

As Felicity started the engine and rolled past them, Shasa caught a glimpse of him. She wasn't sure he could even see her through the tinted window, yet the longing in his eyes made her insides hurt. He was all in, and she hadn't given him an answer.

She gave Felicity her address, grateful when she offered to take them straight home.

When they arrived, she settled Lilla in front of her laptop to watch My Little Pony and phoned Marnie.

"Are you sure?" she asked. "Is it a done deal?"

Her friend's voice brimmed with excitement. "Yes! Don't worry. They can't back out. This is happening!"

She finished the call and burst into tears. Because all she wanted was him. All this time, she'd thought she wanted the house. The security. Her forever home. But without Mac, her home would be a pointless building, forever reminding her of what she'd lost and how blind she'd been.

Chapter 34

Mac sat in his ute, staring at the entrance of his house, tall and imposing, lit by two torches. Could he let it go? He'd been so proud of this place, but now it didn't seem to matter. If Shasa didn't want to live here with him, he'd sell the house and buy something else. Something she liked. She'd reduced him to a lovesick teenager, unable to think of anyone or anything else.

Once he got inside, he collapsed on the couch and pulled out his phone. He'd distracted himself all afternoon with the gym and the movies, to give her time to think. Time to miss him. But she hadn't messaged him.

Mac: I miss you already. I know you said we should wait until the deal goes through, but I don't know if I can. I need to see you.

Shasa: ...

He stared at the three dots on the screen for so long they developed purple and pink shadows. Was she still writing? He craved her so much he would have done anything. If she told him to meet her, anywhere, he'd come running.

But she didn't reply. Eventually, the dots disappeared and he dropped the phone, feeling like he'd been punched in the lungs. Did she not feel the same? Did she doubt them? His arms ached to hold her, to reassure them both, to reclaim that feeling. Instead, dread had set in, like ice running through his veins.

He had to stop his thoughts from spiraling.

Mac forced himself up from the couch and attended to his growling stomach by browsing the emptiness of his fridge and eventually ordering a takeaway meal. His mind wandered back to their conversation in his kitchen, feeding him an uncomfortable playback of his own elitist comments. He could hear it now. He'd been talking casually about 30-dollar meals, when she had to feed two people on less than half of that. Feeling a little sick, he logged back into Uber Eats and started a new order, typing in Shasa's name and address. His heart beating faster, he added several of his favorite Japanese dishes into the cart and pushed 'order'.

Would she hate him for this? Should he even confess to it? And if he didn't, would she donate the food somewhere, convinced that it was a mistake? After an agonizing half-an-hour of pacing his kitchen and drinking one beer he found at the back of his fridge, the doorbell rang, and he jumped. He rushed to the door and nearly ripped it off its hinges. His face fell. He'd already forgotten about his own teriyaki salmon order and ended up staring at the receding back of the spooked delivery man.

As he took his food back to the kitchen and settled on a barstool, his phone pinged, telling him Shasa's meal had been delivered. He took a picture of his own food and texted her again.

Mac: I just wanted to share this meal with you.

Shasa: Oh God, Mac. It was you? I can't accept this!

Mac: But you also can't let it go to waste. I know you.

Two minutes went by.

Mac: I love you.

He waited, his heart in his throat. Finally, she replied. It was a voice message. Hearing her voice made his insides wobble, but her words stabbed him in the middle.

"I've been fighting it so hard because it's all wrong, but I love you, too. Please try to remember this moment when everything blows up and you blame me for ruining your life. Because I don't want to. I don't want to hurt you. I never did. I want to travel back in time and undo everything." She sniffed, pausing for a moment. "I don't deserve you. And I won't message you again. Just remember that I'm sorry. And that I love you."

He blinked at the phone, his heart thudding out of his chest. Why was she sorry? What had happened? Was she talking about the property deal? Why was she crying? And did she really love him?

All he wanted was to find her and pull her into his arms and tell her everything would be okay. But he couldn't shake the uneasy feeling. Something was going on, and he had to find out what the fuck it was.

Mac tried to call his parents. They didn't pick up, which was unusual. He left a short message on their answering machine, telling them he'd be around for Sunday lunch. Tomorrow. He'd get their signature and sort out the property deal.

Next, he called Shasa's landlord. He didn't pick up, so Mac texted him, making a higher offer. He should have done it yesterday, right after his phone call with Rick, but he'd been busy planning the balloon ride.

All done, Mac collapsed against the table, sinking his fingers into his hair. His head felt light, like he was on a merry-go-round. Did he even have a brain in there or had it been replaced by a swirling cocktail of hormones?

Just remember that I'm sorry. And that I love you.

He tried to draw comfort from those words, but they disappeared into the hollow pit of fear that had opened up inside of him, leaving behind no warmth.

Chapter 35

Marnie poured champagne into a crystal flute and handed it to Shasa with a flourish. They stood in the middle of Shasa's backyard, eating blueberries straight off the bush. The weather had been ideal, ripening the berries in record time.

"These are delicious." Elsie popped another one in her mouth.

Earl joined her, asking them something about gooseberries. Shasa tried to smile, half-listening. She liked these people, and this was an opportunity of a lifetime. If it weren't for Mac, she'd have been jumping for joy. They'd won.

She could hardly believe it.

Her stomach twisted, ready to disagree with anything she poured down her throat, but she couldn't let her personal heartache ruin everyone else's celebration, so she lifted her glass, mouthing after Marnie. "To our community!"

A cacophony of voices echoed hers, emphasizing the meaning of the word. Marnie had brought her teen daughter, who was pushing Lilla on the swing. Elsie stood between Earl and her architect, who'd spread the building blueprints across Shasa's wobbly outdoor table—one of many things flagged for the skip as soon as they could organize one. The table wobbled under the weight of all the party food they'd brought for the celebratory morning tea.

Marnie had done most of the shopping while Shasa had been useless, blaming poor sleep, then a headache. She couldn't even commit to an excuse.

Marnie clinked a teaspoon on her glass. "I have an announcement." She paused, waiting until she had everyone's attention. "Elsie already knows, but I haven't told Shasa yet because she's been so moody with her headache..." She paused to roll her eyes, and others laughed. "We've just sold the last apartment. We're officially sold out!"

Everyone cheered. Everyone, except Shasa. How could they sell the apartment without consulting her? Were they not in this together?

"Perfect timing!" Marnie shouted as Mac's parents appeared from around the corner. "I was just telling everybody that you're joining our community! Welcome!"

Shasa's mouth hung open as John and Sue introduced themselves, apologizing for being late as they'd just come from church.

"Isn't this amazing?" Marnie gushed, attaching herself to Shasa's side. "We figured you'd be okay with them since they're your neighbors already."

Shasa nodded but felt sick. "Yeah, they're great. But... what did you do? How?"

Marnie beamed. "I paid them a visit yesterday, as soon as we heard from the seller, and told them about our project. I took those slides you prepared. They know you, and they like you. They got excited and said they'd take down the fence and join the two gardens together. Isn't that amazing? "

"Does Mac know about this?" Shasa couldn't help the words tumbling out.

Marnie raised her brow. "I don't know, but it's not my job to tell him. He's their son."

Of course. They must have told him. Shasa's legs shook and she struggled to stand up straight. Mac knew about it. He must have heard about the sale by now. She felt like she'd been holding her breath ever since that last message, waiting for him to call her, or burst through the door, shouting. She'd prepared herself for his anger, almost hoping for it. But she'd heard nothing.

John raised his glass and his voice. "We're excited about this community initiative. We've been looking for ways to help families on this street, and now it looks like we'll be able to do up our old house to rent out to someone in need. There's a family down the road sharing a three-bedroom house with another family. They could use some extra space. We don't need so many rooms. By downsizing, we can create a big, safe yard for all the kids in the street. I know that's also important to my wife, Sue." He nodded at Sue, who blushed.

"I'll drink to that!" shouted Marnie, raising her glass.

"Would you let me lead us into a short prayer?" John asked.

Marnie lowered her glass in embarrassment. Elsie and Earl bowed their heads.

Shasa couldn't stop staring at John. His strong jaw and cheekbones reminded her of Mac. The man she'd betrayed. The man she loved. Craved. Missed. But yes, loved. A tear fell out of her eye. Large and round like a glass bead, it landed in her champagne.

She sniffed, trying to compose herself, but it was too late. She couldn't be part of this celebration. Her fake headache would have to progress to a fake migraine.

"Hey," she grabbed Marnie's arm when the prayer finished. "Do you mind if I lie down for bit? My head's killing me."

"Good idea. I need you to be functional by 3 p.m. for the reporter."

Shasa wobbled away on a deep sigh. She couldn't even think about that yet.

Chapter 36

Elsie edged closer to Marnie, her gaze following Shasa's retreating back. "Where's she going?"

Marnie furrowed her brow. "To lie down, she said. Headache."

"Not … heartache?"

"Hope not. Why?"

Elsie drained her champagne. She hadn't missed the look in Shasa's eyes as she enquired about Mac. For a moment, her face had given her away like a funeral guest in the middle of a wedding reception. "Talk to her. Find out what happened with Mac. She's out of sorts. And it's not just a headache."

Marnie nodded. "You might be right. She's been quite odd lately. I think she saw him last weekend, but she wouldn't talk about it."

"It's over. We got the section, so there's no need to worry about Mac anymore, no reason they can't be together, either."

Marnie's eyes widened. "I suppose. If he can handle the... situation?"

Elsie sighed. Shasa and Mac faced a tricky romance. She quite enjoyed her drama-free relationship with Earl. They'd had a couple of lovely dinners – which he'd insisted on paying for – and had met once for a walk around the lake. She confessed to him her loneliness and shared her regrets. With each word, the dark cloud had lifted higher, until she barely noticed it. Talking to Earl worked better than therapy, restoring her faith in love and life, even in those moments they said nothing, strolling side by side in companionable silence. She was still building up courage to ask him to spend the night. Maybe tomorrow. Elsie smiled as giddiness bubbled up in her chest. She fought to straighten her face when she noticed Marnie's eyes clouded with worry.

"What's wrong?"

Marnie fiddled with her necklace. "Do you really think we can finish the build in four months? The timeframe feels..."

Elsie gestured at Earl. "It's ambitious, but we have everything lined up. Earl's rushing the council approval. And going with a modified prefab saves a lot of time, and money.

A flat section, minimal site works."

Marnie's face split into a wide smile. "I can't believe how quickly it's moving!"

Elsie smiled at her enthusiasm. Marnie had sold her house and the settlement date was four months away. If the new build wasn't finished in time, she'd have nowhere to live. Elsie had offered her guest suite to Shasa and Lilla.

She patted Marnie's arm. "We'll get there."

"Thank you for everything." Marnie wrapped her in a tight hug. "You're the most amazing person."

Elsie froze for a split second, but quickly found her bearings and hugged her back, amazed at the ease of her affection. She'd do everything in her power to make sure the build was finished in time. She hoped the new friendship continued beyond the house building.

Chapter 37

Mac knocked on the open door of his parents' house out of courtesy. He'd arrived early, hoping to catch them before the neighborhood kids showed up. He placed a bouquet of purple daisies on the table and looked around for his Mum. The smell of a roast wafted from the oven, but the house seemed empty. After a quick check, he returned outside.

Distant laughter and chatter caught his ear. The sound carried from next door, from Shasa's backyard. Was there a party? He tracked along the fence, to the missing board Lilla had used as a doorway and peered through the hole. He spotted his parents, along with Marnie, Elsie, and an old guy who looked familiar, with champagne flutes in their hands. Lilla's voice chimed from the swing, but he couldn't see Shasa.

The landlord hadn't replied, and Mac had destroyed any chance of sleep by guessing and second guessing everything. He had to see Shasa. He had to talk to her.

Okay, enough with the hiding. If his parents were there, he had enough of a reason to go over and ask what was going on.

As he entered the gate, Mum rushed to hug him. "Hi! Everyone, this is our son, Elijah!"

"You can call me Mac," he corrected.

Lilla got off the swing and ran to him. He smiled at her, the one person who didn't judge, who accepted him for who he was. He picked her up and swirled her around the yard, then landed her to his hip.

"I want to go in the balloon again!" Her mouth spread into a wide smile.

"Do you?"

Lilla nodded three times. "Can I?"

Elsie stepped closer. "You'll see the balloons when the festival starts." She turned to Mac. "We talked about going next Saturday morning to see the balloons take off."

He suspected it wasn't an invitation for him but decided to humour Lilla. "I'd love to join you," he said with a wink. "You know, this year, they have a pink unicorn one?"

Lilla's eyes looked like they were about to pop out of her head. "A pink unicorn balloon?"

He nodded. "A friend told me."

Elsie studied them, then offered him a surprisingly gracious smile. "It's nice to see you're not a sore loser."

Loser?

She strutted away, her champagne flute held high. A weight landed on Mac's chest, making it hard to breathe. He lowered Lilla down and watched her sprint across the yard.

Mum appeared by his side, squeezing his hand. She spoke in a low voice, her smile unwavering and eyes darting over the yard. "I wanted you to hear this from us first. Your father and I have decided to invest in this cohousing community. We'll move into one of the small flats and rent out our house, maybe to the Mills down the road. That way, we can help more people. I hope you understand. We don't want luxury apartments. It's just not us."

Nausea welled in his stomach and his vision blurred. This was insane. He didn't always see eye to eye with his parents, but he'd never imagined they'd go behind his back and form an alliance with the one person who'd been out to destroy this deal. Shasa. She'd well and truly bested him.

He'd asked her to give them a chance, but she'd never given him an answer. He'd told himself she'd been conflicted by the property situation, but he'd had no idea how conflicted she'd truly been. She'd already known.

"Mum, I'd work with you to build the kind of place you like. As small as you like. I can't believe..."

His mum squeezed his hand even harder. "I'm sorry. We

thought about it, but we didn't want to become a problem for you, lower the value of your investment with our ideas. They're just not compatible. One day you'll understand."

"Mum, no! We can change the drawings to fit in an extra apartment for the poor, whatever you want. I'll fund it myself. Just let me build it. If I lose this, I lose everything!"

Mum turned to him, misty-eyed. "I hate to disappoint you, but we already signed the contract. Surely you can build the condos somewhere else? Plenty of sections around."

She had no idea. Mac buried his face in his hands to keep from screaming. It was over. He'd been wondering what was most important to Shasa, and now he knew. She wanted the house, not him. She'd played him and won. And now she wanted nothing to do with him.

Mac turned around and left. When he got to the gate, Lilla wrapped her skinny hands around his legs. He turned around, trying to rise above the crushing pain in his chest.

The girl's eyes were huge, full of hope. "Can you take me to the unicorn balloon?"

"Maybe one day," he said with a sad smile and snuck through the gate.

If his mum thought he couldn't be trusted to build something that fostered community and wellbeing ... well, lying to little kids was just par for the course, right?

Chapter 38

"I'm not sure about this," Shasa said for the third time, pulling on another T-shirt.

Marnie gave her a weary look. "It's just the local paper. All you have to do is smile and talk about cohousing. You did those two presentations. You know your material."

Shasa gave her a shaky nod. Barbara Bell, the woman who'd joined their first cohousing meeting, was coming over to interview them. It was a great opportunity. They wanted more people to get excited about cohousing and more communities to appear around the city. If only she could get herself excited. In her current state, she wasn't a great advertisement for the concept.

"What if you do it? You'd be so much more... happy, you know? Engaging?" She looked at Marnie, pleading for understanding.

Her friend stared back, a stern expression on her face. "Seriously. What is up with you? We're about to make history! You worked so hard on this. Why aren't you excited?"

Shasa looked into her dressing mirror and caught sight of her own face, morose like a petulant teenager.

Marnie joined her, peering over her shoulder. "And what's up with your clothes? You've gone mainstream!"

She'd put on jeans and a simple tee. "I don't want people to judge cohousing as something 'alternative', you know? If I wear something too colourful or different, everyone will look at the photo and think I'm talking about a commune, an ashram, or something."

Marnie shrugged, smiling. "I'm not saying it looks bad. You're most welcome to join us T-shirt and jeans minions. It just doesn't look like you, you know? Although, you're an actor now so you'll get to wear all kinds of costumes, right? That'll be fun!"

Her friend was trying to cheer her up but thinking about acting brought up Mac. Their next rehearsal was supposed to be this week, on Wednesday night. Was it still happening?

She looked at her friend, who'd worked just as hard to achieve this goal. Marnie deserved to celebrate. Shasa dug deep and found a genuinely happy smile that lasted a few seconds.

"I'll make some tea." Marnie patted her on the arm and left.

At the knock on the door, Shasa glanced in the mirror. She was as ready as she'd ever be.

"I'll get it!" she yelled to Marnie.

She opened the door, ready to smile from the bottom of her heart. Instead, her heart fell to the bottom of her heels.

It was Ollie. All dreadlocks, hemp and golden tan, smiling like he'd won the lottery.

"God, I missed you!" he sighed, enveloping her in a hug that brought up a sense of familiarity, along with queasiness.

She scrambled free, stumbling over the threshold into the house.

Ollie followed her inside, flinging his rucksack on the floor. "It's so good to be home! Did I surprise you?"

Did he ever. "I... wasn't expecting you." Shasa rubbed her forehead, like he was a hallucination she could banish with sheer will.

Ollie took another look at her. "Wow, you've really gone mainstream, haven't you?"

He'd seen her new hair on Skype, but she'd disconnected the call before he could comment. Shasa looked away, her heart pounding. He had no right to judge her appearance. She owed him nothing.

Ollie softened his voice. "Don't worry, the hair will grow back."

"I don't want it back!" she yelled, her eyes stinging.

The truth of it hit her hard. She didn't want any of it back, including him.

Ollie rolled his eyes, smiling. "Okay, chill. Where's the bean?"

"Backyard." Shasa pointed at the back door, hoping he'd go straight there and give her a moment to think.

Ollie jogged past her, calling for Lilla. She heard the girl's incredulous voice, "Daddy?" and imagined her running to his arms. Ollie should have done this a long time ago, but he'd picked the worst timing she could have imagined.

Eyes blurred with tears, Shasa wandered into the lounge. She dropped down, missing the couch by inches, landing on the floor with a thud.

Marnie appeared in front of her. "Was that Ollie?"

"Yeah." Her voice sounded like it didn't belong to her.

"What's he doing here? Why now?"

"Because the universe hates me," she wailed.

"It's peculiar timing," Marnie admitted, rubbing her shoulder. "What do you want to do? Should I ship him back to Indonesia?"

Shasa shook her head. A large part of her wanted to kick him out without further questions, but he was the father of her daughter. She had to hear him out.

Ollie returned from the backyard, carrying Lilla. The girl looked startled, like when she'd sat on Santa's lap at the mall.

He lowered her onto the floor. "I brought you a present."

Stealing lines from Santa, too, Shasa thought, watching Ollie open a side pocket of his rucksack and pull out a necklace made from seashells and twine. Hundred percent natural, no doubt. The twine looked so rough it'd likely cause rope burns.

"Did you make that?" she asked.

"Yes. I've been learning some new skills."

He joined her on the floor, leaning on the couch. Marnie took the hint and returned to the kitchen, pulling Lilla with her.

"I'm sorry, Shasa. I've done a lot of thinking and I don't want to be that guy. The guy who chooses work over his family. No matter how vitally important it is." The way he said the word important made her shiver. Slow and serious. Like it was something she'd never understand.

"What about the other woman?" she asked.

"What other woman?"

"Don't play dumb. It was right there in the subtext."

Ollie looked away, his face twitching, like he was deciding how much to reveal. "Fine, I'll be honest. There was someone else, but I told her I'm going home, so... it's over."

"But if you went back, you'd pick up from where you left off?"

Ollie ignored her and stood up. "Are you saying you've been celibate this whole time?"

Shasa swallowed. If he'd been sleeping with someone on

the side, she'd definitely been celibate.

Another knock rapped on the door. Shasa's stomach lurched. The reporter. This couldn't be happening. Before she made it up from the floor, Ollie opened the door to Barbara Bell in a red blazer. She flashed them a bright smile, a camera bag swinging on her shoulder.

"Afternoon! I'm Barbara Bell. I'm here to interview Shasa Daniels about the cohousing community."

"Cohousing community," Ollie repeated, his voice raising in surprise.

"You're in the right place," confirmed Marnie, appearing at the doorway next to him. She led the reporter inside and seated her on the couch.

Shasa made it up from the floor, and, directed by Marnie, sat next to Barbara.

Ollie took the old armchair, leaning in with curiosity. "You didn't tell me about this cohousing thing," he said pointedly, staring at Shasa.

"Ollie's been away at sea," Marnie told the reporter. "Don't mind him. He just turned up out of the blue." She shot him a sharp look, her jaw tight.

Ollie raised his hands in surrender. "Sorry. I won't get in your way. You carry on. I'll go unpack and leave you to it. If you need more time after that, can I take Lilla to the park?"

Panic squeezed Shasa's throat. She couldn't let him unpack. He wasn't moving in with them, not like this. How could she get him out without creating a scene?

Marnie read her mind and jumped in. "Ollie, why don't you take Lilla out first? That'd be a big help."

Ollie scooped up his daughter. "Okay. Should we go get vegan ice cream?"

"What's vegan?" Lilla asked.

Ollie shook his head. "I've been away too long, haven't I?"

As they approached the door, Barbara jumped up, pulling a camera out of her bag. "Wait. Before you go, can we take a couple of family pics, maybe out on the deck?"

Ollie gave her a charming smile. "Absolutely."

Carrying Lilla, he stepped with Barbara onto the deck.

"Shasa, could you join us?" Barbara called from the door.

"No. No. No." Shasa whispered to Marnie, but her friend gave her a gentle shove.

"It's one pic in a community newspaper nobody reads. You can do this."

Shasa stepped outside like a lamb to the slaughter, taking her place next to Ollie.

"Great. Now, smile!" Barbara commanded, clicking away.

Shasa wasn't sure whether she smiled or not. Barbara, however, seemed happy, and let Ollie leave with their daughter.

Watching them disappear through the gate, Shasa felt ready to vomit. Something about this wasn't right. Ollie couldn't just take away her daughter. But, of course he could. He was the father.

They returned inside and Barbara began the interview,

firing off question after question. With Marnie's help, Shasa made it through the session.

Once the interview was done, Barbara took them to the backyard and snapped several photos of the two of them and the section. She even spent time with the blueberry bush, no doubt trying to frame an artistic shot with ripe berries in the foreground.

"It's been a pleasure," she announced. "You can expect the story in the next issue." She bagged her camera and headed to the street.

Shasa woke up from her stupor and sprinted after her, catching her at the gate. "It's not going to be a big story, is it?"

Barbara looked puzzled. "That's up to the editor, but I don't think so. The balloon festival will likely get the front page. Sorry."

"No, that's good. Also, if you use that photo of me and Ollie, he's not my ... we're not together. He doesn't live here."

"Okay," Barbara nodded. "We'll caption accordingly."

Relieved, Shasa let her go and returned to the house. Now, she just had to make sure that what she'd said remained the status quo. Ollie had to go.

Chapter 39

Mac stepped out of the elevator into the Sky City bowling alley and headed straight to the bar. He had to talk to his business partner, face-to-face. On Sunday nights, Rick often met up with his old buddies for drinks here. Mac had been invited to join them in the past but found their endless bragging tiresome.

He spotted the familiar group on the balcony – two real estate agents and Daryn, a property developer who worked with Rick. From their rolled-up shirt sleeves, he could tell they'd finished work. The fourth guy looked like a newbie, young and smooth like a Ken doll.

Counting on Rick being late as usual, Mac bought himself

a beer and stepped through the balcony doors into the crisp night air. City lights shone below. He suspected the guys liked the bar for its view. From a distance, the human lives faded away, turning property into a game, a Monopoly board of tradable assets.

Except, he could see the faces now. He could see Shasa and Lilla.

"Mac! Haven't seen you in ages!" Daryn pulled out a chair for him. "You remember Dale and Nick? This is their rising star, Jaden. He sold his first house today."

Mac congratulated the grinning Jaden, focusing all his energy into channelling confidence. He had to keep going, fake his way through the pain. Through the confusion gnawing his gut.

"Where's Rick?" he asked.

Daryn pointed at an empty chair. "He went to take a phone call."

Mac took a long sip of his beer and opened a shirt button, letting the night air cool his skin. His heart pounded. He couldn't shake the nausea that had dogged him ever since this morning. He'd lost, but the game wasn't over. There had to be a way to turn things around. He'd talk to Rick, do some damage control, offer an alternative plan. It all came down to mindset. Maybe Shasa could have her cohousing build and he could have his, somehow. They could do a smaller development on another site.

Daryn's eyes gleamed as he returned to the conversation

Mac had interrupted. "We're talking about a struggling holiday park. No beach, no views, no playground. But it's on prime land in the Boys' High zone, and you can fit at least twenty units on it. Hamilton East is da bomb, an easy sell. You guys know how to word that more eloquently on the listings, eh?" He winked at the agents and they laughed.

"Where in Ham East?" Mac asked. "Is Rick in on this?" He drew a deep breath, his fingers tightening around the beer glass. A new development in the right school zone was a safe bet.

Daryn raised his brow. "Rick's driving this. He's looking for a couple more investors. I thought he'd talked to you already?"

"I haven't seen him for a bit. Too busy." Mac tried to keep his tone light.

This could get him back on his feet if he could get the bank on board. He'd sell the city apartments, if necessary, and his Tauranga rental. That way, he could dive into pre-sales and make some quick gains. Without the lakeside condo deposits, he needed something else to generate cash flow. The leaky townhouse renovation was sucking him dry. If he had to sell it at a loss... he didn't even want to think about it.

Preoccupied with calculations, Mac missed the figure approaching him from behind.

"Mac?" Rick radiated stony disappointment.

Mac turned to face him. Blood chilled in his veins. Rick

knew. “You heard about…?”

“I heard.”

“I need to talk to you.” Grabbing his beer, Mac got up and pulled Rick away from the table. They stopped at the balustrade. Mac rested his weight on the steel railing for support.

“I know I messed up, but I have a new plan. I know how to fix this. There’s another section on Alison Street—”

“Shitty school zones.”

The chill travelled down Mac’s spine. “You pitched them this Hamilton East one, didn’t you? The holiday park?”

Rick cast an angry glance at the table. “Daryn told you?” He turned back to Mac, defiant. “It’s a great opportunity. The buyers deserve to know about it.”

Mac’s throat tightened, panic squeezing his every muscle. “I deserve to know if you’re leading our buyers to another property! We’re partners.”

“You deserve nothing! You fucked up a sure-fire deal! You lost us—”

“I’ll make it back. Let me in on this Ham East deal. I’ll work hard, I’ll—”

Rick’s tone was ice cold. “I called the vendor and he told me about the community housing, the tenant pulling together all these hippies to buy the section. Seriously, it’s unbelievable. I tried to offer more, but the deal’s done. He said you never even called.”

“I did! He didn’t pick up. I made a new offer but…” Mac’s

insides clenched. He couldn't explain this away. "I'm sorry. I've been distracted, but it won't happen again, I swear."

"Distracted with that bohemian chick you took for a balloon ride? Felicity told me."

Mac sighed. "Yeah."

"I guess you want me to cancel that date since it sounds like..." His eyes flashed with realisation. "Wait! This hippy chick, is she involved in that community housing thing? Sounds like the same crowd." Mac watched in horror as Rick connected the dots. "She's the tenant, isn't she? She's the one who—"

"She's the one." Mac fixed his eyes on moon. Unbearable sadness pressed against his lungs.

Rick shook his head, stunned. "I thought it was Elsie whatever née Alders who screwed us and you were just incompetent, too busy chasing tail. But it was you. You practically handed over a couple of million... Hope she was worth it."

Mac's gaze dipped to the city lights across the dark river. Exhaustion swept over him. It was over. He couldn't fix it. This show had come to an end.

"She *is* worth it," he insisted, the words rising from somewhere deep inside. Rick would never understand.

Mac drained his beer and closed his eyes. The beer glass slipped out of his hand and smashed on the parking lot somewhere below.

"Shit, mate! Losing it over one tree-hugging hippy. She

must be incredible in bed. Magic mushrooms and witchcraft, right?" Rick huffed. "Did her pussy put a spell on you or—"

Mac's right hook landed squarely on his friend's nose. Rick staggered backwards, colliding with a nearby table.

Mac braced his fist as pain shot through it, immediately regretting his actions.

Two security guards scrambled through the doors to stop the fight, but not before Rick made it back to his feet and launched at him.

A red flash. The shock radiated from his eye socket to the back of his skull. The pain made him feel better, transferring some of his anguish onto his flesh, where it belonged.

He heard the low rumble of shocked commentary as Rick joined the others. Doors slammed as they left the balcony. The guards manhandled Mac into one of the metal chairs.

Remorse set in, as thick and overwhelming as the night around him. Mac hadn't lost it in years but seeing the pity and disgust in his friend's eyes had been too much. Nothing was left of their friendship or mentorship. He had one thing left, one person he cared about, and she wasn't here. She wasn't even his.

Mac shivered from the cool night air, listening to the thumping of music that carried from inside the bar. It seemed the guards had left him out here to cool down, and he had no desire to move. He opened his phone, scrolled to Shasa's last message and listened to it again and again.

She said she loved him, and he wanted to hang onto those

words like a raft that kept him from drowning, but were they even true?

He would have taken care of her. He would have given her everything, had she asked. But she'd taken it, and now he had nothing left to give. She's rendered him a useless husk of a man with no wealth, no prospects. No hope.

Maybe love didn't conquer all.

And how had she done it? He'd gone over it in his mind many times, looking for clues. Shasa had known exactly how much to offer for the house to sway the buyer and get her way. He hadn't left any papers lying around. He'd been so careful. Everything was on his phone, in password-protected PDFs and—dread flushed through him—his email.

He'd left his phone on the table in the restaurant. She must have grabbed it before it locked and read his emails.

Please try to remember this moment when everything blows up and you blame me for ruining your life.

He remembered, and those memories made his heart ache. He'd been planning their future when she already knew it was over. She'd made a fool out of him. Did she expect him to brush it off and move on?

Shasa didn't care about money or status, but she didn't have to strip him of both!

Mac rested his throbbing face against his sore hands and groaned. His mind was split in the middle, one half willing to forgive everything, making excuses for her. He would have done the same, given the chance. They'd been competitors, but he'd never taken her seriously, too confident in his victory. And falling in love was a messy process. Maybe she loved him now, but back in that restaurant, they'd been two people with some stage chemistry, developing a crush.

I've been fighting it so hard because it's all wrong, but I love you. I do.

Love had snuck up on them when the destruction of his life had already been set in motion. She'd known it and held back, careful not to get in too deep. And what had he done? He'd fallen headfirst, hard. And there had been no way to soften the crash landing.

The other half his mind simply howled like a wounded animal, angry and hurt, wishing he could burrow deep underground to never be found again. Never be hurt again. But why hadn't she told him the truth? Nothing could remove the pain of that. She'd kissed him. She'd fucking blown him, knowing that he'd soon have nothing to his name.

I don't want to hurt you. I never did. I want to travel back in time and undo everything

She couldn't undo it, though. The pain was as inevitable as gravity.

Mac got up, swaying on his feet. His face throbbed. He had to salvage what was left of his career and life. Maybe there was something he could save. He'd ignore the heartache and focus on the facts. He'd done it once before. He'd started with nothing and built a portfolio. He could do it again.

Or, failing that, he'd beat his bruised ego into submission and throw what was left of him at her feet. See if she really didn't care about money or status.

Chapter 40

Shasa stared at her sleeping daughter, hoping to feel the sense of accomplishment that the sight usually triggered. Not tonight. Part of her wanted Lilla to get up and make a fuss, so she didn't have to return to the kitchen, where Marnie was making tea and questions hung in the air.

She wanted to confide in her friend, but admitting it out loud for the first time felt like setting yourself on fire to see if anyone had a hose nearby. She was the villain of this story, and she had to own it.

Quietly closing the bedroom door, Shasa padded down the hallway toward the smell of tea and biscuits. How could she smell the biscuits?

Marnie sat across the table, nibbling a gooey chocolate chip cookie, with a whole tray of them steaming on top of Shasa's oven.

"You baked these?" Shasa picked one, inhaling the addictive smell.

"I brought some dough I had in the freezer. Super easy."

Shasa joined her at the table where her hot teacup waited. Her stomach felt almost too wobbly to accept food, but who could resist the smell of fresh baking?

It melted on her tongue. "These are amazing."

Marnie got up and closed the door to the living room, where Ollie had passed out on the couch. She sat a little closer to Shasa and kept her voice low. "Okay. Why are you so upset? Does it have something to do with Mac?"

Shasa's gaze drifted at the living room door. Did she care if Ollie heard everything? She couldn't hold it in any longer. Keeping herself busy during the day only got her so far. At night, the regrets came back like whiplash.

"I'm in love with him. I know I shouldn't be, and it makes no sense, and I've already ruined any chance of us ever being together. But I miss him so much I just... ache. I've been waiting for it to go away. I keep waiting."

She stared at her teacup, eyes welling, afraid to look at Marnie. Her fingers fiddled with the teabag tag and the silence between them stretched.

Marnie reached her hand across the table to hold hers. "Why didn't you tell me?"

The tears spilled out. "I didn't want to be a downer. I didn't want to ruin all the celebration and happiness."

"How would you falling in love ruin anyone's happiness?"

Shasa looked up at the pair of compassionate eyes across the table. "I mean, it wasn't part of the plan."

"Of course not, but that's love. It's unpredictable." She narrowed her eyes, peering at Shasa. "But why can't you be together? The property is sold. It's all done."

"You know what happened. We won because I spied on him. I betrayed his trust. And I didn't know it at the time, but he had a lot riding on this property deal. I made him... I made him lose his house." Uncontrollable sobs shook her shoulders and she buried her face in her hands.

Saying it out loud made it so much more real. She'd destroyed him, and somehow destroyed herself at the same time.

"Did you apologise?" Marnie asked.

Shasa gave a wobbly nod, thinking back to that last voicemail. She'd apologized, but beforehand, when he hadn't known all the facts. Would her apology make any sense to him now? And how could any apology ever be enough?

"I... sort of." She hiccupped. "I've been too scared to contact him. And he hasn't contacted me, so I think it means he's moved on. It's over."

Marnie waited for her to calm down, untangling her earrings from her hair. "I don't think you should assume anything. I can see it would be a big blow for him, and maybe he needs time to regroup. But if he loves you, he'll hear you out."

Shasa lifted her chin, dread and hope and desperate desire coursing through her. "You mean, in person?"

She wanted nothing more than to see him again. Could she face the consequences?

"Aren't you doing that play together, anyway?"

Shasa swallowed. "I don't know anymore. I was wondering if I should just cancel. The next rehearsal is this Wednesday."

"You should go! Face him. Apologise to him. Tell him we forced you to spy on him. None of us knew he was on such thin ice with his finances. I feel bad for him, and I'd hate for you to break up because of us and what happened. I love this cohousing community, but I don't want it to cost you that much. I mean, he's not the guy we thought he was, is he?"

Shasa looked up, her chest glowing like a furnace. "He's not. He's so good to me. To us. Nothing like what I thought. He's hot but he's also sweet and thoughtful and funny and... he's everything, Marnie."

"Sounds like you really love him." Marnie's voice was soft.

Shasa sighed so deeply her whole body shook. "I do."

Chapter 41

Mac never visited his parents during the week, but this couldn't wait. After three gruelling days of phone calls with the bank, investors, builders, potential buyers and non-bank lenders, interspersed by poorly slept nights, he'd sorted out his finances, for now. By some miracle, he hadn't ended up on the street, but he hadn't been far off.

The market was down. It was the worst time to sell. Yet, he'd put his apartments up for sale and agreed to sell his own house to fix cash flow issues. That way, he could pay the contractors working on the leaky townhouse and eventually keep one property. He was still technically on the property ladder and in due time, could start again. After he found his will to live.

Dealing with his house-of-cards finances had left no energy for what his heart craved. But before he could seek out Shasa, he needed answers. She'd kept things from him, and he never wanted to be clueless again. He had to find out how exactly she'd pulled it off. And if he had to fall out of love with this woman, maybe that knowledge would help.

This parent's door was wide open.

"Mac? Is that you?" Mum rushed from the kitchen, followed by the smell of lentil soup, and hugged him against his will. "I missed you! I wanted to talk to you on Sunday, but you left."

"I couldn't stay."

Mum pulled back, taking in the bruise around his eye. "What happened?"

"Stupidity."

She shook her head, eyes wide with worry. "John said you're selling your house, that you're losing all these houses." Her eyes widened even more. "We didn't know. You never told us you were in such a bind! Otherwise, we'd never have signed up for this cohousing thing."

"But you love that idea."

"We do." She gave a sheepish smile.

"Then you should do it," he said, his shoulders heavy as lead.

"But I never meant for you to lose out like that."

Mac sighed. He'd wanted to be the big shot, their clever

firstborn who had his life together. Admitting he'd made bad investments didn't fit that narrative. He'd been too proud.

"It's just money." He knew that's what she wanted to hear – if he shrugged at losing millions, they'd succeeded as parents.

Oh, the high road, how he hated it.

Still, under all the disappointment and hurt, there was a tiny ray of relief. Lying awake in bed with his swollen eye, he'd considered his new reality. He'd been brought back down to earth, down to the level of most people. He had a house, but he wasn't the rising star anymore. He no longer lived in a different world to everyone in his improv group, to his brother, to Shasa... The market was out of control. It wasn't right that he'd been able to make so much money while others couldn't get into their first home, no matter how hard they tried. And the market was turning now. He couldn't ride the property train forever. There was pain in store for everyone, and in all that pain, a hint of justice.

Mum gave him another hug he hadn't initiated. "We're so proud of you. Whatever you do."

He sat at the dinner table and let his mum make him a cup of tea she insisted he needed. He didn't need tea, he needed answers.

"How did you find out about the cohousing?" he asked.

Mum peeked from the kitchen doorway. "Marnie came to see us. I know her from KidsCan and she thought we might be interested."

"Marnie?"

"We tried to call Shasa to ask her opinion, but she didn't pick up," Mum said, placing a steaming cup of tea in front of him.

"When was this?"

"Saturday morning."

Mac stared into his tea. Shasa had been with him. Had she known about Marnie visiting his parents? She must have known about the plan. That's why she'd looked at him like that, with such sadness. That's why she'd pulled away. Mac fought to fill his lungs. He wanted to travel back in time and just hold her. He imagined holding her so tight, for so long that she spilled all those secrets. Would he be angry? Hurt? Betrayed? All of that, but he still couldn't imagine letting her go.

Mum slid into a seat next to him and lowered her voice. "John saw you leaving Shasa's house the other night. Quite late at night. Are you two...?"

Mac shook his head. "No, we're not."

"That's what I told John. She's a lovely girl, but you're very different."

Why was everyone so focused on their differences? "You mean we dress differently?"

"No, I mean she's a single mum and you're... a bachelor."

Mac nodded. He couldn't contest that, but what did it matter? Every cell in his body still called for her, even after everything he'd lost.

"Will you stay for dinner?" Mum asked. "It's just lentil soup, but you're welcome to join us."

"That sounds great, but I have to go."

He glanced at the door, but something on the dining table caught his attention – the local paper, opened on a story titled 'Hamilton's New Cohousing Community'. There were several photos of Shasa and Marnie. The main picture, however, was a family shot. Shasa stood next to a tall man with a head full of dreadlocks, holding Lilla on his arm. He smiled like he'd won a prize. Shasa smiled too, but in a more startled way.

Heart pounding in his chest, Mac read the caption: 'Marama Street cohousing project lead Shasa Daniels with her partner Ollie and daughter Lilla.'

Partner Ollie? Mac stared at the paper, willing the image to change before his eyes. He would have taken anything else, but the photo stayed. The man smiled, his dreadlocks taunting him. 'I'm like her' they seemed to say. 'We're the same. You'll never understand.'

Mac dropped the paper and left, not responding to his mother who was saying something about the coming Sunday.

He climbed Shasa's steps two at a time and banged on the door. He had to see it for himself. Was it true?

The door opened and there he was – the dreadlocks man in the flesh.

"Where's Shasa?" Mac asked.

Ollie leaned on the doorframe, scanning Mac's suit with a mixture of pity and disdain. "And you are?"

"Mac. We do theatre together."

"Theatre?" he raised his brow. "Shasa doesn't do theatre."

"How do you know? I haven't seen you around."

"I just got back. But she's never mentioned theatre."

"Well, we have a rehearsal tonight, so maybe she'll mention it then?"

"Maybe. She's still at work."

Mac glanced at Shasa's car in the driveway.

Ollie noticed. "She walks to work. I thought you knew her?" His voice held a challenge.

"It's fine. I'll catch her later then." Mac raised his hand by way of a goodbye and descended the steps.

So, Ollie was back. That should have been enough to deter him, but he must have been a sucker for pain because he wanted to hear it from her. She owed him that much.

When he reached the gate, Ollie caught up with him, blocking his way. "Look, I don't know what was going on between you and her, but... I'm back. I know I was gone too long, but I'm here to stay. We're a family. I hope you'll respect that." His earlier cockiness was gone, replaced by a flash of fear.

"So, you're back together? That article in the paper..."

"Oh, you saw that?" Ollie voice took on a cheerful tone.

Overwhelmed by the urge to punch the nose ring off his face, Mac buried his fists in his pockets and slipped through the gate. He had to get out of this town.

Chapter 42

Shasa fished about her kitchen for picnic food. If Lilla hadn't been so invested, she'd have skipped the whole thing. But ever since their balloon flight, the girl had been talking about hot air balloons nonstop. Now, the festival was here and she'd agreed to spend Saturday morning sitting on the lawn, watching the balloons ascend.

"Are peanut butter sandwiches okay?" she asked her daughter, although she had no other options.

She'd spent the week sorting out her belongings, hoisting useless items into the big rubbish bin that occupied her driveway and moving the few things she wanted to keep into a storage container. The house had to be empty by Sunday to allow for the house removal company to take it away. Apparently, the old villa still had good bones and original features that made it worth transporting on a back of a truck late at night. It'd probably make a nice home after some extensive renovations.

Shasa hadn't seen Mac all week or heard a word from him. He hadn't shown up for the last rehearsal. She'd stood there with Gareth, unsure what to do. Gareth had tried calling him but couldn't get through. They'd decided to keep trying and stay in touch. The audition was next week.

It had taken three days to get Ollie out of her house. She didn't want to throw him onto the street, so they had to find him somewhere to live. For two nights, he'd slept on the couch and complained about this back. On the third night, he'd climbed into bed with her, and she'd climbed out to sleep on the couch which, she had to admit, wasn't made for sleeping.

She couldn't let him get close. He'd suck her in once again, back into a relationship she'd worked so hard to leave behind. She didn't need him anymore. She didn't want him in her ear, constantly educating her on something else she should feel enraged, shocked, or victimized over. The lectures had already started, from the type of detergent she was using, to the tuna and eggs. Always the eggs. The chickens were never happy enough, free enough, pampered enough. Or maybe she just heard it that way.

What about human suffering? They'd spent the last four

years living in a draughty house that creaked and smelled musty even on dry days. Now that she could see a way out, all those details came into focus. She wished the house would accidentally split into fifteen pieces when they tried to move it.

With Ollie out, it was a bit easier to breathe, even if the pain lingered and her thoughts kept going back to Mac. She'd driven past his house the previous night. There had been no light behind the windows, no truck in the driveway. For what felt like the thousandth time, she'd written a message but hadn't sent it. What she needed to say felt too huge to be contained and transmitted via phone. She had to see him in person, even if it was just so he could scream at her and throw eggs. Free range or battery hen ones, it didn't matter, as long as they hit her in the chest where it hurt.

"Is daddy coming to the balloons?" Lilla asked, jumping up and down next to the bag she was packing, touching every item that went in.

"I don't know," Shasa replied, her throat tight.

Ollie was trying his best with his daughter, and after some initial weirdness, the girl had been excited to have him back. Shasa couldn't help the ill feeling. She didn't trust Ollie's change of heart. This time, Lilla was old enough to understand. This time, she'd really get hurt.

Ollie had already mentioned a friend working on another ship and how much he admired them confronting the fracking in the Pacific. It was a matter of time before the part of him that had responded to that siren call last time reared its head. Whether it took a few months or years, he'd eventually find New Zealand too small, their life too boring.

Ollie could see his daughter, but they couldn't play happy family.

Shasa lifted the picnic bag on her shoulder and took Lilla's hand. "Let's go!"

The balloon picnic was on the other side of the lake, but the distance didn't faze Lilla. She ran ahead, carrying her unicorn purse, which contained another stuffed unicorn.

From the distance, they could see the balloons, most of them already up but tethered to the ground. Sun streamed in from behind the hospital, casting its golden rays across the field. The grass had brown patches from the ongoing drought, but it was gorgeous. She'd always been so happy to live near the lake.

So happy. The words made her choke. If she hadn't betrayed Mac, could they have made it work? Would they have been here together, watching the balloons, holding hands?

Tears blurring her vision, Shasa nearly missed Elsie and Earl, who were set up on a large picnic blanket with a huge basket in front of them. Elsie looked relaxed in yoga pants. Her smile was wide as she leaned on Earl's shoulder.

Lilla leapt to play with the dog and Shasa collapsed on the blanket. "Morning."

"Morning, Shasa! So good to see you! Big day today! Are

you all packed? Do you need help?" Elsie asked.

"We're okay," Shasa assured her, discreetly dabbing her eyes on her sleeve.

Elsie opened her basket. She'd brought food for an army, an army of foodies. Admiring the spread of strawberries, pâtés and cheeses, Shasa didn't feel like revealing her peanut butter sandwiches. She tucked them on the side of the mat and grabbed a strawberry. This was one thing she could get used to. Elsie had a taste for good things in life, and her catering was next level. Soon, they were going to be surrounded by it, staying in her house.

"Have you heard from Marnie?" she asked Elsie. "I thought she was coming, too."

"No."

"I'll check on her."

As Shasa picked up her phone, it beeped.

Ollie: Where are you?

Her heart sank. Lilla had told everyone about the balloons, including her father. So, he was here, worming his way back into their lives.

She texted back their coordinates.

"I'm sorry," Shasa said, turning to Elsie and Earl. "Lilla's father's here, and he wants to see her."

Elsie smiled. "That's perfectly fine. How are things with you two?"

A lump rose in Shasa's throat. "Not great."

She'd already told Elsie that Ollie was back after a two-year absence, and that he wasn't moving into the new apartment with them. Beyond that, Shasa found it hard to talk about him. On most days, she worked actively to forget his existence and the fresh bag of complications his return had brought. She hadn't told Elsie about Mac, either, hoping that Marnie would share about it on her behalf.

As the first balloons lifted off the ground, Ollie arrived. Relaxed and casual in a hemp shirt and worn-out shorts, he'd tied a scarf around his furry mane, revealing a deep tan on his neck and shoulders. She'd always loved his broad shoulders and cheeky grin. Now, the sight of them did nothing for her.

Ollie introduced himself to the others and sat next to her on the blanket. Too close, like he was claiming her. She kept her gaze at the sky, watching the lifting balloons, hoping for an excuse to move away.

Her rescue came in the form of a phone call. An unknown number. It took her a couple of seconds to recognise Gareth's voice.

"Look, I don't know who else to call. I just heard Mac's out of town. Sold his house, moved to Tauranga. He sent me this short, bullshit message. Apologies, whatever. I don't know what's going on, but I feel like you do."

Mac had left town? Shasa's stomach tightened at the thought, the pain spreading from her chest all the way to her toes and fingertips. She got to her feet and hurried away, searching for privacy. There wasn't any, but at least she was surrounded by strangers.

"Why do you think I know something?" She tried to sound neutral but failed. The thought of Mac moving away to another town hit her so hard she could barely stand.

Gareth's deep sigh crackled on the phone microphone. "Please don't bullshit me."

Shasa paused, staring at a red balloon as it lifted off the ground. She had no reason to lie to him. If Mac was gone, there was no audition. No more secrets. "I messed up one of his business deals, he lost a lot of money. He lost his house because of me."

"How?"

"I'm sorry," she whispered. "I know we weren't supposed to get involved. But we kind of were to begin with, through his property deal. And also…" She tried to swallow. She had no claim on Mac, but she couldn't deny her feelings. "I fell in love with him. And I didn't mean to hurt him like that. I didn't know he was in so much trouble. It's all a huge mess."

The line went quiet. Shasa wondered if Gareth had ended the call.

Finally, he spoke. "I warned you about getting involved, because I didn't want to risk you guys breaking up in the middle of this, but it sounds like you already have. Look. Whatever's going on, the audition's booked for tomorrow. I'll be there, the producer will be there. I can't tell you what to do, but I'm going to send you this address I got for Mac. Then it's up to you. If you hurt him, fix it. Apologise. Whatever you need to do. One thing I know about Mac is that if he doesn't show up for this, he'll regret it."

Gareth ended the call.

Shasa shuddered. The balloons were rising in the air all around her. Pink, yellow, blue, green, red. They floated up, getting smaller and smaller, crossing the lake, slowly disappearing on the horizon. She'd never be able to look at a balloon again without thinking of him.

With a heavy heart, she returned to the picnic blanket, her mind on the audition. Mac was so passionate about acting. How could he throw it away like that?

"Unicorn!" Lilla screamed, appearing by her side. "Mac told me about it! He said we can go on the unicorn balloon." Her eyes huge, she pointed up at the sky. There it was, a pink unicorn, floating across the lake.

Shasa blinked at her daughter. "Mac told you? When?" A pointless question. Three-year-olds had no concept of time. Either way, what was Mac doing making promises to her daughter?

"What's wrong?" Elsie asked, her face wrinkled with concern.

Ollie stared at her as well. Shasa looked at them. She must have sighed too loud.

"Mac's sold his house and moved to Tauranga."

Elsie cocked her head. "Is that right? He must have taken

a bigger hit than I thought."

"Mac?" Ollie asked, like tasting the sound of his name.

Something about his tone sent a cold shiver down Shasa's spine. "You know him?"

Ollie hesitated for a second, then nodded. "Someone by that name came to the door looking for you."

"When?"

Ollie shrugged. "I don't remember. When I was still there, before you kicked me out. You were at work, and this guy said you had a theatre rehearsal or something. He thought you must be home since your car was there. Like people couldn't get anywhere without a car." He rolled his eyes, but the snipe barely registered with Shasa.

Mac had come to see her. After everything that happened, he'd come to her door. And Ollie had no doubt sent him away.

Ollie smiled. "It's okay. It's been two years. You're allowed to have new friends. Even ones who wear shiny suits and resort to violence."

"Violence?"

Ollie's voice held an air of superiority. "He had a black eye."

Shasa shook from fury. "Why didn't I get that message?"

"What message?"

"You just said Mac came to see me and you never said a word!"

Ollie shrugged. "He came to tell you about the rehearsal.

You went to that rehearsal. What's the problem?"

Shasa sunk her face into her hands, wanting to scream. Ollie was an ass, but it was nothing new. She didn't want to waste another second on him.

Where was her daughter? She found Lilla standing behind them, looking up at the sky. All the balloons were now up in the air, getting further and further away.

"Are you leaving already?" Elsie asked as Shasa stood up.

"We have to finish packing so we can get everything into the storage container when it arrives."

Ollie stood up. "Do you need help?"

"Not from you."

Her voice came out so scathing he dropped back on the blanket, sighing loudly.

"We'll see you around midday," Earl said. He, Elsie, and Marnie were coming to help shift the large items and look after Lilla.

She farewelled Elsie and Earl, grabbed Lilla by the hand and took the path leading home. They had a lot to do. With all the idle moments she'd spent thinking of Mac in the last two weeks, this should have been the easy day, the one so busy she had no time for self-torture. The day she moved on, literally and figuratively.

Pulling her reluctant daughter in tow, Shasa ploughed up the hill, back to the house that was no longer a home.

Once they reached the porch, she dug up her phone and called Marnie.

"Hi! I was about to call you," Marnie said. "Why aren't you here? I just arrived."

"Sorry." Shasa winced. "Ollie is there, and I can't be around him right now... I found out Mac came to see me when Ollie was still staying with us. I wasn't home."

"Oh, dear."

"I know. You can imagine how that went down."

"But he came to see you. That's good, right?"

Shasa took a deep breath, fire burning in her belly. "I need to see him, Marnie. I really need to see him. But he's moved to Tauranga, and I have all this packing to do. The moving truck is coming. I can't go anywhere today."

"Go first thing tomorrow. I'll watch Lilla."

Shasa sniffed. She didn't deserve a friend like Marnie. "Thank you."

Chapter 43

Before ten on Sunday morning, Shasa arrived in Papamoa Beach, one of Tauranga's popular holiday spots. Church bells rang in the distance as she crept along the endless coastal street, looking for the address Gareth had given her. The 80-minute drive had felt long, with her small car struggling up the Kaimai ranges, windows rolled down for natural cooling. Her air con hadn't worked in years.

The quintessential weatherboard house with a decaying, uncovered deck, looked nothing like she'd expected. She was about to double check the address when she spotted Mac's truck. Thank goodness he hadn't downgraded that. It shone as her only beacon.

Shasa approached the door with trepidation. What could she say? It's not like they had a relationship. They'd shared a collection of moments she'd stored in her heart and relived over and over, but that was it. She stopped at the door, hoping for the hot ball of despair to lift off her chest. It didn't. The sliding door was covered on the other side by thermal curtains which gave no way of peeking in.

She knocked and waited.

The curtain behind the window moved, and she saw him. In boxer shorts and a sleeveless tee, he looked like he'd just woken up. The black eye Ollie had mentioned had faded into yellow and light purple. He looked lost, his dark curls a little longer, sticking out in every direction. But he was still Mac, and her heart leapt into her throat.

Mac unlocked the door and opened it a crack, staring at her. She couldn't figure out if he was angry, sad, or indifferent. Of all the things she'd imagined, she'd never expected this stony silence. He was waiting for her to make a move, but she couldn't speak. She stood at his doorstep, frozen like a statue, her heart punching the inside of her ribcage. Why had Gareth sent her here? This had been a horrible idea.

Gareth. Her brain landed on the one solid piece of information she had. "The audition's today."

Mac shifted his weight. "I know." His expression remained unreadable. Gone was the flirty smile and the eyes that lit up and explored every inch of her.

Shasa took a deep breath, closing her eyes. "I'm so sorry, Mac. You have no idea. I hate myself for everything. I keep thinking about you, all the money you lost, what I did... It was ugly. So wrong. I didn't know you had so much to lose. If I'd known—"

"I don't care about that," he said quietly.

She opened her eyes. "You don't?"

"I know you have me pegged as this heartless rich guy, but you're wrong, on both accounts. I have a heart. I've become intensely aware of that because it hurts all the time."

Shasa drew a raggedy breath, her own heart swelling. "I know I can't fix anything, but can we just go to that audition, please? If we leave now, we'll make it before..."

"And what if we get the part? I live here now."

"No, you don't! You just fled here when things got tough!" Why was she yelling at him? This was the opposite of what she'd come here for.

Mac's voice rose to meet hers. "Yeah, things got tough. I had to sell my house. My tenants moved out of this one, so I moved here. I didn't have a lot of choice."

His eyes were the darkest she'd ever seen, and her heart cracked wide open. There was so much hurt and regret she could barely take it in. Yet she wanted to. She wanted all of it because it was him.

"Mac," she whispered. "It wasn't my idea to go to your parents. I didn't know about it. And... I thought we had something. You asked me to take a chance, and I never replied, because I was too scared of how you'd take it if we won. Because I betrayed you. I read your email and found out how much you offered for the section. It was a horrible thing to do, and I hate myself so much for it. But it was before I knew I loved you. You don't have to forgive me, but you should know I'm so sorry I feel sick. "

He looked away, his Adam's apple bobbing as he swallowed. "I figured it was something like that. You did what you had to do."

His voice sounded distant, almost polite. She felt like slapping him, just to make him yell at her. She deserved his anger.

"You don't do that to someone you love," she insisted. "And if I could undo it somehow, I would. I'd give up everything."

His eyes flashed at the words, locking with hers for a moment. The brief connection jolted her, making her crave for more. Until he broke the eye contact and returned to that polite tone. "Don't worry about it. You have a daughter with him. You're a family. Think whatever you want of me, but I'd never break up a family."

She stared at him in disbelief. "My family was already broken! I don't know what Ollie told you, but he's not in the picture."

"I saw the picture of you two in the paper."

That news story! Shasa rubbed her forehead, desperate to erase the image. When she'd seen the caption that identified them as a couple, she'd sent the paper flying across the room. That night, Ollie had finally moved out of the house.

"It's rubbish. I'm not back together with him."

"Why? You guys are cut from the same cloth. It makes sense." He sounded resigned.

The fire that had driven Shasa to his doorstep returned, flaming in her belly. She'd had it with these arbitrary differences. Her nostrils flared as she stared into his eyes. "Let's get rid of the cloth then."

Holding his gaze, she kicked off her jandals, peeled off her tank top and dropped it on the deck. Mac didn't blink, but his eyes dipped to take in her yellow cotton bra. She hadn't dressed for this show, but it didn't matter. Her body vibrating, she yanked off her two remaining bracelets, letting them clatter on the wooden floorboards. Then, she pulled off her harem pants, turning them into a pile of fiery red fabric at her feet.

The church bells were still ringing. The bright morning sun heated her back, yet she shivered in the late summer breeze as she searched his face, hoping to catch a hint of the man she loved.

She scanned his boxer shorts. "I suppose my underwear doesn't match yours, either—"

She was about to take off her bra when Mac grabbed her by the elbow and pulled her inside, manhandling her onto the couch.

"That's enough!" His voice was hard, his touch like an

electric shock.

She burrowed into the couch, hugging her knees. Uncontrollable sobs escaped her throat, and she hid her face inside her arms, trying to hold herself together. She'd lost him. The hot ball of despair expanded in her chest, pushing air out of her lungs.

The couch sunk as he sat next to her. She had to get out of here, fall apart somewhere else.

Drawing a deep breath, she pushed herself upright, planting her feet on the carpet. The sparsely furnished room was small, nothing like his house in Hamilton.

"Where're you going?" His hand gripped her arm.

"Back," she gasped.

His hand remained, squeezing so hard she couldn't move. "So, you come all the way here to tell me about the audition, apologise for ruining a two-million-dollar business deal, and then you strip on my deck... for the enjoyment of my elderly neighbours Patty and Neil who were on their way to church."

She caught a hint of lightness in his voice, an opening, and her heart jumped.

Shasa lifted her chin. "There was nobody in the street," she argued, although she had no idea. She hadn't looked.

"Neil was quite excited. Patty had to grab his walker and roll him away."

Shasa dropped her head, unable to stop the laughter or the tears that immediately followed. "I'm sorry."

"It's okay. Although I'd rather not share you with them.

Or anyone."

She blinked away the tears, to see him clearly. "I came here to apologise and beg for you to reconsider… us. I know I'm doing a terrible job of it."

He tried to smile, but it turned into a grimace. "Look. What you did hurt me. I'm not going to pretend it didn't."

She exhaled, holding his gaze. He let her witness the pain, and she teared up at the privilege. "You're allowed to feel hurt. You're allowed to hate me."

"I don't hate you. I could never."

"I bet you hate living here, though." She winced, glancing across the dimly lit, musty lounge at the worn-out dining set.

Mac shook his head. "That doesn't feel important."

"But your house was so nice."

He shrugged. "I could have ended up in my brother's basement flat. A house is a house. And I've learned that there's a cheap alternative to almost everything I'm used to buying. I even went to an op shop here in Tauranga. Bought some more pots and pans so I can cook at home. Can't afford takeaways."

Shasa squeezed her eyes shut. "Oh, God. Mac. You can hate me. I'll understand."

"I'm saving odd socks now, for future use." Mac leant forward, elbows over knees.

The cheeky tone of his comment cut through Shasa's inner turmoil. She wiped her eyes with the back of her hand.

"Really?"

"I have a high need for stress balls these days."

She let out a wobbly laugh, her heart in pieces. She gently touched the side of his eye where the bruise faded. "What happened?"

"I punched Rick. He hit me back."

"Oh, Mac." She traced the shape of the bruise, tears flowing.

His eyes were sad, but a hesitant smile tugged his lips. "I couldn't let him insult you."

Shasa hung her head. "But I deserve it. I ruined everything."

His fingers caught her chin, forcing eye contact. "No, Shasa. We were both playing to win. I took risks and I lost. I can live with that."

He gazed into her eyes, waiting for her.

Shasa's heart fluttered. This was her chance. "You haven't lost me. Not unless you want to. I'm all in."

"You don't mind me being broke?"

"No!"

"Or living in a house like this?" Mac gestured at the room.

"I mind you living this far away, but we can figure it out."

"Good. Because I've missed you so much. I thought about calling and texting you a million times. But I thought you'd made your choice. I couldn't risk breaking up your family. So, I waited, and hoped." His voice caught. "Shasa, I've never hurt this much in my life. But you're here. If you're really here, and you're serious..."

She caught the hungry intensity in his eyes, just before his mouth closed on hers. Every nerve in her body fired up, and she matched his fierceness, climbing onto his lap and pushing him against the couch. If she could have him, she'd never let him go. Blood rushed in her ears as warmth flooded her body, relaxing every tense muscle, slowly melting away the fear and pain.

"I'm really here," she whispered, looking at him through wet eyelashes. "There's nowhere else I'd rather be."

Mac's hands slid lower on her hips, sending a shock of sensation to her lady parts. His hard-on pushed against her thigh, straining against the boxers. She slid her hand on it, gasping from pleasure, and kissed him again. His body tensed and he grabbed her shoulder, pushing them apart.

His eyes were inky black as he brushed a strand of short hair from her eyes. "We do this, and you're mine. Do you understand?" His voice was gruff as he held away from her, waiting for an answer.

Shasa tried to speak, but her voice had disappeared somewhere down her throat. She nodded, her heart beating so fast she feared it would give out. "I'm all yours."

Mac relaxed his hand, letting their bodies mould together into another kiss, deep and needy. She swept her tongue into his mouth, opening up, giving him everything. Eventually, they ran out of air, hot and panting.

"Do you have a bed?" she whispered. "If not, I don't mind

the couch. Fuck. I don't mind the floor."

Mac pushed them upright, then up to standing. The room was warm and stuffy, but she shivered against him, her arms locked around his waist.

"Do you mind the table?" he asked, lifting her on the small dining table, stepping closer as she spread her legs, drawing him in.

His erection pressed against her, stretching the boxers out of shape. He unhooked her bra and dropped it on the floor, lowering his mouth to her breast, sucking each one in turn. A sweet sensation shot down her spine. His hand slid down, grazing her wet panties, then sliding inside to circle her. Oh, God. She'd been waiting for this for so long, replaying the moments under the fallen balloon, fantasizing about his touch. Shivering from head to toe, she opened her legs wider, digging her nails into his back.

"You didn't let me take care of you." He kissed her neck, his fingers grazing her again.

That feather-light touch made her back arch and she moaned. "More."

"But I'll take care of you now, and you won't run away."

"I won't run away," she panted.

She'd never run away again. Even if she didn't deserve the hot, delectable pleasure pouring through her, blurring every thought and turning her into a vibrating bundle of need. She tried to reach for him, but he pushed her hand away, lowering himself between her legs. Pulling her soaked underwear to the side, he licked her swollen flesh, letting out a growl that almost jolted her off the table. She held onto its edges, her knuckles white. "Don't stop."

Mac gripped her thighs, holding her in place as he buried his face between her thighs. Bloody hell. She was already on the cusp, shaking. The table let out a loud creak.

"I need you, Mac," she whispered. "Do you have protection?"

"Wait." He left her onto the wobbly table, aching and desperate and ran to fetch a condom. Scared that the furniture would give out, she hopped down and followed him into the bedroom, her legs jelly. A mattress lay on the floor, covered in balled up sheets and clothes.

He gestured at it, apologetic. "I'm sorry, it's not—"

"I don't care." She pushed him on the sheets, her body vibrating from an unmet need.

He kicked off his boxers and she helped him roll on the condom.

She peeled off her undies, sitting next to him, fully naked. "What do you prefer?" she asked, expecting him to the take the lead. She deserved to be punished, not pleasured.

"I want to see you come, Shasa. Whatever you want. Whatever you need."

His thick voice made her throb and her insides flooded with warmth.

She eyed his impressive erection, giving him a coy smile, before she climbed on top of him, guiding him inside of her, inch by inch until she ached in the sweetest way.

Mac's gaze locked with hers, reflecting her own hunger and need, along with tenderness. "Anything you want, Shasa. I love you."

Her throat tightened. He loved her. After everything, he loved her. Nothing had ever felt this good. Her hips moved as if they had free will and he groaned, his hands gripping her buttocks, letting her set the pace. With her orgasm building, she forgot everything else, chasing the mounting pleasure. He matched her gasps with grunts, calling her name.

It was too much. She wanted the moment to last forever, but she couldn't hold it any longer. The perfect friction built up with every thrust until the tsunami of pleasure flushed through her. She felt his release, moments after her own.

She laid her head on his chest, shivering. "We'll do the kitchen table next time, okay?"

He laughed. "I don't care about the table. I just didn't want to show you the mess in here. I put most of my things in storage in Hamilton because I need to renovate this place first."

Shasa looked at the open suitcase in the corner of the room, its contents spilling across the floor. She thought of the day they'd first met. "My house was worse than this, when we first met."

He laughed, wrapping his arms around her. His chest rose as he inhaled deeply, then exhaled into her hair. "Next time, we'll take it slow, I promise. Like ... hours."

Would they ever have hours? What time was it, anyway? Shasa bent her arm to look at her wristwatch. Oh, no. "The audition!" she gasped. "We can make it, if we leave now and ... speed a little."

Mac groaned. "But I don't want to get up."

Shasa peeled herself off him. "You want the part. I know you do. I can't let you..."

Mac took a deep breath, following her example. "Okay. Put some clothes on!"

He reached for the nearest shirt.

Shasa ran to the front door and peeked out, checking the street for passers-by. Wincing at the thought of Patty and Neil, she grabbed her pile of clothes off the deck and dressed quickly.

When she was slipping on her jandals, Mac appeared in shorts and a T-shirt, holding a hoodie.

"We'll take my ute," he said, unlocking it remotely. "It's faster and won't fall apart on the way."

Shasa stared at him in confusion. "I can't leave my car here. How will I get it back?"

"We'll sort it out. Meanwhile, you have me and my ute."

"We could take both," she said.

It made sense, but suddenly, she didn't want to make sense. She wanted their lives together, tangled and inseparable.

Mac clasped her hand in his, pulling her toward his truck. "Come on. I don't want to drive alone. I want to be with you."

He playfully shoved her onto the front seat, stealing a kiss. She loved him for taking charge. She didn't want to be without him, not even for one hour, regardless of practicalities.

Sitting next to him, her mind kept replaying the previous moments, her body still gently throbbing. Mac drove decisively, taking every curve so tight that Shasa slid on her seat, the fabric of her pants catching under her, tightening against her crotch. Every move sent a delicious shock wave through her. She couldn't wait to touch him again, to be with him again.

But as they passed the signs for Hamilton, she couldn't contain the thoughts that popped up. Real life, with all its complications, waited for them.

"We're moving house! Everything's in storage and the house removal company is coming late tonight. Marnie has Lilla, I have to pick her up after the audition and then we're moving into Elsie's guest room." Her breath caught in her throat.

She couldn't bring Mac into Elsie's house, could she? She couldn't be with him. They didn't have hours, not even minutes. After the audition, they'd have to say goodbye.

Mac's hand squeezed her thigh. "Don't worry about it. I can crash somewhere else. Then we'll drive back here when you're free. We'll bring Lilla with us, go to the beach, make a road trip out of it. That house is basic, but the location's great."

He was making plans with her, with them. Hope flooded her heart. She leaned her cheek against Mac's shoulder, enjoying the low hum of the air con. His truck was a lot more comfortable, but she wasn't with him for nice things. She'd happily live in his half-furnished Papamoa house if it were close enough to work.

On the motorway, Mac called his brother and confirmed that he could crash on Izzy's couch. Shasa's stomach tightened at the thought, but she couldn't suggest anything better, at least anything that allowed them to be together. The future opened in front of them like a terrifying jigsaw puzzle.

They spent the rest of the ride rehearsing the play and listening to music on the radio. Shasa could feel the nerves waking up in her gut as they approached Hamilton and the theatre. Mac went quiet.

Finally, he turned into the theatre parking lot. Shasa had texted Gareth from the road, confirming they were on their way.

At the door, Shasa froze, grabbing Mac's arm. "Are we ready? I mean, we slept together. Isn't that going to kill all the tension?"

A cheeky smile spread across his face. "I'm hotter for you than ever. We'll be fine."

He took her face in his hands and captured her lips in a kiss that was full of promise. A surge of pleasure swooped between her thighs, making her pulse with need. When he broke contact, she tried to catch her breath. "Yeah, okay. We're good."

The tension between them hummed like music playing on a frequency that was out of range for human ears. He opened the door.

Gareth stood in the middle of the room, talking to a woman. When they entered, he rushed to greet them. "You're here! Thank God. Nice special effects." Gareth pointed at Mac's bruised eye. "Was it you?" he asked Shasa.

Shasa let out a nervous laugh as Mac shook his head. "I accidentally punched myself."

Gareth introduced them to the producer, a middle-aged lady in blue-rimmed glasses called Iris. Without a hint of a smile, she gestured at the stage. "Are we ready?"

Something about the stage, now in broad daylight, called to Shasa. She longed to return to the world of make believe where she'd had the first taste of Mac, a safe space where real life couldn't reach them.

She climbed on the platform and lowered herself on the cool floor, allowing it to transport her away from here, into the story. She was the princess, waking up in the reporter's apartment in Rome, the dream of him still lingering in her mind. The dream. She stretched her arms over her head, waiting for the director's cue. She was ready.

As she opened her eyes, she saw him. The Mac she knew, the one she loved. Without the pain and hurt that had hovered between them, making everything murky. His eyes lit up, and he studied her with curiosity.

They kept to their lines, with a good dose of innuendo. Mac stayed in character and she was desperate to match his commitment. The director and producer faded into the background. Only Mac existed, the brown eyes she wanted to drown in, the hands she longed to feel on her again. But she was a princess, she reminded herself. She belonged to another world – one where he couldn't follow.

When the scene ended, Shasa peeled herself off the floor, blinking like she'd just woken up. Beside her, Mac shuffled his feet.

"Thank you," Iris said, her voice a mask of politeness.

Gareth thanked them with a quick smile. "I'll see you out."

Had they completely bombed?

Shasa forced her feet to move, to follow Mac and Gareth to the doors. She cared about the play, but she cared more about Mac. If this was important to him, she wanted it to work. And if it meant he had to move back to Hamilton, even better.

As they approached the front door, Shasa noticed a faint rumble. Rain. She couldn't remember the last time it had rained. Mac and Gareth stopped in their tracks and stepped back to stay under the small cover. Shasa joined them, hugging the wall. She could hardly see the other side of the street from the steaming waterfall.

Gareth's voice rose over the rumble. "Thanks for coming,

guys. I appreciate it."

"I hope we did okay?" She hated sounding so needy, but she had to know.

"You were fantastic. I'll have a chat with Iris and see what she thinks. Although, I don't know if we can risk casting someone who doesn't live locally?"

Mac met his gaze. "I'll see what I can do."

"Very well. Thank you for coming. I'll be in touch." Gareth slapped them both on the back and retreated into the theatre.

Shasa's heart pounded in her ears. The audition had been such a thrill that she hardly wanted to return to real life, especially as they had to part ways.

Mac wrapped his arms around her. "Thank you for dragging me here. I'm glad we auditioned, even if it doesn't work out."

"No problem."

"And whatever happens, I'll find a way to be closer to you, I promise."

Emotion welled in Shasa's chest. "You have to. I need you here."

They stood for a long time, breathing each other in, holding onto each other like lifebelts. Eventually, the rain eased, turning into slight light drizzle.

Shasa turned to look up at the sky. "We should go."

"Where's Lilla? At Marnie's?"

"Yeah."

"I'll give you a ride." Mac nodded towards the carpark, still holding her against his chest.

Shasa didn't move. She wasn't ready. What if everything between them disappeared as soon as they left this theatre? Elsie didn't even know about them. She'd told Marnie she was going over to apologise and fetch Mac for the audition. Her friend knew she was madly in love with him, but nobody seemed to believe they had a future.

"I'm scared," she whispered. "How do we make this work? What do we tell everyone?"

Mac tightened his arms around her. She caught a whiff of his deodorant, mixed with the dampness of the rain.

"We'll make it work. I'll sell the Papamoa house and move here. And I don't know about you, but I'm going to tell everyone I'm in love with you and want to spend every waking moment with you. Every sleeping moment, too."

He slid his arms around her bottom and lifted her off the ground. She wrapped her legs around him as his hot mouth landed on her neck, ear, cheek and eventually, her mouth. The kiss was so tender, so demanding, that she barely noticed when he lowered her down and her feet touched the ground. He grinned at her, lowering his head to hers so that their foreheads were touching.

She breathed in his scent. "So, we're together? You and me?"

"Yes, you and me. I don't care what anyone thinks. We fit together like... mac and cheese."

"I'm the cheese?" She giggled.

"Well, I'm Mac."

Strength returned to Shasa's legs. Maybe they'd carry her into those new challenges. They descended the steps, entering the warm drizzle. Blindingly bright sun peeked through the heavy clouds, illuminating the tiny raindrops like crystals dancing in the air. Shasa opened her mouth at the sky, soaking in water and light.

Mac took her hand and twirled her on the pavement like they were dancing. An uncontrollable smile split her face.

"So happy," she said.

"So happy," he said.

It was the happiest she'd been in years.

Four months later

"Do we have more baked beans?" Shasa asked, tapping Lando on the shoulder.

The community house hall was packed with volunteers assembling donation boxes for struggling families. Lando cut the plastic wrap around the last pallet and peered inside.

"No, this is all tomato and creamed corn."

"We'll just have to substitute." Shasa blew onto her freezing fingers and rubbed them together. The hall was difficult to heat in the winter.

She went to check on the volunteers. She didn't want to be seen to be playing favourites, but it was hard to ignore Mac. In a puffer vest and a beanie, he blended in but worked harder than anyone else, making sure both his and Lilla's boxes were filled correctly. The girl wanted to help but had the attention span of a squirrel.

"Wow, you're almost finished!" Shasa gushed.

She'd been grateful beyond measure when he'd turned up early to help them out. She'd sent Marnie home after the first half hour when she noticed her friend struggling with the cardboard boxes, visibly in pain. Shasa hoped there wasn't anything seriously wrong with her.

Mac lifted the packing tape dispenser with an empty roll. "Is there another one somewhere?"

He got back to work, humming. At first, Shasa had thought he'd volunteered to impress her. But lately, she'd seen the spark in his eyes as he spoke about the families they were helping – the same families he'd wanted to help into home ownership. That plan was now on the back burner, but in the meantime, Mac seemed to enjoy connecting with people and helping in a tangible way, even if on a smaller scale. Shasa was so proud of him she got a lump in her throat every time she thought about how far Mac had come, from losing his house to new focus and determination. If only she were able to share her life with him. Between busy schedules and complicated living arrangements, they didn't see each other that much.

For the past four months, Shasa and Lilla had stayed in Elsie's guest suite while Mac rented an apartment in Hamilton. He'd decided to renovate the Tauranga house before selling it to get a better price. Since he was doing the work himself, he spent a lot of time over there.

She felt grateful for the play. Some weeks, the rehearsal had been her one chance to see him. Working with a large group of other actors wasn't exactly a date night. A couple of times, they'd snuck away for dinner afterwards, but it felt like their time together was a series of stolen moments.

As Shasa entered the small office, looking for packing tape, her phone beeped. She pulled it out of her jacket pocket, struggling to tap on the message from Marnie with frozen fingertips.

> **Marnie:** I forgot to ask about the lunch... are you bringing anything? Sue keeps saying 'just bring yourselves', but I'm pretty sure Elsie will bring some super expensive flower arrangement, and if you take something amazing, and I turn up empty-handed, I'll feel horrible!

Shasa chuckled at the row of terrified smiley faces following the message. She was even more terrified. Mac's parents had invited them to Sunday lunch many times and now they were all going.

She texted back to Marnie.

> **Shasa:** I know how you feel! We picked up some daisies on the way. Mac says they're Sue's favourite.

Shasa stared at the word 'we'. She still wasn't used to talking about herself and Mac as a couple. Putting her phone away, she located a roll of tape on the desk. As she turned to go back, she nearly ran into Mac. He stepped in the office, blocking the doorway.

He smiled, sliding his hands around her waist, pulling her against him. "Found you!"

Shasa gasped. Okay, she'd allow herself a ten-second break. Fine, twenty-seconds. She slipped her hand through the roll of tape, the world's ugliest bracelet, and wrapped her arms around him. Her body responded to Mac like it had a secret on-off switch, going from zero to a hundred in seconds. He kissed her with passion and intensity, aware that their time was short.

Mac's raspy voice was hot in her ear. "Can you ask for someone to babysit so I can take you on a proper date? Or a weekend away?"

He loosened her purple scarf and bent down to kiss her neck, lingering for a delicious moment. Shasa wanted to, badly. Now that she knew how he could make her feel, she craved it even more. Since that first time in Tauranga, they'd only managed to get together in private four times, usually after the theatre rehearsals and once on a long hike after Lilla had fallen asleep in her pushchair. Every time she thought about that secluded spot behind large trees, her body flushed with heat. It was so good, but it wasn't enough.

"I will," she promised. "I just want to give everyone time to adjust. With us living at Elsie's..."

Mac groaned. "Why can't we ask Marnie?"

"She's already babysitting for every rehearsal and next week for the premiere."

"Let's pay someone. Or ask my mum. She loves Lilla." Mac brushed a strand of hair behind her ear. "It's almost like you don't want to date me."

Shasa bit her lip, her throat tight. He was right. She was holding back. She loved watching Mac bond with Lilla, but it also terrified her. She feared Mac didn't understand what he was getting into. The child would always be there, competing for their attention, complicating their lives. Everything required planning. Mac insisted he was okay to take it slow, but what if he got frustrated with all her baggage and moved on? Ollie had already sailed away to fight fracking in the Pacific Ocean, just as she'd expected. She had to protect her daughter. She had to protect herself.

If she was completely honest, dating felt wrong – something fun and casual that childless people did. For her, it had to be all or nothing. What if it ended up being nothing?

"Have you thought about moving in?" she whispered, breath catching in her chest.

Mac's smile was guarded, his lips tightly sealed. She'd asked him before, but he'd insisted Shasa focused on finishing the house to her liking. But how could she do that? She thought about him at every turn, wondering if he liked the colours and materials she picked. She'd included a lot of the charcoal and sandy tones she remembered from his house. They worked beautifully, although it would look different with her Pakistani cushions, chipped yellow teacups and the pink bedroom light.

Most of her stuff – the mouldy curtains, dream catchers with spider nests, and half-burned candles, had ended up in the skip. It had felt like an overdue cleansing ritual. Shasa didn't want her new home to look like a student rental that Ollie would feel comfortable bringing his ganja pipe into. No. This time everything would be higher quality, more considered. On a tight budget, it meant going without many things until she could afford them. She'd have to fight those urges in second-hand shops and learn to choose well. Maybe in time, Mac would be there to choose with her.

She placed her hands on his chest. "I know it's a huge decision, but it makes sense. Once you sell the Tauranga house, why pay rent for that place in town? I want you over every night ... If you want to be with us?"

A pang of pain clutched her chest as she searched for an answer in those deep, brown eyes.

Mac placed a quick kiss on her forehead and took the roll of tape off her hands. "Let's get this wrapped up so we can make it to that lunch."

She followed him out of the office, back into the hall. They worked as fast as they could, packing, prepping and cleaning. Once everything was in order, Shasa thanked the volunteers, locked the doors behind them, and they piled into Mac's truck.

It was a crisp winter's day with blue skies. Mac turned up the heater, but it hardly had time to make a difference before they arrived at his parents' house.

The sight on the adjacent section took her breath away.

"The house is ready!" Lilla yelled, jumping on the backseat.

"Wow!" Shasa stared at it, her mouth open.

With fresh paint and timber accents, their new cohousing community now looked like a real townhouse, dwarfing John and Sue's brick house. The fence between the two properties had been taken down, creating an enormous yard.

Shasa knew it wasn't quite finished inside. She'd opted for installing the kitchen and lighting fixture herself to save money – Mac's idea, like so many others. He'd also be the one to do the installations as she had no idea what that entailed.

Whether he admitted it or not, Mac was already involved. They'd gone with the builders Mac had used for his own house and he'd done extra site visits, making sure they stayed on schedule and the work was done right.

"Do we have time for a sneak peek?" Shasa asked, glancing at the new house.

Mac smiled. "Absolutely. In fact, I asked Tony to meet us here.

Shasa's eyes widened. "The site manager? On a Sunday?"

"Don't worry. He's happy to since he gets to hand over the

keys. In record time."

"The keys?" Shasa squeaked, her voice nearly drowned out by Lilla's excited sounds. "I thought it was going to take another week?"

Mac looked out the window. "I lent them a hand to make sure it was finished a bit earlier. Come on!"

They got out of the truck and approached the last unit, the one furthest away from the street that Marnie had promised to Shasa. Its yellow door beckoned her, happy and bright.

Tony appeared from around the corner, holding a white folder. "Welcome to your new home!" he called, stroking his grey beard. "It's not quite move-in ready yet. We still have to finish the driveway and fencing. But you can certainly have a look."

He handed Shasa a shiny key.

Shasa gasped. "Wait! Shouldn't we wait for Marnie and Earl? Shouldn't we do this together?"

Mac shook his head and exchanged a look with Tony, who retreated down the driveway towards his car.

Mac nudged Shasa towards the door. "Come on!"

Confused, she unlocked the door, letting Lilla sprint in ahead of her. The girl ran from one room to the next, letting out high-pitched yelps at every detail she noticed.

"My room!" she called from upstairs.

Shasa followed her up into the single room right beside the master bedroom. It was pink.

"Did you already paint this?" Shasa asked Mac, who

appeared behind her.

As far as she knew, Mac had arrived from Tauranga early that morning, getting behind the wheel before six a.m. She'd texted him twice, worried that he might be too tired to drive. Had he been lying to her?

Mac wrapped his arms around her, nuzzling her neck. "I got back a bit earlier. Well, a lot earlier. The Tauranga reno was done and I had some time. I've been staying at my parents and it's quite handy to this building site as you know."

Lilla threw herself on their legs, her eyes dancing. "I love my room! I love it!"

Mac released Shasa and picked the girl up for a hug. "We can paint the unicorn on the wall later." He let her down, and she skipped away to explore the rest of the apartment.

"So, this morning you weren't driving from Tauranga?"

"No," he admitted sheepishly. "I'm sorry I lied. I just didn't want to ruin the surprise."

Shasa whipped her head in astonishment. The curtain rods still waited for curtains, but the walls were painted, the kitchen installed. She shot a desperate look at Mac. "You can't do all this, it's too much. Especially if you're not moving in. It's just... wrong."

Mac took Shasa's hands. He stared at her and his eyes shifted darker, just like they did on stage, right before a scene. "I don't want to be your flatmate."

Shasa held back tears as he dug into his pocket.

"I want to be your husband." He held open a small velvet box with a ring.

Shasa blinked several times, but the image remained. A vintage gold band with a small green stone.

"It's recycled," he explained with a quick smile. "I can make up a story of someone amazing it used to belong to if you'd like. Will you marry me, Shasa?"

She hadn't expected it. Ollie and she had never discussed marriage – he didn't believe in biblical covenants, or even legal contracts of that nature. Could she marry Mac? Shasa stared into his eyes and down at the ring. The scratches on it tugged at her heart. Staring at it, the shock began wearing off, replaced by conviction. It felt right, so much better than him moving into a house that was essentially hers. She wanted it to be theirs. She wanted to share everything with him.

Mac lifted her chin, forcing her eyes off the ring, back onto him. "I'm going to need an actual answer here. Even if it's no."

"No! No! I mean it's not no. The answer is not no. It's yes! Sorry, I'm … in shock."

He laughed and kissed her shaky lips. "Wow, you nearly gave me a heart attack."

Shasa shook her head, laughing and crying at the same time. "I know! That was the worst response in the history of proposals. But I do love you."

He took her hand and slid the ring on her finger. Shasa

didn't expect it to fit, but it did. Her legs trembled as they descended the stairs. They picked up Lilla from the laundry room and crossed the yard to his parents' house.

Shasa paused at the door. "Wait! How are we going to tell them?"

Mac didn't respond. Instead, he opened the door. Sue, John, Marnie, Elsie and Earl all sat at the dining table, engrossed in conversation. As they noticed Mac and Shasa, a deep silence fell.

Mac lifted Shasa's left hand. "She said yes!"

As if on cue, everyone started clapping and whistling.

Marnie was the first to rush in, hugging Shasa so tight she struggled to breathe. "Congratulations! I'm so happy for you both!"

"Congratulations!" echoed Elsie and Earl, both coming in for a hug.

John and Sue followed, smiling widely. Sue had tears in her eyes.

"What's happening?" she asked Mac, blinking in confusion.

Mac's hand curled around her waist, pulling her closer, claiming her. "I may have prepared them a little."

He winked and Marnie erupted in giggles. "I'm so relieved you said yes! We were all in knots over here. I know it's a big decision, especially when you have a kid... but we've all got to know Mac." She glanced at Sue and John. "Well, some of us have a head start, but we've all got to know him and can't wait for him to join our cohousing community!"

"We held an emergency meeting, and I officially applied," Mac explained.

"To be honest, we're quite excited about the idea of living next door to Elijah," Sue said, her cheeks burning pink.

Mac nodded, pulling a face. "Yeah, that part is exciting for sure."

"We can take the unit on the roadside," John smirked. "That'll give the newlyweds a bit of privacy."

Newlyweds? He'd just proposed. Had everyone else known about this but her? All this time, she'd thought Mac didn't want to live with them, that he wasn't ready for that kind of commitment.

Shasa looked at the ring on her finger, her mind spinning from the sudden turn of events. She retreated out the door, circled the house and sat down on at the outdoor table to catch her breath. For the past couple of weeks, Mac being so busy she'd thought he was pulling away. All the while, he'd been here, working long days at the construction site, lying to her about his whereabouts. Shasa stared at the ring on her finger, so absorbed by her thoughts that she jumped when Mac sat down next to her.

"Are you rethinking it?" he asked.

"No." The answer burst out of her chest. She wanted him, but if this was going to work, they'd have to stop sneaking behind each other's backs. "I'm just trying to catch up with everything... I thought you were going to break up with me.

I—"

"I'm sorry. I never meant to make you think that! I was so focused on creating this perfect surprise that I got carried away."

"Yeah, I get it. But no more surprises, okay? Or secrets." She swallowed but couldn't stop the tears. The uncertainty and worry, followed by the shock of his proposal, all poured out, turning into relief. And snot.

He stroked her back. "No more secrets. Or spying. Or running away before I get to make you come."

She laughed, her face flushing with warmth. Mac got up and pulled her up from the chair, against his chest. Her arms wrapped around him like a slap bracelet, activated by the contact. This is where she belonged.

"Sorry I messed up your proposal," she whispered.

Mac's arms tightened around her. "No, you didn't. As long as your answer is still 'yes'?"

Shasa nodded against his chest, a relaxing warmth spreading through her. "It is. I just didn't mean to snotty cry."

Mac stroked her hair. "All good. Besides, it's not over yet. We still have to tell Lilla and ask for her blessing. She might say no."

Shasa buried her face into his puffer vest. It warmed her heart that he wanted to ask her daughter. This is how it was supposed to be. Them on the same page, considering things together. Mac wrapped an arm around her and guided her back to the house. They found everyone around the dining table, waiting for them.

Marnie studied them with caution. "Are you still engaged?"

"Yes," Shasa said, a smile bursting through.

Lilla ran over to hug her legs. "Where did you go?"

Mac turned to Lilla, who stared at them, her eyes wider than Shasa had ever seen them. "Is it okay if I marry your mum and live with you? I promise I'll take good care of you both."

"Will you take me up in the unicorn balloon?"

"Oh, Lilla." Shasa sighed.

Mac gave her a grave nod. "I'll try to organise that."

"Then it's okay," Lilla announced with an exaggerated shrug. She turned around and sat at the table.

Shasa stood at the doorway, her body humming with happiness.

"Come on, guys. We're starving!" Elsie called from the table, making everyone laugh.

The thick smell of roasted lamb lingered in the air. Mac turned to Shasa, cupping her face in his hands. She held her breath. He was going to kiss her here, in front of everyone, in bright daylight. No more sneaking around.

Shasa closed her eyes, letting out a deep exhale. As his lips found hers, her feet anchored on the flowery carpet. She was no longer floating, no longer lost. She was home.

BONUS EPILOGUE: The Premiere

The theatre premiere Mac and Shasa have been working towards is under threat as an old feud emerges. However, they have different ideas of how to fix things. Can they turn things around before it's too late?

Download here:

dl.bookfunnel.com/wq37lcmk6s

Ready for book 2 in Love New Zealand series?

Hidden Gem

Newly diagnosed with chronic illness, Marnie is planning to hide away in a remote cabin. But fate has other plans. A surprise invitation to a gala, along with a makeover, and she's swept into a Cinderella story of a lifetime.

Rising political superstar Jason is on a mission to fix New Zealand's housing crisis. If only he could sleep. Haunted by guilt, he stares at the ceiling every night, his goals slipping away with his health and sanity. Until hope enters his life in the shape of a woman. She seems to remedy everything – his insomnia, career… and libido.

Then she vanishes.

Jason scours New Zealand to find her. But as he falls for the woman of his dreams (pun intended), he discovers how much really stands in the way of their happily ever after.

Available wide: books2read.com/hidden-gem

About the author

Enni Amanda is a graphic designer moonlighting as a rom-com author, or maybe it's the other way around. In 2006, she and her husband moved from Finland to New Zealand and fell in love with the gorgeous islands and their laid-back people. They spent eight years traveling between the two rather inconveniently located countries, studying filmmaking and running a film festival. Through all the filmmaking, Enni discovered a passion for screenwriting, which eventually led to writing books (a slippery slope). Her heart-warming, funny stories explore real-life issues like identity, found family, and the housing crisis. These days, she lives in the Waikato, close to the rolling hills of the Shire, raising two cute, rambunctious boys while writing away and ignoring housework.

Books by Enni Amanda

A Tiny House on Wheels (2019)

Coffee on Waihi Beach (2020)

Christmas in July (novella, 2020)

Love New Zealand series

Nest or Invest (2021)

Hidden Gem (2021)

Night and Day (2022)

Love Istanbul series

My Lucky Star (2023)

My Turkish Fling (TBC)

Visit **enniamanda.com** for more information